A NOVEL

BY RUSTY HODGDON

The Eye

Coming soon, to a location near you . . .

This book is a work of fiction. Names, characters, businesses, organizations, places, events and incidents are products of the author's over-active imagination or are used fictitiously. Any resemblance to actual events, locales or persons, living or dead, is entirely coincidental.

Published in the United States by Create Space, a subsidiary of Amazon.com

KEY WEST, FL

OTHER NOVELS BY RUSTY HODGDON

~SUICIDE

A new arrival to Key West, Dana Hunter only wanted to be left alone to write and enjoy life after raising children and a divorce. But a brief argument in a bar, and the later witnessing of a suicide, lower him into the hellish depths of facing murder charges and police corruption from which only a good lawyer and the love of a woman can resurrect him.

~THE SUBWAY KILLER

Anthony Johnson is a handsome, charismatic pimp who is suspected of murdering several college co-eds. When Mark Bowden, a young, impressionable Public Defender is assigned to represent him, he quickly finds himself cajoled by the beautiful women of Johnson's stable into going far beyond the bounds of ethical legal conduct.

~INSANITY

The denizens of a small town in California start engaging in strange, aberrant behavior. When a young health inspector begins to suspect the cause could be attributed to the spillage of an hallucinogenic chemical into the town's water supply, his efforts to disclose that fact expose him to fatal retribution.

ACKNOWLEDGEMENTS

This novel, like many, is the final product of many individual efforts, not just one. First and foremost, I want to thank the love of my life, Joyce, for her patience in dealing with my long bouts at the computer, and her excellent editing and advice. I'd also like to thank my good friends and fellow writers at the Key West Writers Guild, who gave me such excellent critique, especially my good friend Eddie Goldstein. Lastly, I need to acknowledge the fine men and women at the Key West National Weather Station for their time in giving me guided tours and sitting down with me to explain in layman's terms the complex factors that govern the formation and strength of major storms.

PRELUDE

The cicadas moaned. The hot breath of air lapped at the tall, dry grasses and tree limbs of the Acacia savannah in the Sahel region of Burkina Faso near the west coast of Africa. It was the interminable month of September. A small herd of wildebeests hovered unsteadily by the remnants of what was once a small spring, now only hard packed clay surrounding a barely discernible, waterless hole.

Then as the winds slowly increased, the natural flora and fauna roiled with the blast of the 120 degree furnace. The air then rose skyward, as if funneled through an invisible chimney, and formed a broad stratum of disturbed atmosphere. Inexorably the mass moved westward at an altitude of ten thousand feet, over the dense jungles of southern Mali, east Guinea, Sierra Leone, and into the Atlantic Ocean toward the Cape Verde Islands, sucking up moist heat as it went.

CHAPTER ONE

Thomas instinctively knew that something was very wrong. The Harmattan – the hot, dry wind blowing in from the distant Sahara Desert – had never lasted this long or been this intense. As he stood at the open doorway to his tiny mud and thatched roof hut, his dark eyes surveyed the purple sky to the east. It appeared almost bruised, with black pockets accentuating its inner realm. The wide open savannah still retained its intrinsic beauty: splashes of tall grass rustling with the soft breezes, spotted as far as the eye could see by the light green acacia trees.

As he turned and walked inside, he looked lovingly at his sleeping family: Miriam, whom he had married eight years ago, and little Geoffrey, just six now. His wife still retained her youthful beauty even after living in this hard, unforgiving land all her life. Her features were soft, her color mulatto, the remnants of the European influence that descended even this far south into the dark continent.

But it was her eyes that had first attracted, and still fascinated him – clear, large orbs, the black irises and pupils set in sharp contrast to the surrounding white. Luckily Geoffrey had taken his mother's looks, not those of his very African father, with his thick lips and flat nose and broad, muscled shoulders that unceasingly worked their small farm.

His wife and son had not been in the sun for two and a half weeks. The inside of their small abode, designed for maximum ventilation with large spaces between the rafters and roof, was barely tolerable, but certainly preferable to the intense direct blaze of the sun.

Thomas himself spent as little time as possible outdoors, just enough to ensure the trickle of water from the nearly dry stream behind their home emptied into the trough for his three goats and four pigs. He had given up seeking liquid nourishment for his small plots of sorghum, millet and maize. They had been harvested early, a week into the Harmattan, and the puny store placed into wooden crates which now formed temporary interior walls in the hut.

Miriam had talked him out of taking the long trek to Ouagadougou, the capital of Burkina Faso, to purchase some beloved Banji, or Palm Wine, made from fermented palm sap. The last time he had a bottle, he hadn't worked for two days.

She also insisted, as the heat steadily built up in the hut, that he do something to appease the Harmattan. Their prayers to the Mother Mary had thus far gone unanswered. So as his mother had taught him, he took clay from the banks of the small stream and formed two figures: one of the fiery red clay from deep within the murky water, and the other of the cool blue clay from the surface. The red figurine he pierced multiple times with sharp thorns, and tossed harshly on the ground. The other he raised to a prominent location atop the harvest boxes, and lit two small candles on either side.

Now he felt he had done all he could to ensure that the cool breezes from the west would overtake the hot winds from the east. When little Geoffrey, used to attending Mass, asked him what he was doing when creating the clay shapes, Thomas recited the well-known proverb of the region: "Geoffrey, remember, half of Burkanabe are Muslim, half are Christian, and all are animists."

It was late at night, possibly around midnight, when Miriam started awake as the suction of an unseen vacuum snuffed their two lanterns and pulled the air out of their home. It began slowly, then rose to a crescendo of screaming winds as an enormous air plume, miles across, blasted upward. Portions of the thatched roof tore off and leaped upward into the inferno. The board, upon which had been painted the "All Seeing Eye" to protect the household from danger, was ripped from its position at the entrance. Thomas awoke as his ears popped with the differential in pressure, and Geoffrey screamed in fear and pain.

It was over in a minute, as the cool air supplanted the hot at the surface of the scalded earth, and the Harmattan joined its legion far above and moved away westward.

CHAPTER TWO

Thomas spent the morning doing some quick repairs to his home. It didn't take much. The sudden storm had been mercifully brief, and had given way to a cool, damp hazy day. A few hours were spent re-thatching the portions of the roof that had been sheared off and re-nailing some of the underlying slats. Geoffrey was carefully lifted up to sit next to his father while the work was being done. Miriam regularly brought up chi, the strong tea imbibed in the area, and water as the morning was heating up rapidly.

When the repairs were completed, Thomas told Miriam he was going to take Geoffrey into town. It was a long walk for a six year old, but Thomas knew better than to coddle his youngster. Life was hard in this country. Miriam insisted they don the standard garb for the trip: pressed short-sleeved cotton white shirts, long black pants, and sandals made from the hides of the all pervasive water buffalo in the land.

The road, unpaved and full of large potholes, cut through thick jungle which lay just past the edge of the savannah. Two hours into the trip, Thomas began to realize the destructive forces of the storm had largely bypassed his small farm and instead had unleashed their fury farther south toward the town. They began to come across large branches and palm fronds littering the roadway. Many trees had been topped off or razed.

As they passed the first few white stucco and concrete homes forming the outer perimeter of the town, the havoc became more apparent. Some structures had been totally leveled, others were simply beyond repair. People were milling about, most with empty expressions, the rest with sheer panic contorting their faces. Thomas was now sorry he had brought Geoffrey with him, fearing the sights would be traumatic for the young child. Injured men, women and children were lying on cots in makeshift triage structures, mostly ramshackle stick huts covered with canvas roofs.

Entering the small town, they headed toward the center where the inhabitants would normally gather. Thomas was struck by the fact that a throng was scurrying in the opposite direction, passing in hurried strides and hushed whispering.

Thomas finally stopped a man he knew vaguely from some of his infrequent visits. He had a crazed look, his white hair wild, disheveled, his face pockmarked with bits of stone and dirt. Thomas placed his hand gently on the man's arm to stop him so he could ask what was happening. The man turned and screamed at him: "Who are you? Who are you?" and then continued on.

Thomas, unsettled by his encounter with one he had thought to be at least an acquaintance, considered returning home, but felt compelled to see for himself the source of the consternation. Holding tightly to his son's small hand, he pushed through the increasing frenzy of the exiting crowd. At the very center of the town square, an area that would normally be bustling with energy and activity, a large circle of people had formed around an object laying on the ground. Thomas could not see at first, and struggled to make it through the crowd. Most of the women were fingering their prayer beads and chanting, others were wailing incantations.

As he arrived at the inner perimeter of the assemblage, he could finally see what had caused the widespread panic. For there, in the very epicenter of the square, was a large water buffalo, lying in a pool of crimson blood. It had been nearly decapitated by a long piece of shattered wood. To his horror, Thomas saw that it was the sign that had adorned the entry to his home – ripped off and catapulted miles to this very spot – the now bloody eye protruding grotesquely from the sorry animal's neck.

CHAPTER THREE

Aircraft Commander Charles Rogerson, a seasoned veteran of the 53rd WRS Hurricane Hunters, could tell by the satellite data that they were coming into a big one. They were flying the venerable workhorse of the Hurricane Hunters, a Lockheed WC-130J, and were now six hours out of Kessler Air Force Base in Biloxi, Mississippi.

Carrying a reduced crew of three to lower their gross weight, the sturdy craft was capable of staying aloft for almost eighteen hours at a cruising speed of more than two hundred miles per hour. Major Aaron Hotchkiss, his Aerial Reconnaissance Weather Officer, stood behind him and his copilot, Richard O'Conner, in the now crowded cockpit of the plane. Just back from them was Harry Masterson, the first civilian who had ever accompanied them on a reconnaissance flight. He was a reporter with the New York Times who had been sent by his employer to check out this massive, brooding storm.

Aaron was relatively green, having served in his present capacity for only six months. This was his first reconnaissance mission – a "check ride," as they called it – to the eastern Atlantic. He had already displayed technical knowledge and leadership abilities far in excess of his twenty-eight years. The Major was strikingly handsome, a pleasant blend of Tom Cruise from the nose up, and Ryan Gosling from the eyes down. At 6'2" he had to stoop slightly in the low cabin. They were now two hundred nautical miles southeast of the Cape Verde Islands.

"I believe we should release the dropsonde in just about ten minutes. We'll be about one hundred miles from the center then," Aaron suggested. "I really don't think we should venture any closer than that."

"Roger that," the Commander responded. "I can already tell by the disturbance that we'd be safer with this baby well outside the vortex."

The copilot nodded his assent.

Even though they were high above the maelstrom at nine thousand feet, the old plane creaked and groaned with the constant buffet of the winds. The air was clear around them, but below was the enormous circular cloud formation they were studying. Although not yet a named Atlantic cyclone, all the indications were that it had a high probability of developing into one.

"This guy is forming well,"Aaron interjected. He knew its name would be Daemon, the fourth storm to be christened this year if in fact it developed as expected. "See the way the inner cloud structure is rising up. That's the stadium effect we'd expect from a big one."

Rogerson looked down and perceived for the first time that, at the center of the cloud mass, a bubble was beginning to form which even now had the suggestion of a circular domed football stadium.

Harry spoke up: "I've heard that storms like this that come off the coast of Africa can be the worst of them all. Is that right?" He was quite bookish looking, with thick, black horn-rimmed glasses and a pasty complexion.

O'Conner was the first to respond: "That's correct. In fact the five largest Atlantic cyclones on record were from the Cape Verde region. They've also been the longest lasting. It's mostly because they almost always head straight westward, which gives them a vast expanse of warm water to feed off of."

Aaron then added: "Hurricane Faith, the third longest lasting hurricane on record, was a Cape Verde hurricane. It lasted sixteen days total, and was a hurricane for fourteen. We're usually not sent this far east to check out a storm, but this one caught someone's attention, and here we are."

It was time to let the dropsonde go. Aaron readied the cylindrically-shaped instrument, and moved it toward the rear door of the plane. It weighed only a little over two pounds, so it was not laborious work.

"What exactly is that thing?" Harry asked.

"It's a Dropsonde Windfinding System," Aaron responded.

"A what?"

Aaron repeated the full name of the device, and said: "This little baby is equipped with a high frequency radio and other sensing devices. We drop it right through the inner perimeter of a storm. As it descends, it measures and relays back to us an atmospheric profile of the storm's temperature, humidity, barometric pressure, wind speed and direction. A small parachute will deploy ten seconds after it leaves the aircraft to slow and stabilize its descent."

Masterson watched as Aaron unhitched himself from his safety harness and walked to the rear of the plane, a distance of about twenty feet. He passed the four passenger seats, gently placed the dropsonde in a chute located on the right, and pulled a handle. The apparatus made a loud *swooshing* sound as it was ejected into the atmosphere. He then went immediately to a bank of instruments that lined the starboard wall of the plane.

"Now we're gonna see what's really up with this guy," Aaron proclaimed excitedly.

The Commander had come back from the cockpit to check things out, leaving the piloting to Richard. A half minute passed in complete silence, until Aaron let out a low whistle. "Chuck. Take a look at this, will ya? Look at that drop in pressure. I've never seen anything like that. And the wind speeds. I never would have expected them."

Commander Rogerson stared at the readings in disbelief. He was not specifically trained in analyzing the data, but he had been on enough missions to know he was looking at something special.

Aaron addressed no one in particular, his full attention on the dials and gauges in front of him. "It's getting worse as it drops through the storm. The barometer is showing an extraordinarily low pressure area. And the wind's blowing at over a hundred miles an hour at some levels. I think we can now class this on the Saffir-Simpson scale. It's no longer a tropical depression. This has advanced quickly into a Cat 2 hurricane. I've never seen a storm progress so quickly."

Just as those words left Aaron's mouth, the large plane lurched to the left, then dropped precipitously as if a phantom floor had collapsed beneath it. Masterson let out a sharp cry. Aaron and Chuck braced for the next blow. It came in the form of a terrible shuddering which started at the nose of the plane and worked its way to the tail in a matter of seconds.

Then, without explanation, the port engine caught fire, sputtered for a few seconds, and went silent. The big bird could fly with only one engine, but not in these conditions. Aaron grabbed the radio microphone, but was unable to utter a single "Mayday" when again the disabled craft careened into a deep nosedive toward the center of the storm.

CHAPTER FOUR

It was just past sunrise when Pedro stepped out the front door of his small, whitewashed stone home on the tiny island of Fogo in the Cape Verde archipelagos. A slight man, he had the wiry build typical of the Portuguese ancestry of the island chain.

As was his custom, he spent some time staring at the summit of Pico do Fogo, the only remaining active volcano among the Cape Verde Islands. It had given the name to the island: Fogo, meaning "fire" in the native language. Even though the volcano had not erupted since 1995, Pedro did not want again to be awakened late at night and have to flee with his family to safety from the molten rocks which catapaulted indiscriminately from the fiery blast. He knew it was being monitored constantly by the government, but he also believed his well-honed senses, sharpened and passed down through the centuries of his family's residence on the island, would be a far better prognosticator of the behemoth's intentions.

The summit was quiet, as he expected. But an occasional wispy plume of light gray smoke meandered from the apex, something he had not seen for years. He would have to keep an eye on that.

Turning to the land flowing down from the peak, Pedro smiled to himself as he viewed its stark beauty. The island was essentially a volcano, the tiny towns perched on its sides like fleas on the back of a huge anteater. Although the ground was nearly devoid of any trees or larger shrubs, at this time of day the rising sun illuminated the igneous rock until it shone and sparkled like a sea of gemstones.

His attention was quickly drawn, however, to the scene beyond the landscape and mountain. He hadn't seen it at first, focusing more on the volcano and the majesty of his immediate surroundings. But there, unmistakably, far off in the southwestern sky, was a massive blackness, as if night were creeping forward out of turn to usurp the incipient day. Pedro had never seen the horizon covered by darkness like this. More, even though the monstrous cloud cover was at least fifty miles away, he could still discern the swirling motion above.

It had never been this ominously large, yet he knew what it was. Pedro calmly entered his tiny hut and awoke his aging wife. Her features, worn by the sun, salt air and hard work of their environment, still maintained the glow of a kindly inner spirit. *Thank God the children, Joaquim and Julio, are grown and living safely in America,* he thought.

Marcia protested at first, turning to the far side of the bed to delay her arising. But Pedro would not be deterred, as he lifted her bodily from the covers. Sensing her husband's urgency, she quickly dressed and went out to the rusting bicycles leaning against the side of their home. Without a word, they rode the short distance to the one school house and only shelter in their small town of Sao Jorge. It had been built on the highest point, and was made of native stone, three feet thick throughout.

The couple had weathered more than one storm here. A gaggle of their neighbors had recently arrived, and more could be seen streaming along the rocky paths that crisscrossed the land. Already the winds were picking up slightly, driving jagged grains of sand and stone into the eyes of the travelers.

"Mi Bonita," Pedro said, addressing his wife with his favorite nickname for her. "I'm worried about this one. It's too large. The largest I've ever seen."

Marcia nodded in agreement, her eyes still fixed on the increasingly darkening sky. Just then she pointed to an object that seemed to be ejected precipitously from the purplish maelstrom. At first it gleamed silver, with a fiery tail. Pedro and Marcia stood transfixed as they watched the seeming missile focus into a large airplane, streaming smoke and flashes of yellow-orange flame from one wing. It wobbled uncontrollably from side to side, as if a novice pilot were overcorrecting with each dip of the wings. It blasted almost directly overhead of them at an altitude of only five hundred feet, heading toward the tiny airport in the town of Sao Felipe far below them. As it disappeared from view, they caught only one word out of several on its tail: "Hurricane."

CHAPTER FIVE

Ben Harris knew he would not go right home. In fact, the longer he could delay that, he would. There were three places he might stop, but his favorite was always Roma, a very good Italian restaurant with a bar area that closely resembled a mens club. Dark wood and low lighting from chandeliers prevailed. That is where he was headed tonight.

Marjorie, his wife, always thought he worked until after six, and then there was the imaginary traffic. By the time he arrived home, Ben was well fortified to deal with his bored and uncommunicative wife.

Ben caught his reflection in the lengthy mirror which adorned the back of the bar. *Not bad*, he thought. His deep tan set off his recently bleached teeth. The nerdy black horn rimmed glasses that had earned him the moniker "Clark Kent" at work had been exchanged, again just in the past few days, with new contact lenses, colored to accentuate his hazel eyes.

Ralph was there at Roma, in his usual spot directly at the end of the bar, a vantage point where he could check out any free women who might saunter in. Ralph was ageless, and Ben knew instinctively he shouldn't ask. A good looking older gentleman whom the younger women found attractive and safe, Ralph was too smart to go for ladies his own age. He enjoyed his bachelorhood and, after a difficult divorce years ago, was in no mood for any long term relationships. He wore, as usual, the same herring bone sports coat and open collared shirt.

"Hey Benny boy, how's it going?" Ralph's eternal greeting.

"Not bad Ralphie, how 'bout with you?"

"If I was any better, they'd have to clone me."

I never understood that one, Ben thought. *Maybe it was a generational thing.*

Roger, the weekday evening barkeep, brought Ben's usual, a vodka and tonic with a splash of cranberry and a lime. Ralph was still working on his fourth Old Grand Dad as evidenced by the three cocktail straws lying in a neatly arranged order on the bar surface. Ralph usually came for lunch and drank the afternoon away, leaving with Ben around seven. They whiled away a few minutes talking about sports and the weather, safe subjects for two bar acquaintances.

Eventually Ralph asked: "How are the kids doing?"

"Good. They're both still living in Colorado. I like the fact they chose to live close by one another. Evan is in Vail, still working at the ski slope. Patricia lives in Denver. I didn't have a chance to tell you yet. She landed a good job as a social worker. With a private organization. She loves it."

"That's great," Ralph said as he took another sip of his drink. "Do you hear from them much?"

"Not as much as I'd like, but I guess that's a pretty typical complaint. I'd enjoy getting out there more often to visit with them. It's been a year now. They'll be back for Thanksgiving. Keep up mostly through Facebook."

"You do that thing?" the older man asked.

"Yeah. It's the only way I can stay current with what they're doing. They post all the time."

"That's way too complicated for me. I just pick up the phone."

"I used to do that. But it was almost impossible to catch them at a good time. They're both too busy."

"Yeah. That's the problem with today's world. Everyone's so busy."

Then Ben blurted out, but more in a whisper than a declaration: "Guess what? I'm heading down to Miami Beach this weekend. The Miami International Wine Festival is on. It's the biggest wine show in the country."

"Miami Beach? You mean South Beach, and all that? I hear that's a wild place," Ralph responded.

"I don't know about that. I'm just going to see the festivities. But I'm staying right on Ocean Drive in SoBe, as I hear they call it. I'm really excited."

"When's the last time you took a trip without the wife and kids?" the older man inquired.

Ben hesitated. "Never. I do feel a little uneasy about it. But I just feel I've been in a rut so long, if I don't break out now, I never will."

"Well, you deserve it. You never go anywhere, and have worked your butt off all your life. I hope you have a great time."

"Thanks. Just so you know, things haven't been going all that well at home. We used to laugh about the empty nest syndrome, like it was a joke on others when the children flew the coop. Problem is, there's a nasty reality to it. You suddenly learn you and the person sleeping next to you have nothing in common. But we'll work through it."

Ralph appeared slightly embarrassed by the sudden turn to the personal realm. "You'll hang in there. The alternative is far too expensive."

The two men went back to their small talk and checking out every woman who came through the door. Finally they left to the stale reality of their lives.

On the way home, Ben's mind wandered to earlier in the evening. He had just finished his daily routine of tidying up his desk. He never left the office until his work area was organized and spotless, ready for the next day. Being a Senior Accountant at Smith & Ford had its few perks. He could leave with impunity any time after five in the evening, abandoning the young Turks to toil away far into the evening.

He had been there once. He still cringed at the thought of the long hours over ten years he spent in that windowless office just down the corridor. Then he had only been promoted to Junior Accountant, a stinging blow after the hard work he had put in. He was next passed over twice for the Senior position, until, and Ben knew it, someone at the top felt pity for him and finally relented. But that was only three years ago, hardly enough time to accumulate the wealth he knew he would need for his retirement until his forced exit at age sixty, just two years hence, a Smith & Ford mandate for all but the tenured partners.

Ben's thoughts were interrupted by a call on his cell from Phil, one of the few childhood friends he had stayed in touch with over the years. They spoke once or twice a month, and tried to get together every few years, even though they lived many states apart.

"How goes it?" Phil asked.

"Good, how 'bout you?"

"Same ole, same ole. Just waitin' for retirement in a couple of years. Anything new with you?"

"The only thing is I'm takin' a little trip this weekend. To Miami Beach for the wine fair. Goin' all by myself."

"Hey, that's fantastic. The old lady's lettin' you go?"

Ben paused for a moment. "Ah . . . she doesn't actually know I'm going. Booked a room at the Tides. It's very expensive, but right on Ocean Drive, the main drag on the beach. The pics on the internet of the place are unbelievable. Art Deco everywhere. I've decided I'm just going to step out a bit. For once in my life."

"Oh you ole dog," Phil snickered. "I hear they got some really pretty Cuban ladies down there. Gonna try to taste some?"

"Look my man, I'm just going down there for some sun and relaxation. And I hear the wine festival is one of the best in the world. Of course I don't have the money to buy much, but I feel I need something different in my life. So I'm just going, that's all."

"Well, be careful. All kinds of diseases down there," Phil added, knowing full well his old friend would never come close to contracting anything. "Also, watch out for this storm that's heading across the Atlantic from the Cape Verde Islands. It's a monster. Right now it's on a path straight to South Florida."

Ben admired his good friend's weather prophesying. Phil was an amateur climatologist with a dizzying array of equipment at his home. Ben had learned over the years to listen to Phil's prognostications, as he was rarely wrong. But he felt he had to say, more for his own benefit: "Oh, those things never hit where they're supposed to. I've got nothing to worry about."

"Only wanted you to be aware of it," Phil warned.

CHAPTER SIX

Mark Johnson looked up from the wheel into the sensual curve of the fully deployed main sail of his forty-two foot Beneteau. No sight caught his imagination and thrilled his soul more. It was a sterling day to be cruising in his Bristol condition yacht. The sun danced across the water in no more than a two foot chop. The breeze was steady and sufficiently strong to drive the craft at the maximum hull speed of nine knots.

He had been sailing on and off for the past fifteen years, first with much smaller boats: a twenty-two foot Hobie monohull, then a twenty-eight foot Corsair catamaran. He had picked up this used 1986 Beneteau just two years ago, coinciding with his retirement from his psychology practice and receipt of a moderate inheritance from his mother's estate. He had spent every day since then molding it into its present superb condition.

It was a stunning craft: schooner rigged with a large jib and mainsail, the exterior generously adorned with teak, and two staterooms below with head and spacious galley. He had honed the topside bright work to a lustrous, deep sheen. A nine foot Zodiac inflatable with a six horse Honda outboard hung from davits at the stern, ready for action.

This had been his dream for the past five years since his divorce from his first and only wife: to cruise the British Virgin Islands for a year, or as long as the vessel remained in good condition and needed no major repairs. His ample pension would cover the financial end of things.

He had left Newport, Rhode Island a week before, heading for his first stop, Bermuda. Needing real blue water experience, he never entered the safer intercoastal waterway. There had been some tough days – as there always are in sailing – but he, the boat and his single crew member had made it through with flying colors.

Mark had no kids – that he knew about, anyway. A whole succession of girlfriends since the end of his marriage. None that had hung around longer than a few months. He was very content in his bachelorhood.

So that meant when it was time to get really serious about his trip – the repairs had been done, the luxurious hours poring over charts and nautical travel guides had been spent – it was time to find someone to join him. He could not single hand this boat for any more than short outings of coastal cruising.

Mark had seen enough classifieds in his many boating magazines to know how to do it. The ad in Cruising World read as follows:

READY FOR A LIFE-CHANGER?

First Mate needed for long-term cruise in the BVI. Need at least a one year commitment. Beautiful Beneteau 42'. Have your own cabin. Receive room and board for your efforts – anything else is on you. Females only between the ages of 35-45. Relationship level is up to you. Leave for Bermuda in early August. Respond to Mark Webster, P.O. Box 286 Newport RI 02840

He had included a recent – and truthful – photo of himself, showing his mostly salt and pepper hair and close-cropped beard and suntanned face, with just enough wrinkles to reveal his fifty-five plus years.

Mark received over a dozen responses from all across the country. Most he was able to toss immediately – they were clearly frauds – enticing photos of buxom beauties with a request for an advance for their travel expenses and time to come for the interview. One instantly caught his attention. It was a short letter written on plain paper, accompanied by a passport size photo.

Dear Mark:

My name is Jennifer. My friends call me Jenn. I am 38 years old and recently divorced. I have no children, and am drifting here in southern New Hampshire. I say why not drift into sunnier climes? I'm not an experienced sailor – have done some – but am a ready learner. As far as a relationship, let's meet, discuss, and see where the trade winds take us. OK?

Jennifer La Valle, Concord NH

The picture revealed a wholesome looking woman – not stunning or beautiful – but cute, with a pleasant smile and sparkling eyes. Her personality oozed out of the pixels. Mark thought, however, he detected a hint of sadness in the slight darkness under the eyes.

Mark answered, and they met at the Black Pearl in Newport. It was an instant attraction. The best part was that she looked *exactly* like her photograph. *Now when did that ever happen*? An hour lunch turned into three – with the assistance of a couple of glasses of wine – and after a few e-mails over the ensuing days, the deal was cemented.

Jennifer came down every weekend over the next two months for some trial runs. She turned out to be a natural, a quick study with a taste for the salt air and lively breezes. He also liked her fastidiousness with coiling the lines on the dock and wiping down every splotch on the gleaming white fiberglass. They slept on board during the nights, each in their private staterooms, with only brief moments of slight embarrassment as they coincidentally passed each other at night on the way to the head.

By the end of the last Sunday, Jennifer had learned the names of each sail and line, and could respond with alacrity to any orders when tacking or jibing. She arrived around nine o'clock on that final day of practice sailing to see a tarp covering the stern of the yacht.

"What's that, Mark?" she asked.

"Well you know you didn't like her name."

"I wasn't really serious about that. And then you told me it was bad luck to change a boat's name. 'Matilda' wasn't so horrible, I could have lived with that."

"Let's see what you think of this."

Mark jumped on the swim platform and gently lifted off the cover. There, in beautiful blue and gold script, was the new name, "Trade Winds."

"Mark! You're wonderful. What a great name!"

"It's what you put in your first letter to me. I think it's appropriate."

"More than appropriate. It's beautiful you remembered. Thank you."

They picked a departure date – September 10 – and amidst a flurry of last minute preparations, they actually cast off only a day later. The circumstances were most propitious, a day almost like this day, but cooler and a tad rougher. The forecast over the next four days was stellar.

They motored out of Newport Harbor, and once leaving the moored and sometimes anchored boats, set the main sail and shut down the engine. Then commenced their short journey through one of the most beautiful channel entrances in the world. The Newport Harbor Lighthouse on Goat Island was slightly behind them and to their starboard side. Soon they passed the stocky Lime Rock Lighthouse built into the side of the rocks bordering the channel to their port side, then by Fort Adams and Rose Island Lighthouse.

Their vessel cut smoothly and briskly through the deep azure water, the late summer sun dancing in kaleidoscopic fantasies around the slightly whitecapped sea. They were exhilarated, even drunk on the beauty and inspiration of the sights.

Once out of the harbor, they slid by mile after mile of the reflective white sand beaches of Narragansett. Surfers, many from the nearby colleges, bobbed like black seals on the surface. It was not long before they passed Point Judith, and keeping Block Island to the east, headed for the blue waters of the vast Atlantic.

Their schedule had been so hectic, Mark, uncharacteristically, had not checked the long range forecast for their trip beyond Bermuda. If he had done so, he would have seen the beginning warnings of a large tropical disturbance, now five hundred miles due west of Cape Verde.

CHAPTER SEVEN

The National Hurricane Center (NHC) occupies a low, squat but expansive building on the campus of Florida International University in Miami, Florida. One's comparison upon viewing the structure for the first time is that of a porcupine displaying its bristles in expectation of an attack. Antennae, domes, dishes and slowly spinning radar blades seemingly cover every available spot on the roof.

Robbie Stewart had labored in a small, square cubicle deep in the bowels of the Center as a member of the Hurricane Specialist Unit (HSU). The HSU is charged with the responsibility of maintaining a continuous watch for areas of disturbed weather and tropical cyclones, and preparing and issuing analyses and forecasts. He loved his work, but yearned to advance into the educational arm of the Unit. Robbie was a natural born teacher, and often went in, with all of his charts, models, and slides, to the local elementary school to teach climatology whenever he had the opportunity.

He was surprised to see Gary Welker, the Unit chief, approach his work area this early Wednesday morning. Gary had never graced the sweat hogs, as Robbie and his compatriots referred to themselves, with his personal presence. Robbie respectfully addressed his boss, which was not the approach the sweat hogs took in his absence. The chief was largely seen as a political hack and appointee, with a bare minimal knowledge of severe weather and its meteorological origins.

"Good morning, sir. It's nice to see you here."

The chief was abrupt and rude. "Cut the crap, Stewart. I know what all of you think of me, and I'm not here to engage in small talk. But Oscar is on vacation, and he tells me you're the man in the know when he's away. I need some information and I need it now."

Robbie didn't really expect any other attitude, and was now sorry his direct supervisor, the Unit Assistant Chief, Oscar Rodriguez, was not there to deflect the coarseness of the Chief.

"I just got an e-mail from Henry about a storm that's brewing off the Cape Verde Islands. He's very concerned. It's apparently the biggest storm he's ever seen coming from that area. I need you to be my eyes and ears on this one. The potential for devastation if this baby hits the coast is huge, and damn if I'm going to be blamed for any lack of advance warning."

Robbie was certainly aware of the existence of the storm. The entire team was tracking it closely. It was highly unusual for Henry Williams, the Director of the NHC, to become personally involved in and concerned about a single storm. Robbie had never been asked to report directly to Gary, and realized Gary must be very worried of the possible negative impact this one could have on his career if it was not properly and accurately tracked.

"No problem, sir. We're all over this one. We've been waiting for the word from above to put a name to this gargantuan. Do we have that permission, sir?"

"Not yet. Let me confirm that with Henry. What's the next name?"

Robbie consulted his updated manual. The NHC, in conjunction with the World Meteorological Organization, publishes six lists of names for confirmed hurricanes, one for each of the next six years. After six years, the lists are recycled, except that the name of a particularly devastating hurricane, in the opinion of the NHC, is retired, and never used again in deference to the sensitivities of those whose lives were traumatically affected by the storm.

"This will only be the fourth hurricane this season, so the name is Daemon."

"Well Stewart, just stay way on top of this, and let me know at every important stage where this thing is going and how powerful it is. Got that?"

"Yes sir."

CHAPTER EIGHT

Commander Rogerson hunched over the controls, expertly pumping the rudder and pulling the elevators to restore the big bird's flight to some semblance of normalcy. With one engine completely gone and flinging scalding oil and jet fuel over the rear of the plane, and a section of the tail fin badly damaged, it was everything he could do to guide the plane onto the runway at Sao Felipe Airport.

None of those aboard had uttered a word since the port engine had expired, sending them into a nosedive toward the storm. Miraculously, Rogerson, with the help of his copilot O'Conner, had been able to bring the disabled vessel out of its descent and steer it toward the airport. They touched down with a loud bang and screeching of tires, and turned toward the tiny terminal.

Aaron finally broke the silence: "Gentlemen. That was amazing. Good job!"

The Commander was the first to respond: "I really don't know how we did that," nodding in the direction of O'Conner. "Good work Richard."

Richard just raised his right hand in a thumb's up gesture. Aaron noticed it was visibly shaking.

"We've got to get our report to the NHC pronto," the Commander said. Pointing to the craft's radio in the instrument panel, he added, "We'll have to do that from the tower. This weak box won't get us anywhere. Richard, why don't you go and find the chief of operations here at the airport. We're going to need some repairs and supplies. Aaron, you come with me to the tower."

Harry Masterson, who had not moved from his head down position since the dive, began peering out the small porthole beside him. His face was a lime green color, and drawn into a grimace. "Whatever we do, I think we ought to get out of this plane and find some cover. That storm looks like it's almost right on us."

Acrid black smoke quickly began to fill the cabin. "We've gotta get out of here, pronto. That engine is still burning," the Commander yelled. It took only moments for the four of them to scoot down the short ladder that lowered from the belly of the plane.

"Run! That baby could blow at any time!" Aaron shouted.

Sure enough, after they had traveled only thirty yards, the left wing exploded in a torrent of sparks and metal pieces. The flames took but minutes to devour the entire craft.

An expansive, roiling wall of gray-black clouds occupied the entire eastern sky. Already the ground winds were picking up. Chuck and Aaron quickly made their way to the tower, whereas Richard and Harry headed toward the terminal. Harry found refuge at the one tiny bar in the airport.

It took only a few minutes to reach the top of the tower, which was still accessed by a set of iron circular stairs, rather than an elevator. After showing their identification, Rogerson asked the tower chief if he could use their radio. Once he was set up in a chair with headphones, he dialed in the emergency frequency number that he knew would directly pinpoint the head of the NHC Emergency Unit. Just as the crackling radio tried to find it's target, a blast of hot, moist air, joined with tennis ball size hailstones, struck the tower. The unprotected structure groaned with the onslaught, and as the lights flickered and extinguished, the brief connection Rogerson had established died.

"Chief, I've lost them. Do we have another radio, or phone system available? I've got to get through."

"It looks like we've lost primary power." The chief's words were interrupted by the sudden ignition of the backup grid. The lights and control panel flickered back into existence.

"OK. I think we're back on. Try it again."

The Commander donned the headphones again, and once more attempted to reach the Unit. Nothing happened. The radio was stone cold dead.

"Aaron, come over here for a minute please. Can you give this a try?" Rogerson knew Hotchkiss was an experienced communications guy, and could fix almost anything.

Aaron went through several systems tests on the unit. He had to speak loudly to overcome the intensifying pounding of the hail and the screech of the wind. "I don't think we're going to get, or transmit any audible on this box." He held his tongue on commenting on the antiquity of the system. "But once I saw one of my instructors use the on-off button to send Morse code signals. Let me try that."

Aaron pressed the switch to make clicks representing a series of shorts and longs, or dots and dashes. He repeated the message, having no idea if it was getting through or to whom.

Alone at the bar, Harry had set up his laptop and was on his third Bloody Mary. There was no internet connection. His anxiety was mounting with each incremental decibel increase in the impact of the hailstones and the whipping of the rain and wind.

Finally the barkeep said: "OK Buddy. We're going to pack up now. We just received notice that the airport is closing, and I'm going home."

Harry began to protest for a fourth drink, when the plate glass window behind the bar and looking out over the runways imploded with such force that jagged shards of glass flew twenty feet in the air. The two at the bar ducked instinctively as the glass covered them, forming a morass of crystal blood on their bodies and the floor.

CHAPTER NINE

Pedro held his wife under her left arm up the steep, boulder-strewn path that led to the steps of the small, whitewashed structure. The stragglers below quickened their pace as, without warning, the wind gusted to over fifty knots, almost knocking over the lighter of them. The couple entered the school house and took two of the only remaining seats on a bench against the west wall. They exchanged greetings with their neighbors, some of whom they had not seen in months. Worried expressionss filled the dim, dusty inside air. With the tiny shuttered windows and thick walls, little could be gleaned of the happenings outside.

Pedro picked out Antonio across the room and walked over to him. Antonio was a town administrator and had been a good friend for many years.

"Mi amigo, it is so good to see you. It has been far too long," Pedro said. "How are Marcel and Marta?" referring to Antonio's children.

Pedro was Marcel's godfather, and his children had grown up with Antonio's. As with Pedro, Antonio's offspring had found their way to America and were prospering. Both men had resisted the pleas of their children to join them. They were born on Fogo and like their parents and their parents before them, would die on the island. It was not an easy life, but the men could not imagine awakening to a different landscape and sea.

"They're doing well, even though I don't hear from them enough. I go to the library every Sunday after church and use the computer to check the e-mails from them. We also try to talk once a month but it's so expensive. Yet I'm content knowing they have good jobs and are loving their lives. I am waiting for the moment I get a call telling me one of them is marrying, and when the grandchildren come, then I will go . . . only to visit, of course. How about Joaquim and Julio?"

"That is so good, my friend. You did a great job with those kids. I still remember the time when Marcel jumped into and swam across that filthy pool next to the tannery on a dare. That boy wouldn't back down from anything."

"He was a handful. There were many nights I stayed awake worrying about him. Now he has channeled all that youthful energy and bravado into his engineering job. He got a huge bonus just last month. None of the other employees received anything."

"Joaquim is also thriving," Pedro said. "He just married, but I haven't heard anything about children. Let's pray, my dear friend, that we receive the announcement around the same time, and can go to America to visit our grandchildren together. Wouldn't that be great!"

Antonio's response was muffled by an ear-piercing cracking sound. As the occupants jumped at the noise, a section of the western part of the roof ripped off and flew away, leaving a jagged tear above. Those on that side of the room instinctively scurried to the opposite side. Torrents of driving rain poured through the gaping hole, forming immediate pools of water on the floor. Pedro huddled over Marcia in a protective response. Screams filled the room, vying with the screaming wind which now could be easily heard despite the cacophony within.

Pedro yelled to Antonio, who had moved to his side to avoid the elements: "My good friend, we've got a big problem here. I've never seen the school damaged by a storm. This one isn't like the rest. Let's stay together and pray to God that we be spared."

Antonio moved to form a small circle with Pedro and Marcia. They hugged without embarrassment. The tempest outside did not abate; indeed, it renewed its intensity, sucking ever larger portions of the roof into it's insatiable gullet. The plaintive cries of the islanders were instantly silenced when the massive wooden roof beams collapsed downward, crushing whatever was in their path below.

CHAPTER TEN

At thirty-five thousand feet and two Margaritas under his belt, Ben started to relax. He had a volume of travel guides on his lap. It was highly enjoyable to leaf through them, each emphasizing the sapphire ocean and pure white beaches with glossy photos. Scantily bikini'd, lithe women were often superimposed on the idyllic scenery.

Getting out of the house unscathed had been a little more difficult than he had imagined. For the first time, Marjorie had questioned his deepening tan. Ben had decided he wanted to be able to get right out on the beach without fear of a burn, so he signed up for a month of sessions at a tanning parlor. He found the standup booth, called the "Turbo," to be relaxing. It blew cool air at high velocity around his body so he couldn't feel his flesh cooking.

Not only that, he had joined a gym for the first time since he was in his twenties. Never letting himself get badly out of shape, he was amazed at how he had been able to hone his contours in such a short period of time. The stuff really hit the fan when she opened his already zipped suitcase to discover a brand new wardrobe of expensive tropical shirts and pants.

"I thought you were going to a conference in Pennsylvania. At least that's what you told me. What's with the new warm weather garb?" she shrilled. "Where are you going?"

"Look honey. I was going to tell you. After the conference I decided I would grab a little R & R in Florida. I got a great rate, and as you know work is slow this time of year. I just need a little time to myself."

"Well what about me, you bastard," Marjorie screamed. "I haven't had a day to do what I want to do since the kids were born. How about that?"

Ben had to bite his tongue. His wife hadn't worked a single day since months before the birth of their children, and now that they had flown the coop, she spent her time lounging about the house, lunching with her friends, and doing occasional volunteer work. *Not a day to do what you want,* he mused? *You've had a lifetime.*

"Well sweetheart, I'll give you the money any time you want to go where you want. That's only fair. Just let me know."

"I won't be sneaking off like you to the tropics. You probably have some little honey on the side that you're going to visit."

"No honey, just some relaxation. I'll call you every day." With that he grabbed his luggage and ran out of the house.

The flight had started off with a bang. They offered him a free upgrade to First Class, which he had readily accepted, never before having flown in that capacity. Then they sat a very attractive young lady next to him. After the takeoff, she commented on his guides. As it turned out, she was raised in Miami Beach and was living in New England.

"Have you heard of Lincoln Road?" She asked.

The name rang a remote bell, but Ben said he had not.

"You've got to go there. It runs from Washington to Alton, in between 16th and 17th Streets. It's one of the first pedestrian malls in the country. It's beautiful, got great architecture, and lots of cool shops."

"I'll definitely check it out. Sounds great. But to be honest, I'll be spending most of my time on the beach. That's what I'm looking forward to."

"Well, don't underestimate the allure of the nightlife in SoBe. Another place I would recommend is Mangoes on Ocean Drive. Great drinks, dancers. A lot of fun."

Ben was inwardly beaming. Imagine a pretty young gal like this actually talking to him. After a while, he offered to buy her a drink, and she accepted. Her name was Samantha. She looked vaguely of Cuban descent. Three drinks later, the conversation became more fluid.

"So, are you married? Any children?" she asked.

Ben considered lying, as he had already surreptitiously removed his wedding ring. But he only fibbed: "Yes, both. But the children are out of college and on their own, and my wife and I have been separated for over a year. I'm sure we'll be divorced by the end of this year, even though neither of us has filed yet. It will be amicable. I'll basically give her what she wants. I'm fortunate to be able to do that."

Ben was surprised by the sense of satisfaction simply telling that falsehood gave him.

"Oh, I'm sorry to hear that. How are the kids taking it?"

"They're fine," Ben explained. "They both live in Colorado. They're very independent. Neither has been home since heading off for college years ago.

"Marjorie – that's her name – and I have done well to keep them out of our problems. But I'm not looking forward to introducing them to someone new. That will be a little awkward."

"Is there someone new?" Samantha asked with a hint of flirtatiousness in her voice.

"No, not really. I've met some women, but I'm being very careful until after the divorce. Don't want to give the ball and chain any additional ammo, do we?" Ben said in like tone.

He was flabbergasted when Samantha handed him a slip of paper with a phone number on it and said, "I tell you what. I know the Beach like the palm of my hand. I don't have many friends there anymore, so give me a call. Maybe we could catch a drink together, or at the very least I can give you more suggestions of places to eat and see. Okay?"

Ben was barely able to utter a "thank you," when the captain announced their descent.

After they had retrieved their overhead luggage and were standing in the aisle, Samantha leaned over and gave him a soft kiss on the cheek, and said, "Don't forget, now, give me a call. And have a great time!"

Again, Ben was only able to mumble that he would. His pulse was gyrating out of control. In fact, he felt the bulge against his pants grow geometrically, a sensation he had not experienced for quite some time. It was nice.

CHAPTER ELEVEN

They had made good progress. Once out of Newport harbor, Mark had set a course of 120 degrees SSE. The autopilot, combined with his advanced GPS system, made the sailing effortless. The ten knot breeze, with occasional fifteen knot gusts, pushed them forward at a pleasant clip. Both were in good spirits and pointed and yelped like small children as a small school of porpoises rode shotgun off their starboard bow.

By late afternoon, they had traversed over fifty nautical miles at an average hull speed of six knots. The Beneteau was performing like a thoroughbred, steady on its course and consistent in its pace. Jennifer had prepared a late lunch of turkey roll-ups with a side of a delightful tangerine salad. Mark was sitting close to the wheel, haphazardously monitoring the electronics, when he heard the weather fax buzz below decks. *Another great invention of navigation,* he thought. *What did we do before global positioning and instant weather reports?*

Steadying himself as a stronger gust caused the craft to lean slightly farther to the lee side, he made his way through the ample companionway. A single sheet of paper was sitting in the tray of the facsimile. He picked it up, quickly began to peruse it, and took in a sudden breath.

Mark reread it to make sure he hadn't imagined it. Pulling out his chart of the central Atlantic from the circular holder above the fax, he began to plot the projected course of the storm the old fashioned way – with compass, ruler and pencil. He then folded, rather than rolled, the chart and set it by the apparatus so it would be conveniently accessible. Quickly climbing the three short stairs to the deck, he went and sat by Jennifer, who was lounging on the cushioned bench on the windward side of the vessel.

"Enjoying the cruise so far?" he asked her. "This is as good as it gets, in my opinion."

"This is wonderful. I've never felt so free. I know we've got some nasty weather coming up sometime, but I'm going to enjoy these times to the max," Jennifer said with a soft smile.

Mark thought he detected several freckles just beginning to appear on her upper cheeks. The bright sunshine and clear air were making their mark on her naturally pretty visage.

"Well I came up to let you know that I just got a weather alert from the NOAA . . . you know, the National Oceanic and Atmospheric Administration. It appears that a large depression is moving west from the Cape Verde Islands. According to the data, it's a huge one, and developing swiftly. I don't know why I didn't see it before we left. It's not a real problem for us now, 'cause it looks like it's heading well south of Bermuda. But we've got to keep our eye on it."

Even though Mark had tried to disguise his apprehension, which was still rising after reading the report, he obviously failed in his mission, because Jennifer's voice was ever so slightly quavering: "What does that mean for us Mark? Should we turn back? I mean, we can delay our trip until the storm passes."

"Jennifer, I don't see it as a problem. We'll be in Bermuda way before it could reach that longitude, and as I said, it's projected to head toward the south Caribbean and Virgin Islands. Don't worry, I'll be tracking it carefully."

CHAPTER TWELVE

Robbie Stewart was at the work station which held the primary radio receiving equipment. It was not his normal location, but he was well acquainted with the apparatus. It was very late in the day, and he was in the middle of a discussion with Bill Weld, a senior member of the group, who was seated at the station a few feet away. They were the only ones still in the office at this hour.

Robbie was talking. "We still haven't heard from our plane. The last transmission was today at 1400 hours. I'm very concerned. This isn't like them. Plus, based on the satellite imagery we've got on the storm, we need a lot more data, quick. This is a gargantuan."

"Well, it hasn't been that long," Bill replied. "I wouldn't be that worried. We'll hear from them in a few minutes, I'm sure."

That few minutes passed, and more. Robbie remained at his post. A quizzical look passed across his face. Finally he turned to Bill, with his ear phones extended in his right hand. "Bill, take a listen to this, will ya? I can't figure out what this is."

Bill took the headset and listened. "Just sounds like some random clicking. I bet it's interference of some kind. I wouldn't worry about it." He handed the unit back to Stewart.

"I don't know. It seems more than random to me." Robbie adjusted the volume and squelch and listened intently for several more minutes, jotting down some letters on the pad next to him.

"Wait a second, Bill. This is Morse code. Someone is clicking their microphone switch to create the dashes and dots. It's been a while since I've had to transcribe the code, but this is what I have so far:

'5RD WRF'

But I think I missed some letters. Wait. It's repeating."

Bill was in the middle of a yawn. Stretching, he said, "That looks like gibberish to me."

"Here we go – it's 53RD WRS – this is our bird!" Robbie shouted.

"Are you sure?" Bill had a decidedly bored look on his face.

"Absolutely sure. Wait. There's more!" Robbie began furiously scribbling now. When he finished, the paper read:

MAYDAY. MAYDAY. MAYDAY. STOP. TROPICAL DEPRESSION AT LAT 14° 15"N LON 24° 60"W. STOP. APPROACHING CAT 4 STRENGTH. STOP. BAR 26.12. STOP. COMMUNICATIONS OUT SAO PEDRO. STOP. HURRICANE WARNING MUST ISSUE FOR SOUTH CENTRAL ATLANTIC IMMEDIATELY. STOP.

"This is the first real data we've had on this guy. Did you see that, Bill? Over Category three winds! And that barometer reading couldn't be correct. It's way too low. I've never seen anything like that."

"Probably a transmission error," Bill said glumly. He was already thinking about the hours he would have to spend at the office if all this was true.

"I don't think so. I'm e-mailing Gary right now on this," said Robbie.

"No. Hold on. I'll do it. Give me that piece of paper."

"Bill, Gary gave me strict instructions to communicate

everything I got on the storm directly to him."

"Look, Stewart. I hate to pull rank on you. I also got the same order. I'll take care of this."

Robbie tore off the top sheet of the pad and handed it to Bill. Instead of messaging Gary from there, Bill retreated to his office. Robbie could see, but not hear him through the glass confines of the office. Bill first placed a call on his telephone, then typed something at his computer. Satisfied that the information was being properly transmitted to his higher-ups, Robbie went back to some projects that had been lingering from earlier in the week.

Robbie left work around six that evening. The late shift was just arriving. He looked into Bill's office intending to say good night, and then realized Weld had headed off to the men's room up the hallway quite some time ago.

On the way home to Coconut Grove he picked up a bottle of his favorite pinot noir. After the day he had, he needed a little comfort drink. Valerie, his bride of three years, was in the kitchen putting together one of her "Val-meals," at least that's what Robbie and all their friends called them. Valerie was an excellent cook, and very creative at putting together ingenious combinations of leftovers. A Val-meal consisted of about seven little treats from past days' meals on a plate that somehow surpassed the excellent taste of the original dishes.

"Hey Babe. What's cooking?" Robbie called out.

"Jus the usual good stuff, sweetheart," she shouted back. Robbie sneaked into the kitchen and surprised her with a quick but light pinch to her ass. Jumping mockingly in shock, Val turned and planted a wet kiss on his lips. She had fallen in love with this man because of his playfulness, spontaneity, intelligence. She had never before been attracted to a redheaded man with freckles covering every part of his body – well, almost every part – but his natural energy and loving nature quickly won her over.

"You're home a little late," she said with a smile. "Anything special going on at work?"

"Well, you know that tropical depression I told you about? We sent a plane all the way out to the eastern Atlantic to take a look at it. We lost radio contact with our guys, and today I received what we think is a message from them. Very strange. Someone was clicking a Morse code signal on the radio microphone. I decoded it and it was a Mayday alert which also described the storm as larger than we could have ever imagined. Very disturbing.

"Then just when I was about to send a note around to everyone, including Gary, Bill grabbed it from my hand and said he'd do it. On the way home I realized I was never cc'd on his message, so I don't know if it was actually sent. Bill's been acting a bit strangely recently."

"Well wasn't there that thing about his wife? Getting caught out with that younger man? It's all rumor, I know, but a lot of people seem to know about it."

"He sure has been glum lately. He's also been ducking difficult work issues. I have this nagging feeling he may have deep sixed the transmission I recorded."

"I can't believe he'd do that," Valerie protested. "That's important information."

"I can't either, but I can't shake this uneasy feeling."

Robbie and Val devoured their Val-meal and watched some TV in bed. The late weather news made passing reference to a huge depression west of Cape Verde, with satellite imagery revealing a well-formed storm. But without hands-on information, the type Hunter planes could provide, no more could be said about it. Robbie and Val were both fast asleep by the time the news aired.

CHAPTER THIRTEEN

Did this storm, moving inexorably west through the south Atlantic to the Caribbean, now hundreds, if not thousands of miles from land or boat, have any noticeable impact on mankind?

Certainly not within its expanding footprint. Yet it ultimately did, because even now, its ferocious, screaming gales were creating steep swells, the first of which were just now increasing the size of the waves on the Bahamian and Southern Florida beaches. The surfers and boogie boarders on the Abaco's, and from Cocoa Beach south to the Florida Keys, were exhilarated at the unexpected surge. Mothers watched more carefully as their brood played innocently along the shoreline.

At the epicenter, the air currents swirled and beat against each other, causing myriad thunder storms. Lightning began to rage within the steaming, humid cauldron. Gravity caused this northern cyclone to turn counterclockwise, just as it would have rotated clockwise south of the equator as water going down a drain will siphon out in different directions depending on the latitude.

As it spun faster, and faster – terrible things, unspeakable things – began occurring within its massive hive of activity. The winds approached velocities that would tear flesh from a living entity. Hailstones, some as large as fist-sized rocks, mixed with the frenzied, driving rain. The clouds built, forming an impenetrable barrier around the eye. And if God were peering through that orb, She/He would see the surface of the vast ocean frothing into a satanic maelstrom, the denizens of that world diving deeply into the lower depths to escape its wicked retribution.

Then, as if by divine command, the storm stopped its westward march, and paused, maybe deciding to feed on the hot sea, building its strength for further devastation, soon to be exacted upon its upcoming prey.

CHAPTER FOURTEEN

The small, low tower groaned with the pummeling winds. Hotchkiss and Rogerson had sought refuge under the sturdy desk holding the radio. Their attempts to S.O.S their weather counterparts in the United States had been interrupted when a large pane of glass in the tower had blown outward with the power of the suction. Everyone in the structure immediately dove for cover.

"I'm guessing this is one of the safer places to be right now," Aaron shouted to Chuck over the scream of the gusts. "Any aerial tower is supposed to be reinforced with steel columns."

"Yeah, but are you sure the Cape Verde government has the same building code?" the Commander responded dolefully.

The two men were cramped in a small elbow formed by the junction of their desk and the adjoining one. Their bodies were forced against one another, their faces merely inches apart.

"I just hope if they find our corpses here, they won't get the wrong idea," Hotchkiss replied to lighten the moment.

They had no idea where the other occupants of the tower were. They could not see or hear anything inside the cramped space. The lights had long since been extinguished by some unseen event, and the noise of the storm obliterated any other sounds.

Two hours into their ordeal, a strange quietness descended upon them. "What's going on?" the Commander asked. "Is the storm over, do you think?"

"I doubt it. I'm afraid the eye might be passing over us. It'll pick back up soon."

When after a few minutes of relative calm the winds had not increased, the older man said, "I wish we had been able to contact our families, at least."

Aaron had no problem making out his words so close to his ear. "Yeah. But we will later on."

"I hope so," Chuck said as he turned slightly in the cramped space.

"I haven't asked you in a while about your wife and great kids. Too bad it takes situations like this to make us realize what's really important." Aaron had been invited over once for dinner. He found Rogerson's wife delightful and an excellent cook, and the children, all three boys, well-behaved and comfortable with adults.

"They're doing great. Sally is a wonderful mom, and the little rascals are the light of my life. I'd be nothing without them. Hey, when are you going to find the right lady?"

Aaron shifted a bit, and was able to get up on one elbow. "I know she's out there. I'm ready for a longterm commitment. But not gonna rush into it. Playin' the field for a while ... although I hate to admit it, I haven't had a date in a couple of months."

"Well this job of ours is a jealous mistress. You've gotta find just the right woman: independent, but there for you when you need her. Having a flair for the culinary arts certainly doesn't hurt either."

Their conversation was interrupted by the screams of the gale as the eye passed over them and the back end of the storm lashed the shaking structure. They lay there, moving in tiny increments to redirect their weight off a pressure point on their bodies when it arose.

Giving up on any further banter, they waited for hours in their tiny prison as the structure swayed and shivered. At one point sea water began to lap at the base of the tower. That gentle wash soon turned into a two foot chop which battered the foundation. Aaron wondered exactly how long the building could survive.

After what seemed an eternity, but was in reality just over eight hours, the storm began to subside sufficiently that they felt safe to start the process of extricating themselves from their den. It was not easy. At some point a wooden girder – a two by six inch beam – had caved in from the roof and partially blocked their exit. Aaron, the younger and stronger of the two men, was able to twist his position to allow him to exert some force against the obstruction. Finally, after substantial effort, he was able to move it about a foot. He squirmed through the small opening.

Turning to offer a hand to Rogerson, Aaron jumped at the sharp report created as the tower finally gave way to the onslaught. He watched helplessly as the section of the building which had offered him refuge for so long, and still imprisoned his good friend, separated from the main portion of the tower and collapsed thirty feet to the ground. As he peered down, himself now standing at the edge of a newly formed precipice, he could not make out the Commander's body amidst the splintered studs and plywood. No sign of the steel they had hoped would protect them, he observed in horror.

Aaron turned and observed for the first time the wreckage around him. The remainder of the structure was still intact, or at least still standing. His eyes were first attracted to a pair of legs sticking out from the rubble on the other side. By the panty hose he could tell they were female. Any shoes were of parts unknown. No other humans, either dead or alive, appeared to be with them.

He feared the worst for this lady. Quickly, but carefully traversing the floor, he began removing debris from atop the gradually emerging body. Soon he could see her face. Despite the blood and purplish bruising, he could tell she was quite attractive. Feeling for a pulse, he was surprised when her eyes fluttered open and a gasping sound rasped from her throat.

"Hey there. Can you hear me?" he asked.

When he received no response, he gently took her hand, and while stroking it, inquired again: "Can you hear me?"

She let out a gentle moan, and then her lips were able to form the word "yes."

"Okay. I'm going to try to get you out of here. Are you hurting anywhere in particular?"

She was clearly trying to struggle to consciousness. After a few seconds, she said: "All over. Can you help me?"

"I can, and I will. But I don't want to move you if you have a back or neck injury. Where do you hurt the most?"

At this point the lady was able to roll partially over. Sheet rock dust, mixed with a little blood, covered a good part of her body.

"My ankle. My left one. I think it got twisted. But I'm alright."

Aaron reached behind her and gently pulled her up to a sitting position. She did not protest.

"We need to get you out of here pronto," he said. "I don't know how long it's going to stand," motioning with his arm around the perimeter of the structure.

When she agreed to try it, he again, with extreme care, lifted her up to her feet. She let out a soft cry when her left foot touched the ground, but as he put her arm on that side around his neck to take the weight off, she appeared to be okay.

They made their way slowly to the exit doorway leading to the stairs. Opening it, Aaron put his weight with one foot on the first landing. It trembled slightly. Then Aaron saw that the bolts holding the entire metal stair set to the tower had been twisted and partially pulled out.

"I don't think we have a choice but to give this a try," he said.

Both of them looked down again at the twenty or so foot drop to the ground.

"Maybe we should wait a little while to see if someones comes to rescue us," the lady responded.

Just then a particularly strong gust shook the structure again, and some loose boards on the side opposite them crashed to the ground with a loud "bang."

Aaron took her hand firmly, and with her arm still draped around his neck, led her without protest down the teetering stairs. Twice the tower tilted to the right when they failed to keep their weight balanced in the center. Finally they made it to the tarmac. The water level had lowered to six inches. The stranger put her other arm around him and kissed him on the cheek.

"Thank you, thank you! You're my savior. And I don't even know your name!"

"I'm Aaron. How about you?"

"Zoe. Zoe Johnson. Do you think we can get into the terminal?" she said, now looking around them for the first time and seeing the arrival section of the building no more than a splintered mass of wood, glass and metal.

"Let's give it a try," Aaron replied, "But first I've got to see if my Commander is still alive. Can you walk on that ankle?"

"Yes, unless we're going to do a marathon. It hurts, but I can make it."

He took her hand and directed her to the pile of debris which was only a few minutes ago Aaron and Chuck's safe haven. They could just make out his body partially obscured by sea water and several large planks.

They had only made it ten feet, when with a grating, ripping sound the stairway they had just traversed came crashing down a few feet from them. Zoe gave out an involuntary cry and jumped, luckily landing on her good ankle. It fell directly upon the spot where they were headed, and to their mutual horror, a sharp-edged segment of the metal railing drove directly downward into the Commander's torso.

Zoe fell to her knees, trembling. Aaron ran over and very carefully leaned into the quagmire of shifting materials. He placed his fingers on the man's carotid artery, and held that position for a few moments.

Shaking his head sadly, he returned to Zoe and whispered in a quaking voice, "If my friend was alive before, he isn't anymore. There's no further aid we can give him."

He lifted her to a standing position and led her towards some low structures to their left which still remained intact and looked like offices.

CHAPTER FIFTEEN

Pedro's eyes fluttered open for a few seconds, then closed again, as if his brain was reluctant to grasp what had just occurred. Finally he forced them open once more. The air in the room was choking with dust. He could barely take a breath. His other senses slowly came into being: the smell around him was acrid, almost sooty; his ears detected quiet moans about the enclosure; he could now feel the weight of some heavy objects across his legs.

Gingerly he tried to move aside what was on top of him and pull out from underneath at the same time. It was painstaking work. Finally he was able to sit up, then rise unsteadily to his feet. The carnage around him was unspeakable. Large portions of the roof had collapsed and were now covering unmoving torsos.

His first thoughts went to Marcia. She had been right next to him when the frenzy hit. Desperately he began moving debris from around the area where he had lain while at the same time frantically shouting her name. As he lifted a jagged piece of plaster about the size of a card table, his beloved Marcia's face appeared. He quickly removed the other small bits of wood, stone and plaster that covered her, and felt for a pulse. At that moment her eyes opened. Seeing Pedro's concerned countenance brought a wide grin to hers.

"Meu querido," her husband exclaimed with joy. "You're alive! Are you hurt? Can I raise you up?"

Marcia mouthed the word "si" and Pedro lifted her to a sitting position. Through the gaping hole in the roof they could see the clear blue sky, polka dotted with fluffy alto cumulus clouds.

Marcia exclaimed, "Look, meu amor. The storm has passed, and we are safe. Thank the Mother Mary for sparing us!"

Her spouse looked up carefully again, and then out the shattered window across the structure. "No meu pequedo," referring to his wife in the colloquial way as "the little one." "The storm is now all around us. We are in the eye. It's only a matter of time before it comes around again. We must make our way to the hills. I know a small cave a few minutes from here. Let's go there now. Can you walk?"

"But what about the others?" she said apprehensively as she now, for the first time, looked around her. An occasional arm or leg could be seen protruding from the wreckage, but there was no movement.

"There is nothing the two of us can do alone," Pedro responded. "We need to seek refuge before the storm returns."

He helped her to her feet, and she took some preliminary small steps. They then slowly made their way up the steeply inclined hill and found the small cave, barely a cleft in the rocks.

CHAPTER SIXTEEN

Ben retrieved his bags, and took a cab to the hotel. As they exited from MacArthur Boulevard onto 5th Street, he was overwhelmed by the mass of humanity, the bright colored lights and buildings and the noise of blaring electronic music. Even though it had been late summer at home, no one in his suburban neighborhood seemed to venture out, except by car, and that normally the soccer mom version.

In Miami Beach, by contrast, everyone was out in the street, walking, jogging, rollerblading, biking. Izod shirts were replaced by skimpy halter tops and short-shorts. As they took a left onto Ocean Drive, the dazzling displays of art deco architecture, illuminated in soft pinks, blues and greens, bedazzled his eyes. In the park bordering the Drive, palms rustled in the gentle, warm breezes. Ben had never seen anything like it. His senses were both stimulated and overwhelmed.

Pulling up to the Tides Hotel, Ben was greeted by two attendants and escorted up the terraced steps leading past the front patios and into the lobby. He passed huge, overstuffed couches and chairs, covered in light brown and cream colored damask, occupied by attractive couples laying across each other under the starry sky.

He almost tripped as he went through the front entrance, as he was gaping at a particularly sensual couple who were all but copulating on a corner settee. At first he averted his eyes, but as they progressed through the lobby, he sneaked a couple of quick glances. *Did they really allow this type of thing to go on?* he thought.

When the attendant opened the door to his suite for him, Ben was astounded. *No wonder this cost him six hundred dollars a night!* The room was massive. The king size bed to his right, centered against the back wall, took but a small fraction of the floor space. To the left was a low-set circular glass table with several enormous leather chairs around it.

At the back was an entertainment center holding an expansive flat screen television and the usual complement of DVD player, stereo and speakers. He would later find out that he could access porn 24/7 on six channels. Although the furnishings were largely of art deco design, the bathroom was outfitted with the latest in modern Kohler fittings, including a six by ten foot open shower area with dual heads which emptied directly onto the tile floor. His accommodations looked out onto Ocean Drive from the fifth floor and down upon a throng of beautiful people dining, walking, drinking and generally partying below.

Ben generously tipped his bag bearer. He had decided from the onset he was going to play the role of the big spender, even if it meant going deeply in debt. He would face the music, and his wife, when he returned. He had to call Phil right away.

"Man, you're not going to believe this place. It's going to break the bank, but it'll be well worth it. I'm just going to step out of my comfort zone this time and experience life like I never have before."

"That's great! It's about time. I knew you had it in you. Have ya gotten laid yet?"

"Not yet, but soon, I'm sure," Ben joked. "I heard there's this restaurant down on the 100 block of Ocean where people actually get up and dance on the tables after dinner. I might check that place out."

"Well don't go falling off drunk now. I don't want to have to fly down to bring you home."

"No chance of that, my man. I'll take it easy. Just want to experience something completely different. I'll be a good boy."

"Well not too good, I hope. You need a little break."

"By the way, anything new on that storm out in the Atlantic? I haven't been watching any news or weather. I don't want to the entire time while I'm down here. Want to escape from that whole thing."

"Well, it's still there," Phil answered. "And it's huge. For some reason it hasn't been rated on the Saffir scale."

"The *what* scale?" Ben asked.

"The Saffir-Simpson Scale. It's basically a classification system for hurricanes. Developed by an engineer and the former director of the National Hurricane Center in 1971."

"Oh yeah. Think I've heard of that."

"It's based on the intensity of the sustained winds in a storm. Five categories, 1 being the lowest, 5 the highest."

"What do you think this one is?"

"Hard to say. But based on the satellite images I'd say it should be at least a 2, maybe 3 by now. Which means winds ranging from a low of ninety-six miles per hour, to a high of one hundred and twenty-nine. A Category 3 is a major hurricane. It's growing faster than any I've seen before. The NOAA seems to be behind on this one. Don't know why."

"Well keep me posted . . . . no, I take that back. I don't want to hear a word about it. What do I care about some stupid storm. I'm in

SoBe!"

With that, Ben ended the call.

CHAPTER SEVENTEEN

They were into their third day, and still the good weather persisted. They had made three hundred and seventy nautical miles since leaving Newport, with only two hundred and sixty-five left. Their spirits were high.

Mark was standing at the helm, enjoying the tension of the wheel against the sea and wind, when Jennifer came out from the galley with a tray of small tuna fish sandwiches. She was wearing cutoff jean shorts which were cuffed high on her thigh, and the top to her leopard skin patterned two-piece swim suit. The past days' sun had browned her to a rich golden hue, and the small freckles dotted randomly around her nose and checks were even more apparent.

So far Mark had purposely looked upon her as a co-sailor, someone there for the pragmatic purpose of assisting with the chores of blue water sailing. That was becoming more difficult with each passing day.

"I thought you might be hungry. I know I was."

Mark gave her a toothy smile. One of his trademarks. His teeth were straight and white, never having been a smoker. "Thanks Jennifer. I sure can't complain about the food service on this cruise line. I really didn't expect you to be the cook, but I'm definitely enjoying it. Just remember I don't take it for granted."

"I love to prepare food, especially when I have the time, like now. It's a great joy for me."

They sat in silence for a few minutes while they ate. Without warning Mark stood up and studied the sea in front of them.

"What is it?" Jenn asked, with a tinge of alarm in her voice.

"I think we're already approaching the Gulf Stream," Mark replied. "See that whitish fog up ahead? It's also called sea smoke. That's caused by the warm water of the Stream clashing with the cooler Atlantic to its north."

"I hate to sound so naïve, but what exactly is the Gulf Stream?"

"It's a current. One of the most powerful on Earth. It's actually a river in the ocean. It starts as a jet of water known as the Florida Current that rips eastward between Cuba and the Florida Keys."

"So the warm water travels all the way up here from the Keys?" Jenn asked.

"Yes. It can reach speeds as high as seven miles per hour this far north. It's the Stream that allows Parisians to forget they share the same latitude as Fargo, North Dakota."

"You mean the Gulf Stream warms the climate all the way over in Europe?"

"Yep. But scientists are getting worried. The rapid melting of the ice in the Arctic Ocean produces such volumes of fresh water that it could act as a barrier to the Stream, triggering another ice age in the northern hemispheres."

"That's sure a doomsday prophecy."

"It is, but unfortunately it's happening right now."

They pierced through the fog bank. For a few minutes they could barely see the bow of the boat. Then the fog quickly dissipated, and they entered into a new world, the icy steel gray of the cold Atlantic giving way to the cerulean blues of the Stream.

"This is awesome," Jenn said, with wonder in her voice.

"Yes it is."

To their right a pod of porpoises burst from the sea like a fusillade of torpedoes, and took up station on their bow wave.

"Mark. My God. Look at that. They're beautiful!"

"The sea comes alive in the Stream."

They watched in total joy as the mammals dove and surfaced with abandon, then veered off and disappeared to worlds the humans could never grasp.

"How do you feel the trip has gone so far?" Mark ventured.

Without hesitation, Jennifer replied, "Are you kidding? This has been the best! I know we won't get weather like this all the time, but I'm going to enjoy it while I can. How 'bout you?"

"Ditto. I think it's been going great, especially weather-wise. But more importantly, I think we've gotten along famously. You're very easy to spend time with."

"I feel the same, Mark. You've become a great companion. You just don't have any of the underlying issues I've faced with so many men in my life."

"And just how many is 'so many?'" Mark asked with a smirk.

"Oh you know what I mean!" Jennifer replied with a slight blush.

They continued to eat in silence, their eyes wandering only to catch the deep blue of the sea cast against a baby blue horizon. At one point their gazes met . . . and lingered. Each stared deeply into the other's eyes, with no embarrassment. It was Jennifer who broke the hypnotism of the moment.

"I guess we've developed some feelings for each other, huh?"

"Sure seems that way," Mark said without removing his eyes from hers.

"It's kinda nice . . . I mean, I didn't know which way this would go."

"Either did I. I think you're sweet, kind . . . and very sexy. I couldn't have asked for a better person to travel with."

"Ditto, all over again," Jennifer said demurely with a twinkle in her eye. "I'm glad we broke the ice on this. I think we can move forward now. Nice and slow, of course. But forward."

"I agree." With that, Mark bent over and gave her a small peck on her right cheek. She responded in kind. They left it at that . . . for now.

When Mark turned to go back to the wheel, he espied for the first time the bank of brooding storm clouds that had coalesced on the southern horizon.

CHAPTER EIGHTEEN

Robbie arrived at work very early the next morning. He had not slept well. His dreams, although not rising to the level of a nightmare, were disturbing, at best.

In one, he, for whatever reason, came to the office late at night. He was able to gain access to the building, but could not find a light switch anywhere. As he made his way carefully in the twilight corridors, a sense of impending doom enveloped him Not a soul was present.

Proceeding into the Operations Room, he saw that every computer was on, reflecting reddish-orange hues on the walls and ceiling. To his astonishment, each screen was segmented into eight squares, each square containing a separate and distinct satellite view of a massive storm, swirling, malevolent, growing in size. He woke up in a cold sweat.

Entering for real into the work area, he had a sudden flashback to the dream. No one was there. Going from cubicle to cubicle, he finally found Sam, an intern he did not know well. Relieved to find someone around, Robbie poked his head in to say hello. Sam was turned with his back to the door and was busy playing a video game on his IPhone.

"Hey Sam. Where is everyone?"

Without turning around, Sam muttered,"Damn if I know."

Robbie could not help but think that this guy wasn't going to be around all that long. "Have you seen Bill?"

"Nope."

"Or Gary?"

"That's another nope."

Giving up on Sam, Robbie turned back to his office. He checked his voice messages, and found one from Bill Weld, explaining that he was feeling under the weather, and probably wouldn't be making it in today. *With Oscar away on vacation, that sure left the office understaffed,* he mused. *At a pretty critical time.*

Robbie turned to his computer and dialed up the latest satellite imagery of the new storm. Surprisingly, he found the storm had only moved a few nautical miles to the west since he had checked it the prior evening. Instinctively he gave the screen a sharp whack with the palm of his hand, and then had to laugh at his atavistic attempt to reset the picture. Refreshing the screen twice with the appropriate clicks of the mouse, he realized that the original information had been correct: the storm had traveled a very short distance in the past twelve hours.

Robbie got up and ventured out again to see if he could discuss these latest developments with anyone. Sam was still the only one he could find, and he didn't waste his breath this time. He decided to return to his station and shoot an e-mail to Gary to confirm he had gotten Bill's message. Within seconds of his first steps toward his work area, the emergency fire alarms in the building erupted in a screaming frenzy, so piercing and loud that he had to cover both ears immediately with the palms of his hands. Red lights spun from the alarms, throwing bizarre patterns about the room.

Robbie had only been through an emergency practice run once, and that was when he was first hired almost three years ago. It just hadn't been a priority for the present regime. But already he could smell the acrid smoke of burning cables and electronic components.

He knew the drill well enough to check all the offices for any injured personnel, but it was unnecessary, as Sam, the only one present, slowly lumbered out of his space. He was carrying a large stack of CD's, video games, and food – candy, cookies, and peanuts.

"C'mon Sam. Get rid of that crap. We've got to get out of here!"

Sam did not respond, and only clutched his cache more closely to his body. Robbie grabbed him by one arm and hurried him along. The air was filling with smoke at an alarming rate. As they entered the main hallway, Robbie looked to his right, the opposite direction to their escape, and saw the heaviest smoke pouring out from underneath the door to the lavatory.

Once or twice on the way out the intern dropped a few items, tugged against Robbie's restraint, then gave up as the firm hand pulled him on. It was a long way to the nearest exit – at the front of the building – and there were many doorways to pass through.

When they finally emerged from the front of the building they were greeted by a chaotic scene: fire engines, ambulances, and other emergency vehicles with lights flashing and sirens wailing, were everywhere. Hoses were just now beginning to be connected. They were directed by a Miami policeman away from the doorway to a grassy area about fifty yards from the entrance.

As they turned to face the building, a large explosion ripped through the back half of the structure, right where the HSU was housed. The roof collapsed with a roaring sound, and flames leaped from the new opening.

Sam let out a gasp, and Robbie said, "Man, we just made it out of there. How'd the fire travel that quickly?"

Sam only muttered, "There goes that job."

Robbie watched in abject terror as the flames quickly advanced, even against the onslaught of water now being rained down on them by the firemen. The inferno forced the two of them to retreat another dozen yards. Amazingly it took only twenty minutes for the conflagration to devour every computer, every weather instrument, all remnants of a detection system that would have allowed the Hurricane Specialists to warn of the formidable force of nature now venturing across the Atlantic and toward the small island of Bermuda.

CHAPTER NINETEEN

The squall came upon them quickly. After seeing the weather to the south, Mark had started barking orders at Jennifer. So much for the sweet talk. Survival on a boat depends on the person in charge. Trim the mainsail, secure everything below, have the storm jib ready. He helped where he could, but he had to stay close to the wheel. Jennifer performed admirably.

The vessel heeled radically when the first gust hit. Thirty-five knots according to the instruments. Mark steered sharply into the wind, but not so much as to start luffing the sails and losing control. That would have been disastrous.

Then the rain came. Huge droplets at first, then in hard, driving sheets. Mark had forgotten to ask Jennifer to retrieve their rain gear below in the first flurry of commands, so he was gratified to see her burst out of the cabin with their Gull jackets. They quickly donned the all weather coats and tightened the hoods against the cold needles of water.

"Good job, baby," he yelled above the scream of the wind.

She answered with a slight nod of the head and a warming smile. Another gust pummeled them, this one the strongest of the lot. The mast creaked as it strained against the hull. Jennifer had already trimmed the main sail one reef, and Mark shouted to her to do another.

It was not easy work with the boat dipping its starboard gunnels. Mark was able to loosen the main sheet from his captain's station, but it still involved Jennifer moving along the boom and pulling the sail down as she went. Once she slipped while atop the cabin and fell crookedly against the deck. Mark moved instantly to help her but she bounced up and continued the task, seemingly immune to the pain of the landing.

The gale force winds whipped and whirled the small boat into submission, and Mark, with a warning word to Jennifer, started the engine, put it in gear, and dropped the main sail. It flapped in a frenzy until Jennifer could wrap a line around it.

They motored for three hours at a forty-five degree angle into the now five foot swells until the storm began to calm. Finally the sea diminished into a three foot chop, and Mark had Jennifer take the wheel while he cut the engine and put up the storm jib in the event some of the stink came back. The vessel bucked and reared for a while, then settled into a smoother canter through the slowly ebbing surf.

Exhausted, and with nighttime coming, Mark engaged the autopilot and they retired below. Cold and wet, they stripped off their outer and inner clothing without embarrassment. Mark could not help but steal a quick glance, and saw, albeit briefly, a slim, well toned woman with nicely shaped breasts of just the right size. They wrapped terry cloth towels around themselves and Mark started the kerosene heater. Soon the orange glow of the wick sent warming waves of air into the cabin.

Jennifer put together some more sandwiches, this time of ham and cucumber, and they toasted their first bad weather with a glass of merlot.

"That wasn't as bad as I thought it would be," Jennifer said while keeping a straight face.

"Yeah, right honey. But you were magnificent. I can't believe you've caught on so fast. Sometimes it takes an emergency to bring out the best in people. You took quite a fall there. Are you okay?" Mark had noticed that Jennifer was favoring her right leg while undressing.

"Oh I'm fine. Just a little bruise."

It was then Mark saw the blue-black shadow growing across Jennifer's thigh and knee. "Jennifer. That looks bad. We're going to put some ice on that right away."

Despite her protestations, Mark got some ice from the refrigerator, wrapped it in a towel, and held it against the side of her leg.

"Is that too cold?"

"Not yet, but I'll be able to put up with it. Thank you."

After eating, Mark set the radar alarm which would alert them if any object larger than a rowboat was within a three mile circumference of their boat. He also turned off the radio fax so they would not be interrupted. They retired to their respective bunks.

Mark thought it was around midnight when he felt a warm, soft naked body cuddle up to to his back under the covers. He groaned contentedly and reached over and patted Jennifer gently on her hip to let her know it was okay. They slept deeply and contentedly that way throughout the night.

If he had been receiving radio generated weather reports that night, Mark would have seen that the large depression, which had hovered atypically in the same spot for almost thirty-six hours, had now started charging northwesterly at the amazing speed of nineteen miles per hour. The cone of its anticipated pathway held the small island of

Bermuda directly in its crosshairs.

75.

CHAPTER TWENTY

The stone enclosure quickly began to feel like a tomb. Pedro and Marcia were forced together in a space no larger than five by three feet. They waited apprehensively for the return of the tempest. The couple largely whiled away the first several minutes by reminiscing about their children.

"Remember that time Julio was playing around that herd of goats and the billy chased him all the way home? I've never seen that boy move so fast!"

"Yes, and how about when Joaquim made that concoction of all the spices in the cupboard and poured it on the ground. The neighbor's dog lapped it up and was sick for two days."

The wind began to shriek around them. As the heavy rains returned, little leaks from the chinks in the rock added to their misery. Water started dripping on their heads and bodies.

Marcia spoke about their deaths: "My sweetness, we've had a good life. Raised wonderful children. Some would call it simple, but it's the way we wanted it. If we don't make it out of here alive, I just want you to know that I love you, and have always loved you. Since that first day we met at church, over twenty-five years ago."

"My love, we *will* make it out of here. I promise you that. And you know I have also loved you more than life itself over these years. I could not have asked for a better wife, mother to our children, and companion. You may not know this, but I swear I have thanked our Lord every day that he sent you into my life."

"I as well, my darling."

Gusts beyond their wildest imaginations buffeted them. The very stones surrounding them, each one weighing tons, seemed to shake. A horrible blackness enveloped them so they could not see each other even though only inches apart. Marcia began whimpering. Pedro held her tighter despite his rising fear. They held that position for about ten hours as the storm raged around them.

Finally they sensed the storm was abating. The rainwater seeping through their cave had subsided to mere occasional droplets. And the wind, while still gusting strong, had certainly waned.

Slowly and with great difficulty they managed to squirm, one after the other, out of the enclosure. Their clothes were soaking wet, and mud caked every inch of their bodies. Once outside, they were so stiff from their cramped quarters it took them a few minutes to be able to stand.

The panorama that greeted them was hardly encouraging. Both let out a collective gasp. The sky was a putrid gray. Although there had been few trees on this side of the island, those that had existed were broken like twigs and skewered the landscape. The stone foundations and walls of the scattered homes remained, but the roofs were of parts unknown. Everything was desolation.

"Meu Deus," Pedro muttered.

Marcia could only weep silently. They made their way slowly back to the school. It was tough going, the path having been reduced to mud and rubble. When they arrived, they found things even worse than before. Some of the smaller stones that had formed the top layer of the walls had been blown off, most inward to add to the chaos inside.

They walked gingerly around the perimeter of the structure – it was far too dangerous to enter within – calling out to any who might have survived the ordeal. They received no response. They could see lifeless human limbs poking out here and there from amidst the pile of rock and wood, but heard no sounds.

"Let's go home. I'm afraid of what we'll see, but we have to go," Pedro said.

It took them twice as long to get home as it had to bike to the school, even though the way was downhill in this direction. As they rounded the small hill behind their abode, their worst expectations were fulfilled. The roof, including all joists, slats, and thatch had been blown completely off the structure. Approaching closer, they could see their meager furniture, appliances, and knickknacks had been tossed about and now lay in broken heaps around the interior. They remained mute as they observed the carnage.

Marcia finally broke the silence. "There's nothing we can do here alone. Let's go into Ponta Verde and see if we can get some help."

"If there is any help available. But it's our only choice. Let's go."

The adjacent and slightly larger town of Ponta Verde was an hour's walk away, toward the coast. It had, besides Sao Felipe, the only other navigable harbor on the island. Once they got to the one asphalt road the going was easier. Not a single vehicle passed them. Not one structure remained intact. And not a soul came into their view.

They arrived at the outskirts of the small town. To their

amazement, now the homes appeared to be in relatively good shape. Roofs were largely intact, foundations and windows secure. They knew from prior experience that most would have taken shelter in the immigration building by the main dock. It was constructed of solid brick, and had never been significantly damaged in any prior tempests. They quickened their pace in the hope of finding many of the townsfolk alive and well.

Unexpectedly a woman, old, haggard, her brittle hair streaming across her face, walked out of the open door to a small hut. Her eyes were crazed and bloodshot. Pedro and Marcia stepped back at the sight.

Pedro asked, "Where is everyone?"

The woman pointed her boney finger toward the shoreline, and muttered, "All. All gone. Nothing."

The couple backed away in fear. They then ran, slowly given their age and time spent in the cramped cave, the rest of the way. On a hillock entering and above the town, they stood transfixed. Not a single structure remained. Not even the immigration building. Seaweed, sand, and small rocks had been pushed far up the hill. The sea, urged on by unimaginable winds, had reclaimed her own.

CHAPTER TWENTY-ONE

Aaron carefully led Zoe to the only structures they could see that remained intact. As they walked, for the first time he was able to grasp the magnitude of the destruction wrought by the storm. Only smaller planes had been left behind, and they were scattered like balsa wood around the runway. Those that had been tied down at the landing gear or wings had been stripped down to those essential parts, the fuselages, tail wings, rudders having been carried off by the winds.

They now realized the buildings ahead of them were once used for immigration purposes. Some of the signage remained intact, and as they entered they could see the plexiglass enclosure where the officers checked passports and other papers. Not a soul could be seen. Aaron took note that this particular building was constructed of thick concrete blocks with a reinforced roof.

Pointing to a row of plastic chairs connected together, Aaron turned to Zoe and said, "Let's rest a spell here. I'm going to take a look at those vending machines and see if any still work. I'm starved. How about you?"

"I could certainly eat something."

Aaron always kept loose change on him, and was especially glad now that he carried on that routine. The machines miraculously worked. At one he purchased two bottles of water, and at another some Doritos and chocolate bars.

Approaching Zoe, he commented, "I think even if there were a nuclear war, those damn vending machines would work. They'll probably survive mankind."

"Today, I say that's a good thing," Zoe said as she hungrily took the water and snacks and started gulping the precious liquid.

They drank and ate in silence for the time it took them to finish their repast. Zoe guiltily looked up and said, "Sorry to be such a pig. I should have asked if you wanted more."

"No, I'm fine. This will satisfy at least for now. But in a while I've got to see if I can find a telephone, or radio, or anything to communicate with the outside world. Why don't you rest here while I go off and explore. I'm sure that ankle could use a break."

"Thanks. I think I might just do that. But please let me know if I can help in any way and I will."

"I really appreciate that. But let me see what I can find. I'll be back within the hour."

"Okay. But be careful out there. It still looks dangerous with all the debris."

"I will. And thanks for caring."

Aaron set off for the main terminal building. It was a pile of rubble, but he was hopeful that he might find something of value. The main entrance, even though it tilted precariously backward, afforded an ingress of sorts into the interior. Aaron kept his eye carefully on the groaning, shifting, studs, sheet rock and joists. He turned a corner, and came upon what could barely be discerned as the original bar area. The bar itself looked as it some frenzied drunk had taken a heavy maul to it. Pieces of splintered wood protruded at crazy and awkward angles from the once smooth and glossy surface.

Aaron looked to his right, and saw Harry Masterson and two others lying in a crimson, gory quagmire of glass shards, some sticking out of heir bodies like grotesque displays of blown glass art. He didn't need to proceed closer to see if there was anything he could do for them. They had obviously been dead for some time.

Aaron walked the perimeter of the small airport. It was all the same. Everywhere, Armageddon had been waged, and lost. He was still amazed no one living was amongst their ranks. *How could that be?* he thought with growing consternation. He assumed most had left at the beginning of the storm to attend to loved ones at home. But some would have remained. *Were they all blown away*? There was no sign at all of their copilot, Richard O'Conner.

En route back to the immigration buildings, Aaron caught sight of something moving down the road leading to the airport. He squinted against the descending sun, and finally made out what looked like two people coming toward him. As they came into focus, he could see it was a native Cape Verdean man and woman, both older. When they came within hailing distance, he shouted, "Hello. Do you speak English? Are you okay?"

The man yelled back in very good English, "We've survived, but need food and water badly. Do you know where we can get some?"

Aaron motioned for them to follow him into the building. They were covered in mud and some blood, and appeared to be exhausted and dehydrated. He led them inside by holding each under the arm, and sat them next to Zoe who was napping. She awoke at the sound of their entry, and appeared glad to see other extant beings.

"Aaron, where did you find this nice couple?" Directing her attention to them, she added, "Are you hurt? Is there anything we can get for you?"

The man responded, "Just some sustenance, if you have any. We've had nothing to eat or drink for many hours."

Aaron immediately headed for the machines, and using his last bit of change, bought more water and snacks. The two, as had their younger counterparts, consumed the drink and food voraciously. When they had finished, he asked, "What are your names? Where did you come from?"

The woman said her name was Marcia, and her male companion Pedro. Aaron and Zoe also introduced themselves. Pedro then related everything that had happened to them, starting with their seeking refuge at the schoolhouse, and continuing to their long trek from the now nonexistent town of Ponta Verde.

"Did you see anyone else as you traveled?" Zoe asked.

"Only one, and she was crazed from the storm," Marcia answered.

"Crazed? How so?" Aaron asked.

"It looked to me that the storm had stolen her soul. She wasn't even human anymore. More like a wild animal," Pedro said.

"I think we'd be smart to stay together here tonight," Aaron said. "Then go out tomorrow and see what we can find."

The four nodded in mutual affirmation, their eyes betraying their fear.

CHAPTER TWENTY-TWO

Ben decided to take a walk down Ocean Drive to find a place to eat. He headed south out of the Tides. He soon found the sidewalk mostly blocked by tables with umbrellas filled with diners of every nationality. It was difficult to make his way through the narrow corridor left between the tables, especially with the mass of humanity coming the other way. He was not able to make more than a block every few minutes, but he didn't care. He was like a small child in a candy shop – wide-eyed and nearly drooling. The women were beyond gorgeous, most of Hispanic origin. All wore slinky, low-cut dresses, usually with spiked high heels. Multicolored lights and booming music surrounded him.

About five blocks down, he saw a hotel with a restaurant and bar on his right. It was called "Casablanca." The bar looked just like the one in the movie of the same name: spacious; open; slow moving overhead fans with long, wide blades; almost a dusky look. He was mesmerized.

Taking a seat at the long mahogany bar that covered the entire length of the back wall, he took a menu from the prompt barkeep and ordered a Mojito. As he imbibed the cool, minty drink, he noticed two women sitting together at the far end of the bar. They were in their early thirties, it seemed, and very attractive. The closest one to him was a dark brunette, with red painted lips that offset her deep black hair and eyebrows. She was well-tanned, and dressed in a floral dress that came appropriately, for this area, only slightly above the knee. The other was the opposite: clearly bleached blonde, but with fine, almost aquiline features. Her attire was more provocative: a white halter top, low slung, revealing well-formed, tanned breasts, and a black skirt, hoisted well above the thigh.

It took a moment for Ben to realize that the soft, jazzy saxophone music he was hearing was actually coming live from a corner of the restaurant. A dark haired man, around forty, probably Cuban, was executing the keys with amazing dexterity. The song at the moment was "Georgia on my Mind," played with a slow, drowsy, very tactile beat.

Ben perused the extensive menu, and finally decided to try the Cuban pork with rice and black beans, a Miami staple. After ordering, he discretely paid a little more attention to the two ladies. It appeared they were saying their good-byes, and in fact the blond left her seat and exited the establishment.

After a few minutes, the dark one moved a couple of stools down toward him. Ben felt mildly titillated, yet also slightly uncomfortable. She said, in a very sweet tone: "You look new to this place. Is this your first time here?"

Ben was a little taken aback, and said in a slightly high-pitched tone: "Do you mean here, at the restaurant, or in Miami Beach?"

She giggled at herself. "Foolish me. The question could be taken both ways. So let's do it. How about Miami first, then Casablanca."

"Well, that's easy, first time to both. How about you? You look like you belong here."

Ben felt pretty good about his calm demeanor. It had been years since he had held a conversation with a good-looking younger woman at a bar.

"Yes, I've lived in southern Florida most of my life. Moved to SoBe three years ago. This place," and she motioned around the restaurant, "has become my home away from home. I love it. It helps that Casablanca is one of my favorite movies."

"Mine too. But I guess that can be said about most people. It's certainly a classic."

"It is. And this restaurant captures the ambiance of the movie setting like no other place I've ever seen. Let me ask Marty to play '*As Time Goes By*' and you'll see what I mean."

With that, she slipped easily away from the bar and walked over to the horn player. A brief conversation ensued, and before she had sat down again, he was renditioning a perfect version of the song. Ben did not fail to notice her lithesome waist and butt.

"I *do* see what you mean. This guy is good! How long has he been playing here, do you know?"

"Ever since I've been coming. You really ought to buy one of his CD's. They're great."

"I think I will. Thanks."

The two sat in silence as they listened to the music. As Ben's food was being served, she said, "Why don't I leave you alone to eat."

Ben quickly responded. "Please don't go. I'm really enjoying your company. I promise I won't chew with my mouth open. But I can't believe how rude I've been. Would you like something to eat, or drink?'"

"I'm enjoying our conversation too. I ate earlier, but I would love a drink." She turned toward the barkeeper and ordered a double scotch on the rocks.

Dewar's, an expensive beverage, Ben noticed.

"By the way. My name's Angela" She extended her hand to Ben.

He held it briefly, and said: "I'm Ben. Very nice to meet you."

They bantered about while Ben finished his meal. He learned she came from a family of five siblings. Her dad was a contractor and apparently made a good living for them. She was very close to her two sisters, not so much with her brothers. She now worked for a small advertising company in town.

Ben knew it was his turn to recite a bit of family history. His fabrication was now fully practiced. His wedding ring was off his finger. He told her essentially what he had said to Samantha on the plane, emphasizing that the divorce was imminent. She accepted this blatant lie without any apparent reservations.

They ordered another round of drinks, and then a third. Ben was getting quite buzzed. He wondered how she handled that much strong liquor so gracefully. Their discussions became quite animated as the booze spoke.

Angela said: "Let's go back to the Tides and have a nightcap. I haven't been there in a long time. It's so beautiful. What do you think?"

Ben thought it was a wonderful idea, and they walked together on the less crowded ocean side of the street. Angela grabbed his arm. Even at this late hour, Lummus Park, the broad expanse of palm trees, grass and sidewalks separating the Drive from the ocean, was populated by roller bladers, strolling lovers, and bums.

When they arrived at the Tides, they ordered some fifteen year old Cognac at Angela's request, and settled down into a large, cushy couch covered in a soft white canvas on the main veranda. She snuggled closer to him. Her crossed legs exposed bronzed, shapely limbs. With this proximity he could now detect her pleasant scent of jasmine.

They again engaged in small talk, acknowledging the beauty of the night and of the other patrons around them. Ben felt slightly conspicuous, and was glad he had spent the requisite time at the tanning parlor and the gym. He almost fit in.

As their drinks were drained, Angela said, "Ben. I've never seen one of the rooms. Would you mind taking me up to yours? I've heard they're as outstanding as the exterior of the hotel."

Did he detect a slight wink out of her left eye when she said this? He could not believe this young, very attractive woman would have any romantic interest in him. He agreed, and they headed upstairs.

When the entered the room, they walked to the window to look upon the darkness of the sea and the reflection of the aqua, light green, and pink neons emanating from the buildings. Ben noticed the lights in his room had been set, apparently by housekeeping, to a low, sexy luminescence, creating a mysterious atmosphere. He instinctively put his arm around Angela as they stood watching.

She turned to him, and, even though no one else was there, whispered in his ear: "Baby. I want you too. I want to do everything to you. Three hundred dollars will buy you an hour of ecstasy."

Ben couldn't speak. His abject astonishment must have shown on his face, because Angela continued: "C'mon Ben. What did you think this was? I thought you knew. I'm sorry. Maybe I should have said something first."

Ben had recovered enough from his shock to say, "No, it's my fault. I'm just too naïve. I wasn't thinking that . . . well . . . that this was that kind of situation. I'd love to. I really would. But I don't have that kind of cash on me."

"Cash is not a problem Ben. You must have a credit card," and with that she reached into her purse and pulled out her cell phone, which had a credit card swiper attached to its top. He had never seen anything like it.

"I can slide your card through now, and we can have a great party together." She leaned up and kissed him lightly on the lips.

Ben had no clue what to do. It was a lot of money for him, but he was also smitten and nearly trembling with anticipation. "Well, I guess we can do that. It will only be three hundred, right? But how will it appear on my statement? I'm afraid my wife might see it." He realized his mistake immediately. He had told her he was separated, almost divorced.

She didn't hesitate. It was obvious she was used to lies from married men. "Not to worry darling. I've got it set up so that it will appear as an entertainment expense: 'Angela's Lair.' You can say you met some guys and had a nice dinner at an expensive club. Very simple."

Ben looked again upon her shapely hips, and said, "What the hell. You only live once. Right Angela? Let's do it." He took out his wallet and gave her his Visa card. She ran it through her phone, he tapped the "Accept Charge" box on the display, and she put the phone back in her purse.

She then gently took his hand and led him to the edge of the bed. "Let's get those clothes off, baby." She helped him undress, unzipping his fly and removing his belt. As he took off his shirt, shoes and socks, she stripped down to a bra and panties. She looked like a goddess to him: a perfect body, trim, tanned and buxom.

"Lay down, honey, and let me pleasure you," she purred.

He complied, and she immediately took him in her mouth. She was a pro, he thought: a perfect movement of the lips and the hand in unison, maximizing the sensation. When his oh's and ah's reached a fever pitch, she abruptly mounted him and began gyrating on his erect penis. Ben noticed for the first time that there was a condom on his member. *How did that get there?* he thought amid his moans.

It took only about a minute, her movement was so provocative. He orgasmed in a paroxysm of pleasure, yelling, "God! God!"

Angela slithered off of him. In one minute she was fully dressed. "Baby. That was great. I'll be looking for you around town." With that she was out the door, leaving him still panting and wasted.

CHAPTER TWENTY-THREE

Robbie felt a strong, male hand on his shoulder. "Stewart, what the fuck is this!" It was Gary Welker, the Unit Chief.

"Gary. What are you doing here?" Robbie replied.

"I got a call just thirty minutes ago from Henry. Said I had to get over here A.S.A.P. I feared the worst when I got within four blocks and smelled the fire. This is a goddamn disaster."

"Sam and I barely made it out alive. The smoke was horrible. Very acrid. I can still taste it in my mouth."

It was only then that Robbie noticed that Sam was sitting on a curb ten feet away, doubled over and retching. "We should get him some medical attention," Robbie said to Welker. "Help me get him over to that ambulance there."

"Screw that," Welker yelled above the bedlam. "We need to get an emergency team together and decide what to do."

Robbie ignored him, walked over to Sam, and assisting him to a standing position half-carried him to the closest emergency vehicle. He saw Welker out of the corner of his eye take a call on his cell. By the looks of it, the conversation was animated.

Welker ran over to where Robbie was standing. "That was Henry on the phone. He wants us to send a team down to NWS Key West. They're the closest, best equipped office to help us track the storm. Stewart, you're the team. I don't have the time to contact anyone else, and I have to stay here to determine the extent of the damage. You need to get down there first thing tomorrow!"

Robbie had visited that office once about a year prior. He knew it had a reputation for being well-managed and staffed. "Okay, Gary, I'll run home and get packed up and be out of here in the morning. I'll call you when I get down there. It's about a four hour drive."

"Well, make it down there pronto and report back to me. I'll call Larry Grimes, the Unit Chief down there. I've known him for years. Look him up when you arrive."

"Will do."

"Also, Henry ordered another Hunter out to take a look at the storm since we can't màke contact with the first one. We've got to see what this monstrosity is doing. The latest satellite info shows it's stalled on a northerly track, and almost appears to have turned west back toward us. This is a strange one."

"It is at that." Robbie took one last look back at the smoldering building while heading for his car. He couldn't believe the extent of the damage. Most of the roof had collapsed inward creating an erector set jumble of metal dishes and antennae that had once adorned the top of the structure. Occasionally flames still licked upward from the ruins.

At dinner that night, Val was astonished to hear what had happened. "The entire building was destroyed?" she asked. "How could that happen? I thought they'd have state of the art fire protection."

"I can't explain it either," Robbie replied. "All I know is after the alarms went off, we barely had enough time to make it out alive. It was the smoke. It was so caustic. My throat's still burning."

"Honey, maybe we should take you to the emergency room," Val said with concern in her voice.

"No I'll be fine. Really. It's not that bad. I only breathed in a little bit. I can't imagine what happened to anyone who got caught in there longer."

After eating, they turned on the evening news. The incident at the NHC only captured a small segment of media time, being eclipsed by a triple murder and suicide that had occurred in North Miami Beach. The brief broadcast showed fire engines and ambulances circling the front of the building and the smoldering debris behind them. Amazingly, only two minor injuries were reported.

Later, as they turned off their bedroom light, Val turned to her husband, gave him a kiss on the cheek, and said, "Baby, I'm really bothered by all this. What the heck is going on? First the plane goes incommunicado. Then you get a strange signal that suggests the depression is much worse than anyone expected. You get no further information, and now the NHC burns to the ground. I've got an uneasy feeling in my stomach."

"I wish I could tell you I didn't, but I'd be lying. It's almost as if God – or some other cosmic force – has intervened to prevent us from finding out what's going on out there. But I'll learn more tomorrow once I get to Key West, and can get some eyes on the matter. Get some sleep Honey. It could be a long week."

They both slept restlessly, strange, inchoate dreams invading their subconsciousnesses.

CHAPTER TWENTY-FOUR

Mark was awakened by the early morning light as it first began to sneak across the hatch above his bed. Shielding his eyes, he remembered the human companionship he had enjoyed that night. He felt for Jennifer, but she was no longer lying next to him. The sweet smell of freshly brewed coffee explained her absence.

He quickly pulled on a pair of jeans and flannel shirt from behind the stateroom door. The air had a twinge of a chill to it. Going out to the salon, he saw the percolator on the gimballed stove and Jennifer curled up on the bench seat reading. She looked luscious in her faded, slightly ripped at the knee dungarees. He felt again the softness of those knees pressing gently against his buttocks throughout the prior night.

"Hey there. You got up early."

"Around six. How'd you sleep?"

"Beautifully. Especially with my little visitor last night."

Jennifer blushed ever so slightly. "I hope you didn't mind that. I just started feeling very lonely being all by myself. I know I shouldn't have, but it sure felt good."

"It did at that. I didn't mind at all. In fact, I should say I rather enjoyed it. What are you reading?"

"'The Perfect Storm'. It's really good. But probably not the novel to read on a trip like this."

Mark walked over and began to pour himself a cup of coffee

while he said: "That *is* a good one. Shows the hubris of mankind. And greed. Those guys had all the warnings in the world, yet they kept on going 'cause they thought they could beat the odds . . . and of course wanted to make more money."

"Well, what's scary is that the forces of nature can unite like that and form something so horrible, so destructive. Just makes you realize how small and puny we are."

"Yeah, it does. But if we use our brains, and don't unnecessarily tempt fate, we can increase our odds. I'm going to go on deck and check the lines."

"Okay. I'll be right up to help you."

"No hurry. I'm sure everything's alright."

Mark climbed the stairs of the companionway and opened the hatch. He noticed immediately the pleasant light blue skies of the two previous days had given way to a steel cold gray.

He worked his way into the cockpit and checked the attitude of the mainsail. The autopilot was still working perfectly. The wind was blowing at a sweet twelve knots, and the vessel was following pace at six. Everything seemed to be in order.

Then he saw it. At first he thought someone had spilled pink paint on the forward deck. As he approached the spot along the port gunnel, a shape could be discerned amidst the splash of color. It was a bird. From the looks of it, the creature had flown head first into the mast during the night and dropped to the deck. Its neck was twisted at such an odd angle that the head was actually facing backward, viewing him with two unseeing, black eyes. From its distinctive plumage, Mark knew immediately it was an albatross. He shuddered momentarily at the meaning. All mariners knew it was extremely unlucky to have such a bird die on a ship.

Not wanting to have Jennifer exposed to the gruesome scene, Mark picked the bird up by its legs and flung it into the sea. He then retrieved the bucket and sponge, which was permanently ensconced under the starboard bench seat, and wiped up the mess.

Jennifer appeared from the main hatch, and turning toward him said, "What 'cha doin'?"

"A bird must have run into the boat overnight. I was just cleaning it up."

"Oh. The poor thing. What kind of bird?"

"Not sure. Just a seabird. It's okay. I'm going to go below now and check our position. Would you mind wiping down the bright work?"

"Not at all." Then she looked at the bloody bucket and sponge. "But not with that!"

"No, I'll wash it out with the onboard hose."

"Mark, I can do that." She grabbed the pail from his hand and went to the stern wash-down.

Mark went below, turned on the weather fax and GPS, and sat down to chart their location. The fax sputtered into action, reeling out several pages of information. He idly started reading.

"Holy fuck!" He reread the first two pages again. There was no mistaking it. Daemon had made a sudden turn northward, and was now heading directly for Bermuda.

Mark grabbed his compass and protractor. Based on the storm's speed and present location according to the fax, and their own, Mark quickly ascertained that, absent any radical change in conditions, they could beat the storm to the island by about twenty-four hours. That would afford them the time to find a good hurricane hole and hunker down.

He had an uneasy feeling in the core of his stomach. His thoughts trailed to the dead albatross. *I've got to find the right way to tell Jennifer,* he thought. *So she won't be unduly alarmed.*

As she returned from her chores atop ship, he casually said, "Looks like we're in for a blow. That storm that was supposed to go west into the Caribbean is now heading for us. But we've got plenty of time to make it and get ready before it hits. We'll be fine." Mark hoped she didn't notice the quiver in his voice.

She did. "You sound worried. How bad is this, Mark? Can we divert to some other port?"

"No. Bermuda's actually our closest shelter by far. If we start heading for the coast, there are no guarantees it won't come that direction, and then we'll have no shelter at all. I've calculated the time it will take us, and it, to get to Bermuda, and we're well ahead of it. I'm confident of that. What we will do is this, though. Let's tweak every knot we can out of this baby. That'll mean taking her off auto-pilot as much as possible and really sailing for a change. Are you up for that?"

"Of course Mark. Just tell me what to do."

Mark got up and put his arm tenderly around Jennifer's shoulders, saying nothing. She gently leaned into him, accepting the gesture of comfort.

CHAPTER TWENTY-FIVE

The four castaways on Fogo found a suitable place to sleep in the immigration building. By placing series of padded chairs in a row, they created narrow beds for themselves. They were also able to wash up in the public restrooms off the main hallway. Miraculously the water was still running – at least for now. Aaron pulled down four curtains from the windows as bed covers. They made do as best they could.

As night descended upon the group, and they were settled in their makeshift berths, they began to talk in low tones.

"So Pedro, how is it that your English is so good?" Zoe asked.

Marcia answered before he could speak. "We always wanted our children to learn two other languages beside Portuguese. One of those had to be English. The Cape Verdean government offered many languages in the schools."

Pedro cut in. Both seemed to be proud of their abilities. "We learned it as our children did. Now they've moved to the States, and come back every year, so we get to practice."

"Well, I'm impressed. I don't speak a word of Portuguese. A little Spanish, but that's it," Aaron said.

"You've heard our story, Aaron and Zoe. How about you? How did you get here?"

Aaron briefly described his professional position, the problems with the plane, and his harrowing survival through the storm. When he had finished, Marcia said, "It must have been your plane that we saw. It was on fire, heading towards the airport."

"I guess it was," Aaron answered. "I'm amazed I'm here to talk about it." Then realizing he knew nothing about Zoe's reason for being in the tower, he asked her, "Zoe, we haven't had a chance to talk about you. How did you end up here?"

"I'm an intern with the FAA." Then for the native couple's benefit, when she saw a flicker of confusion in their eyes, she added, "That's the Federal Aviation Administration in the United States. It's a government agency that oversees the civilian airways throughout the U.S., including all airports. When I graduated from college in Aviation Science, I was fortunate enough to get this job, which meant I had to pack up and move to Cape Verde for a year. My job was to act as a liaison with the Sao Felipe airport and U.S. Government."

"How long have you been here on Fogo?" Aaron asked.

"Six months now."

"Where do you live?"

Zoe pointed in the direction to the east of the airport. "There's some housing about a half mile from here. When we were walking from the tower, although it was hard to see for sure, it looked to me that my apartment had been blown away, together with the rest of the buildings."

"I'm sorry, but I have to agree," Aaron responded. "When I walked around, it didn't look like anything was intact as far as the eye could see. But we'll explore tomorrow."

Pedro added, "Let's also thank God that he spared us from this terrible storm. We never thought we would make it out alive. And both of you also survived. But many have been lost. So we must pray for them as well."

The four took turns murmuring brief prayers. With that, and some "good nights," the pairs settled down for a restless night of sleep.

Zoe was awoken – at 3:00 AM according to her wristwatch – by a violent shaking. She had to hold on to the edge of her makeshift bed to keep from being thrown to the floor. "What the heck," she yelled.

Aaron was already on his feet in a defensive posture, but no adversary presented itself. "Something's happening. Did the storm return?" Aaron shouted out.

Pedro was now in a sitting position. "Wait. Hold on," he said. The trembling subsided. "I'm afraid of what this is." He motioned to the three – Marcia had gotten to her feet as well – to accompany him out the door. As they exited, an eerie, orange glow filled the sky. "Meu Deus," Pedro muttered. "Fogo has awakened from her slumber. Look." He pointed to the summit of the volcano.

Small rivulets of glowing hot lava were creeping over the lip of the serrated edge of the monster's cone.

****

At that very moment, some seven hundred miles to the northwest, the storm paused again. It hung, stationary, as if undecided, postponing its onward onslaught toward Bermuda. Sucking up the warm moisture from the eastern perimeter of the Gulf Stream, it fed again, growing, seething, hungry for more carnage.

CHAPTER TWENTY-SIX

Ben awoke the next morning with a general feeling of discomfort. The events of the prior evening had shaken him. *How could he have thought a beautiful young lady like Angela would be attracted to him, except in a professional way? How naïve!* He also had a lingering sense of guilt. *What if somehow Marjorie found out about the incident? Well, she couldn't. There's just no way.* Yet he knew what he had done, and it wasn't sitting well with him. He had to be more disciplined in the future.

The day lay ahead of him, with all its infinite possibilities. He would have breakfast, then attend the initial events of the wine festival. That was an exciting proposition.

Ben showered and dressed, and headed downstairs to the front terraced deck where they served breakfast. The day was typical for Miami in September: muggy even at eight in the morning, but bright blue skies with nary a cloud. The Atlantic sparkled in the near distance. Already a dozen or so sailboats were passing by on the horizon. A gentle tropical breeze wafted across the tables.

Ben decided to splurge to raise his spirits, and went for the mango waffles. As the tables around him began to fill, his ears were filled with the sounds of many languages: to his left were a French couple, and ahead a German family, the three towheaded children well-behaved and quiet. These were the two tongues he could identify – of the others he was not quite sure.

After eating, he headed for his first event. During the day all activities were located in large, white canvas tents set up on the beach just in front of the dunes. Each tent measured approximately one hundred feet by fifty, and were over thirty feet high at their apex. They were huge. Ben knew the night affairs were at the Miami Beach convention center.

The specific event Ben had first signed up for was the,"Wines of Napa Valley." It was in a tent across from Ocean Drive and 10th Street. He had been given a lanyard which gave him access and unlimited tastings.

Once inside, Ben could not believe his eyes. It appeared as if every Valley vineyard was represented. There were at least seventy-five booths set up along the inner perimeter and down the center of the tent. Some were quite spectacular. The Inglenook display included a stage with a mini-vineyard constructed in the foreground, set against a photographic backdrop of a tantalizing long-range scene from the Valley. As each patron passed a participating vineyard, the vintners invited them to sample a dizzying array of wines and other delicacies, such as Brie, Italian smoked sausage, and in some cases, caviar.

After an hour and a half of traversing the length of the edifice and back again, Ben realized he was getting quite inebriated. His conversations with the distributors grew longer and more animated. Each gave him a glossy brochure with an invitation to come visit their vineyard. Ben was thoroughly enjoying himself. *If only Ralphie could see me now,* he thought with silent satisfaction.

Out of nowhere he heard a voice – distinctly younger and female – call his name from about twenty feet away. He turned the wrong way at first, and the voice said, "No, over here!"

Ben turned around. To his astonishment, there was Samantha, apparently with another young female and guy. She looked great. White short-shorts and turquoise blue halter top, revealing her ample, tanned breasts.

They approached him. Samantha spoke first. "Hey Ben, I thought I might run into you. When you told me about the wine festival, I gave it some thought, and decided to attend a few functions. Had no idea you'd be here today."

Ben was once again struck by her youthful vitality. "It's nice seeing you again, Samantha," he said haltingly. "This *is* a coincidence."

"Hey. By the way. This is Francois and Katarina. They're from Paris. Can you believe the people you meet down here? It's so exciting."

Ben shook the French couple's hands, murmuring how nice it was to meet them. However, each moved in separately and gave him a warm hug and kiss on the cheek.

"I know," Ben said. "I was at my hotel this morning, and I only heard English spoken once during my entire meal. We might as well be in Europe."

Katarina asked, "Avez-vous déjà été en France, ou Paris?"

Francois smiled at her, and said, "She's asking you if you've ever been in France or Paris. She speaks very little English, and believes everyone should speak French."

Katarina, apparently understanding Francois's translation, flashed her light green eyes toward Ben. Although not as classically pretty as Samantha, she had a "joie de vivre" that transcended any physical defects – of which there were very few.

"We were just heading to the 'Wines of Alsace' exhibit. Francois and Katarina know a lot about french wines. It's over on the third aisle. Wanna come with us?" Samantha asked.

"Oui. Venez avec nous," Katarina added.

Ben agreed, and the four went off together to the far end of the tent. The two women went ahead, and Ben found himself walking next to Francois.

"How long have you been in the U.S.?" Ben queried of the Frenchman.

"We're just here for the week. Got into Miami last Sunday. It's our first time. This is an amazing country. Have you ever been to France?"

"No, but I'd like to go sometime. Especially to Paris. I mean, who wouldn't?"

"Paris is the center of the universe, we think. Culturally, intellectually. There is no better place in the world."

"Well, from what I've read, I think you're right."

They arrived at the exhibit. Two young women were dressed in what appeared to be native costumes for the area: white, low cut blouses tied at the waist with red sashes over short black skirts. They were very pretty. The four began sampling the many wines set out on the bar in front of the exhibit. Francois gave a quick description and history of each. He *was* very knowledgeable, Ben concluded.

They proceeded to taste from many of the exhibits over the next several hours. Even though Ben could only communicate briefly with

Katarina, she was so ebullient and cute it didn't make any difference. He just liked being around and looking at her. Francois turned out to be a consummate guide and oenophile. Samantha was also delectable eye candy, and he could not help but notice how she began to hang on him as the day waned.

"Samantha, I think I'm getting a little drunk here," Ben confided. "I got a head start on you."

She giggled and gave him a quick peck on the cheek. "So are we, Ben. Feels good, doesn't it?" Then to the group, she added, "Hey, let's all get something to eat. What d'ya say? I'm famished."

They agreed, and Francois suggested a Thai place within walking distance. The meal was delicious. Toward the end, Samantha spoke up. "Ben, we've been talking about going down to Key West tomorrow and spend the night. None of us have been. Francois and Katarina rented a car and are willing to drive. Wanna come?"

"Key West? I've never been there either. How long a drive is it?"

"It's about four hours, but we plan to make a lot of stops, so it'll be pretty much an all day affair. Should be a lot of fun. Why don't you come?"

"Sounds interesting, but where will we stay?"

"Oh we'll just get some cheap place. I'm sure there are plenty around."

Ben was secretly stunned that he'd been asked. He also had many reservations, like what the sleeping arrangements would be, how many rooms they'd get. But he was still feeling very good and didn't want to appear to be a party pooper. "Okay. I'd love to go. What time do you want to leave?"

Francois piped in. "Why don't we pick you up at your hotel at eight? We'll pull right up front. It'll be fun!"

"Okay. I'm in," Ben proclaimed.

The waiter left the bill on the table. Ben waited a minute, then picked it up and looked at it. He said to the others, "Rather than do all the math as to who owes what, why don't we just split this four ways?" He noticed out of the corner of his eye that Samantha was rifling through her purse with a frustrated look on her face.

"That's fine with us, and we'll do the same with the gas for the trip tomorrow," Francois interjected.

Samantha kept up her search through her purse, and then said to no one in particular, "God damn it. I thought I brought more cash with me. I must have spent it on the tastings, and didn't bring my credit cards 'cause I didn't want them stolen if I got too blasted. Ben, can I borrow my portion from you, and pay you back tomorrow?" She looked up at him with big, slightly teary eyes.

"Of course, Samantha. Don't even worry about it. In fact, since Francois and Katarina have paid for the rental car and all, why don't I just pick up this check?"

When he heard no objection, he paid the bill and they got up to leave. "Don't forget, Ben. Tomorrow at eight sharp," Samantha said.

The three took their leave of Ben and walked out. Well, I guess that's the end of the evening, he thought, and went back to his hotel.

CHAPTER TWENTY-SEVEN

Robbie made good time through Miami, which, he thought, was almost unheard of. Usually the traffic was horrendous, especially along the Dolphin Expressway, the only major route west. Once he got over to the Florida Turnpike, however, the sailing became clear. It was around nine in the morning when he merged onto US Route 1 in Florida City.

He decided to take Card Sound Road, the alternative to continuing on US 1. He had only driven it a few times, and it reminded him of what the Keys must have been like fifty years ago: isolated, back woods, funky. He'd stop at Alabama Jacks for lunch, the one restaurant along the entire stretch of the road, situated just before the little toll booth which had stood there for decades, collecting a buck from each vehicle.

Behind him, only by twenty minutes, Ben and his new friends were speeding down the same road, maintaining a steady pace fifteen miles over the limit. Ben had felt uneasy during most of the trip, as Francois swerved in and out of traffic with abandon, turning to talk to Katarina most of the way. Ben shared the back seat with Samantha. He was beginning to have vague misgivings about the trip. It appeared to him that his three travel partners might have known each other before the prior day at the wine festival. He overheard Katarina tell Francois that Samantha had not liked the French restaurant where they had dined two days before. But he decided not to pursue the subject, afraid he might embarrass or anger the group.

The same sense of unease settled upon him when Francois suggested they take another way to the Keys. The road, angling off to the left from Route 1, seemed to disappear into the mangroves, with no homes or commercial buildings for miles. Dark thoughts infiltrated his brain. *How well did he know these people?* Ben ruminated. *They could find his chopped up body in one of the drainage ditches, or not find it at all. Wait. What was he thinking? Samantha was still her sweet self. The other couple seemed innocuous enough. Got to put these negative feelings behind him.*

Francois announced they were approaching the restaurant. They had already discussed stopping for an early lunch. Ben first saw what looked like an antique toll booth ahead, and then a meandering, low-slung, dilapidated structure to his right. The sign read, "Alabama Jacks." Ben's initial reaction was that they were taking him to a biker bar, which seemed even more accurate when he observed a half dozen Harleys parked to the side.

"Are you sure we want to go in there?" Ben said hesitantly.

Francois responded: "Oui. We've heard it's cheap., and got great food. A couple of Bloody Mary's wouldn't hurt, either. Let's go."

There were only a dozen patrons sitting randomly at a few tables and the small bar. The restaurant opened its full length to the outside at the west end, allowing great views of a large tidal lake and mangroves. Huge Tarpon, some over four feet long, lounged just over the railing, waiting for the scraps cast by the diners.

They took a table next to the water, and Ben's companions all ordered Bloody's. Not wanting to look stodgy, he did the same. That first round gave way to two others, the three urging Ben to partake and "loosen up," even before any food was ordered. Ben noticed a younger man, well-dressed for the occasion, seated and eating at the bar. He seemed to be paying attention to their discourse.

By the time the food arrived, Ben realized he was three-quarters in the bag. It would have been an altogether pleasant experience except that he became increasingly embarrassed by the loud, and sometimes profane, conversation of his new friends – especially Francois, who, as it turned out, was equally proficient at swearing in both English and French. At one point their waitress came over and asked them to keep it down because some guests were complaining.

Ben excused himself to use the bathroom, which, to his chagrin, he found was a one seater and already occupied. As he waited close to the door, the young man he had seen at the bar came around the corner, obviously with the same purpose in mind. They said a cursory "hello," and then waited in silence. The wait became interminable, and a little disquieting. Finally the young man said, "Looks like we got here at the wrong time."

"If this guy in there doesn't hurry up, I'm going to have to go in the water," Ben said half-jokingly.

"Me too," the man said. "By the way, I'm Robbie," extending his hand. Ben shook it and introduced himself.

"What brings you down this way?" Robbie continued.

"Just a little get away for the Miami Wine Festival. First time I've been away from the family for a lark like this in a long . . . well . . . ever."

"You're a way from Miami. And who are your friends?"

"Just some people I met in Miami. They decided to go to Key West for an overnight, and invited me."

"How long have you known them?"

"Not long. Why do you ask?" Ben said with a little annoyance in his voice.

"I'm not trying to butt in where I shouldn't," Robbie replied. "But I've lived in the Miami area all of my life. You get to know some of the types around the city. If you're new, you have to be careful. There are a lot of con men out there. Or con women, too. The guy – the one with the french accent – bothers me. I've seen his kind. All I'm saying is, protect yourself."

"Oh I'll do that. I'm not as naïve as I may seem. But thanks anyway."

Because they were still waiting, Ben asked Robbie why he was going to the Keys. Robbie explained what he did for a living and what had transpired over the past day. Then he continued, "You need to keep an eye on this tropical disturbance coming across the Atlantic. It headed north toward Bermuda a day or so ago, but there're indications it's turned, and may be heading for south Florida. Just wanted you to know."

"Thanks. I appreciate that, especially from a weatherman. A good friend mentioned it before I came down here. I also heard it was going north, but I'll keep an eye on it."

"I tell you what. Here, take my card. It's got my cell number. Give me a call if you need to."

"Oh thanks," Ben said with little conviction in his voice.

At that moment the bathroom door opened, and the occupant

walked out. Ben went in, used the toilet and returned to the table, with Robbie's warnings still ringing in his ears.

CHAPTER TWENTY-EIGHT

The sailors put everything into maxing out the speed of their vessel. Sailing can be very hard work. They had to keep the sails close, mostly on a starboard tack, as the wind was blowing almost directly from the south. But Bermuda lay more south than southeast, so they had to come about every hour. Mark kept adjusting the lines to goose every knot out of the increasing winds. Each little luff had to be ironed out by skillful seamanship. They made good time, averaging over six knots.

In the early afternoon they decided to take a break from the constant labor, and went below to make some sandwiches. The seas were only two to three feet, so the food preparation went quickly. They took their plates back above board and relaxed for a few minutes.

Jenn took a dainty bite, and opened the conversation: "Mark, I don't mean to get too personal, but I was wondering. How come such a cool, good-looking guy didn't get snatched up after his first marriage? What's it been? Five years?"

"Almost exactly five. I've thought a lot about that. Maybe it's because I deem my divorce one of the biggest failures in my life. I'm not mired in that thought, but I believe it's made me very careful, if not a little gun shy. I also have to add that I haven't met anyone I've come close to wanting to marry. As I told you, a number of girlfriends, but no friends, if you know what I mean. If I find the right person, I'll know it because I'll want to be friends and companions first, lovers second."

"That's the first time I've heard someone express in words exactly how I feel. In the past I tended to become infatuated with a man. Maybe it was his good looks, maybe his intellect. So the sex came too quickly, and the relationship became all about the physical.

"I've now learned what's far more important is finding someone with like interests, with whom I feel comfortable, with whom I can converse easily. And probably the most important thing, a guy who doesn't always have to be right, and doesn't argue over every perceived slight. That was my last one . . . Rick. It got to the point where it seemed we battled over everything. I ended up not even liking myself."

Mark loosened the main sheet a notch. The weather had gradually cleared, and the warmth of the sun was welcome.

"I know that part well . . . the not liking myself in a relationship. Amazing, isn't it? That we can get to the point with someone where we behave like a stranger to ourselves. And probably to the other person as well."

"Yeah it is."

They both became quiet, lost in their own thoughts. It wasn't uncomfortable. The motion of the boat and air and sea offered just enough distraction.

After a few hours, Mark went below to chart their progress, and that of the storm. Several faxes had come in, and the satellite imagery was updated. He poured over the new information, a broad grin forming. In fact, he couldn't believe his eyes.

He shouted up toward the companionway door: "Jenn. Can you come down here a minute? If it's not on auto, go ahead and put it on. I want you to see this."

Jennifer switched on the autopilot and went below, her concern showing in her blanched complexion. She was scared the news was not good, even though Mark's tone was decidedly upbeat.

"What's up?"

"Jenn, you're not going to believe this. First, the good news is that we've made incredible time. But the really good news is that the storm has taken a sudden and dramatic turn back toward the coast. Right now it's heading due west, toward Florida. If it keeps on that track, we've got nothing to worry about. Maybe some rough seas, or storm surge, but no hurricane or tropical force winds."

"That's the best news I could hear," Jennifer exclaimed. "I guess I can tell you now I was very worried. I didn't want to show it so I wouldn't distract you."

"Jenn, I was worried too. There's nothing to be ashamed of in that."

"What are the chances it will change direction again, and come at us? It's done that now. Who's to say it won't do it again?"

"It could. But right now all the forecasters have it maintaining its westerly path and hitting the coast of Florida. In another twelve hours, Bermuda will be well east of it, so even if it heads north again, we won't get a direct, or even glancing blow. For now though, I think we can relax a little. We've worked hard. I'll check its trajectory regularly, but now let's celebrate with a little bubbly."

"Hey, we were going to save that for our arrival in Bermuda."

"We've got two bottles, one cold. This is momentous. Let's have the one on ice now, and we'll still have the other when we get there.

Okay?"

"You don't have to twist my arm on this one," Jennifer said with a twinkle in her eye.

****

Another eye was picking up speed across the ocean, widening its orbit, spewing ferocious winds outward, sucking up and spitting out sea water in torrents. Looking for its next victims.

CHAPTER TWENTY-NINE

The Lockheed WP-3D Orion aircraft barely made it airborne by the time it hit the end of the runway at MacDill Air Force Base in Tampa Florida. There were only two of these craft in the NOAA's hurricane hunter fleet – the civilian counterpart to the military's WC-130J– this one named "Miss Piggy," the other "Kermit." It was distinguishable because of its long, "barber pole" striped nose extension, which housed the highly durable C-Band radar.

"Whew. That was a bit close for comfort," Captain Jay Cross said to no one in particular in the cockpit. "Exactly how much fuel did they load into this baby, anyway?"

The Captain did not have the military bearing of the other pilots in the group. About forty-five, his shaggy, long mane of hair often raised the hackles of the top brass in the NOAA. Yet no one could fly better, or under more extreme circumstances, than Cross. His ability to fix anything, anywhere, was also legendary. The Captain kept a bevy of classic Volkswagens that he had maintained in perfect running condition for over thirty-five years. If a part broke, and he couldn't find a replacement, he'd just go into his workshop and fashion one.

Jack Porter, the Senior Flight Director, who was standing at the doorway separating the cockpit from the fuselage, answered first: "As far as I know they filled us to capacity, almost five thousand gallons. Hope that gets us through the storm and all the way to the Cape Verde Islands."

"That's you and me both, Jack. I've never done a mission like this – a combo reconnaissance and rescue."

"It *is* unusual. But that's where our craft excels. We can fly higher and faster than any of the other weather planes."

"Roger that," Bart McCullough, the copilot piped in.

"I just finished analyzing the latest data on this bohemoth. What I don't like about this one is the wider cone of uncertainty we see," Jack continued. "It has the wildest mix of track models I've ever seen. Looks like a damn bowl of ramon noodles."

"Amazing turnaround, too," the Captain said. "I've only seen a few that have made such a radical shift in direction."

"Daemon has its own personality, that's for sure," Porter said. "Our eye in the sky shows an ever-increasing perimeter. It's at about five hundred miles now."

Jack returned to his station. They crossed over the breadth of Florida in a half hour flying at a speed of almost four hundred miles per hour. The storm lay almost directly to the east at a distance of six hundred miles. It would take them a little under two hours to reach the outer bands, assuming they met no other obstacles in their path. They remained silent as they prepared their instrumentation for the onslaught.

"Okay, boys, buckle up and get ready. We're coming into a pretty good area of turbulence now," the Captain warned.

Jack had already seen the area of magenta in the center of his radar screen, signifying the most vicious weather. "Yep, it's gonna get real bumpy from here on out. I see a lot of energy building here."

There was only one way to gather the information they needed, and that was to locate and fly directly into the center of the hurricane.

On the way they had to try to avoid the "high towers," huge thunder heads that extended far into the atmosphere and contained within their hellish interiors the most intense and damaging winds and weather. If one took a cross section of a hurricane, it would look like layers of consecutive spiral bands of ferocious thunderstorms.

The satellite imagery gave them the general location of the eye: general because the storm was constantly moving, shifting, like an experienced criminal evading the police.

"We're right on target," the Director said. "We should reach the midpoint in about an hour."

The turbulence took on a new dimension as they approached the eye. The craft, as steady and strong as she was, plummeted and lifted up again, sometimes fifty or sixty feet in one or two seconds. It was like riding on an insane elevator where every ten seconds the cart would free fall several floors down the shaft and then shoot back to the top at high speeds.

"Okay men. Just double-checking. All strapped in. The equipment is nailed down tight?"

"Roger Captain," they all reported back in unison.

"What's the barometer reading, Jack?" the Captain asked.

There was a moment of hesitation, and Jack came on the intercom. "I think I'm reading this right. But I can't believe it. It's below nine hundred millibars and falling rapidly. I've never seen a reading that low."

"I hope there's some ice on the transponder," the Captain retorted. "That's impossible. How about winds?"

Again a brief delay in the response from Jack. "Steady one hundred, gusting to one twenty-five. That puts her into category four territory."

A noticeable shuddering of the plane started at the nose and worked its way to the tail. The craft started tipping wildly from right to left and back again. In a moment the plane did an entire three sixty in the air, somehow ending upright.

"Jesus Christ!" the copilot screamed. "What in the fuck was that?"

"We just rolled. I don't think Piggy can take another one of those." The Captain focused on controlling the ship, increasing the speed to get through the mayhem as quickly as possible. "What's our air speed, Bart?"

"Four hundred and eighty knots," he replied. "We're at max speed."

"I couldn't go any slower if I wanted. We're being sucked into the vacuum around the eye."

In only minutes, the bedlam around them slowly quieted. Their speed declined to a comfortable four hundred. There was an eeriness about them. They could now look upward and see clear, bright blue. It was like coasting on a cloud.

"This is the eye, men. Look at that clearing above. Fantastic!"

The plane had entered into a vast, relatively calm circular area, surrounded on all sides by mountainous cumulonimbus clouds extending thousands of yards into the heavens. The onboard radio, and even their intercoms, began emitting a high-pitched cackling sound – almost like some evil being was mimicking the sound of static. It grew louder and louder, then stopped. The four men looked at each other, startled, not speaking.

At almost the same time, the plane lurched forward, as if propelled by some unseen force.

“We're back on the toboggan run, guys. It's kicking us out.”

The Lockheed craft shot out of the eye as a ball out of a slingshot. Air speed increased to five hundred and fifty knots, well above the plane's capacity. A prolonged scream, from four grown men, filled the interior of the craft, as rivets began popping and metal twisted.

CHAPTER THIRTY

Zoe awoke first. She figured she snatched, maybe, three hours of good sleep. But her adrenaline kicked in when she thought about the work they had to do to continue to survive under these circumstances.

The others were still sleeping soundly. The early morning sun was just now coming over the horizon, the new beams falling upon Aaron's face. She realized how darkly handsome he was. His face, now clean of all dirt and debris and relaxed in repose, revealed his sturdy chin, angular jaw, and prominent cheekbones and well-shaped nose.

Her ankle was still throbbing and swollen to twice its normal size. Zoe tore two strips from the curtain Aaron had supplied as bed coverings and bound her foot as best she could. She went into the bathroom and cleaned up quickly – pits, crotch and ass, as her daddy always used to say. When she returned to the room where they had spent the night, everyone was up.

"Hey. Good morning all," she chirped.

A very groggy group responded, "Good morning," or "Bom Dia."

"How'd everyone sleep?" Zoe continued.

Aaron liked the way she maintained her joyfulness, despite the circumstances, without being obnoxious. She simply came across as a genuinely happy and friendly person. He said, "I've had better nights, to be truthful. Some very strange dreams. Of course, I can't remember any of them."

Marcia said, "I'll feel better as soon as I wash up and use the bathroom. Who wants to go first?"

"I just finished. There's still plenty of paper towels left, but all the monogrammed bathrobes are gone," Zoe said with a cute smile.

Now it was Aaron's turn to notice how pretty Zoe was. About 5'3", slim but well endowed in the right places, with short cut blond hair and expressive green eyes. She was quite a package. Then he saw the make-shift bandages. "What's that?" he asked.

"My ankle was a little swollen this morning so I braced it."

"That looks pretty nasty," Aaron said. "It's really blown up."

"I'll be okay."

"Well let's keep a close eye on it." Aaron privately marveled at the girl's fortitude.

Both Aaron and Pedro motioned Marcia toward the bathroom with their arms, and smiled at each other at the fact that they had gestured in unison. Aaron said to Pedro, "What about the volcano? Is it a danger to us?"

"Too early to tell. It could do this for months . . . or it could erupt today. But I think we'll be okay for several weeks. It's just getting warmed up. But we have to keep an eye on it."

"That's all we need. A double whammy of natural catastrophes," Aaron said. "I think we're beyond the point where anyone will care if we break into the vending machines. I don't see any other food or drink around, and we're out of change. Pedro, why don't you come with me and let's see if we can find something that will accomplish the task."

Pedro acknowledged his agreement, and they began searching around the building. It didn't take long for them to find a small toolbox in a utility closet, and inside the box a claw hammer and chisel. It took some effort, but they finally bashed through the locks and latches on the machines and quickly emptied the contents: bags of chips, fritos, cookies and chocolate, together with soda and water. Enough to fill their stomachs for a few days, albeit with little nutritional value.

Marcia was now out of the lavatory, and Pedro smiled at her and said, "Meu bonito. Vem. Vamos comer." She approached the group, famished and ready to eat anything.

They agreed they'd only share several of the snacks at this time, and some water. It was enough to take the edge off their hunger.

Finally, Aaron said, "Okay, we should go exploring. I suggest we stay together, at least at first. Natural disasters like this don't always bring out the best in people. We don't know who, or what is out there. Plus, Pedro and Marcia will be able to communicate with anyone we meet if they don't speak English. Why don't we start with the area around the airport, and then spread out to the town."

The agreement to Aaron's plan was unanimous. He grabbed the hammer and chisel, and gave the latter to Pedro to carry on the journey. As Aaron had already done a reconnaissance of the airport buildings, they did a quick walk around. They detected no living entities, human or otherwise. Zoe observed that Pedro and Marcia were becoming visibly upset.

"Everywhere we look, there's nothing but devastation," Marcia said to the group. "I am so sad for my country and its people. Since leaving our shelter under the rock, it looks like the end of the world has come upon us."

She started sobbing gently, and Pedro moved quickly to comfort her. He said to the others, "We need to get to a telephone as quickly as possible. I'm guessing there will be a lot of news coverage of the hurricane's impact on Cape Verde. We don't want our children to worry about us. They need to know we're safe and sound."

Aaron agreed. "That should be one of our priorities. That, and giving aid to anyone we find who needs it."

They continued into the Town of Sao Felipe, once the home to about eight thousand denizens. Not a single person was seen. Most of the structures were nothing more than piles of pick-up sticks. The combination of raging winds and extreme storm surge had wreaked its havoc everywhere.

The Cape Verdean couple separated themselves from the group and wandered disconsolately among the ruins. Their favorite market, where they used to purchase their bread and milk almost every day, was barely recognizable. They rejoined Aaron and Zoe.

Zoe suddenly shouted: "Look! Down at the end of the street. I see two people!"

From that distance they could not make out whether they were men or women, or how old they were. They seemed to be trying each door of the standing buildings, and shouting into the ruins. Aaron said, "I hope they aren't looters," and felt for the handle of the hammer looped onto his belt.

The four walked more brisquely, and soon Zoe, who appeared to have the best eyes, exclaimed again: "It's two men. In uniform. I think they're police."

Marcia confirmed her conclusion. "Yes, I see. Dois Policia. Hallo!"

The two men, who now clearly could be seen as local gendarmes, approached them with salutations. They spoke in Portuguese, with a little mix of native creole, and Pedro translated for Aaron and Zoe. As they came closer, Aaron noticed their uniforms were ill-fitting and very dirty. They carried no weapons.

"They say all the residents were evacuated just before the storm. All the coastal towns, like Sao Felipe, were emptied, and the people sent to towns further up the side of the volcano. So that's where everyone is," Pedro told Aaron and Zoe.

"Did they say how many people may have died?" Aaron asked.

Marcia asked a question in Portuguese, and after a reply from one of them, said, "There are no good estimates. They just don't know yet. They suggest we find safe shelter for a few days until help, from whatever source, arrives."

"Alright," Aaron said. "Let's keep looking around, especially down by the ocean to see if we can find anyone alive. We should also be looking for more food and water."

They took their leave from the law enforcement officers and slowly made their way to the coast. As they rounded a bend in the cobblestone roadway, the shoreline became visible. Zoe let out a gasp. Marcia just wailed. The men instinctively held the women. Because, there, laid out in stark detail for them, were thousands upon thousands of bloated bodies, some awash on the beach, most still lazily floating in the undulating sea, with millions upon millions of flies covering their exposed flesh.

CHAPTER THIRTY-ONE

Robbie left the restaurant and made a beeline for Key West. Card Sound Road merged with U.S. 1 about five miles south and west of Alabama Jacks, and the road became two lanes in both directions through Key Largo. The way was always slow going because the highway vacillated between one and two lanes, and the speed limit varied from a low of twenty-five through Marathon, to a high of fifty-five south of it.

It was around 12:30 in the afternoon when he pulled up in front of the Key West National Weather Station on White Street. The building was easy to locate with the odd, slanting chrome columns supporting the overhang, and large satellite dish rising some thirty feet high just beyond the station.

He climbed the ten stairs to the front door, which announced the availability of tours in a streaming red neon sign above. He knew from his prior visit that the first floor was specifically designed to rise fourteen feet above sea level, the highest storm surge at that location since such records were kept. He also knew the station contained within its interior a Storm Center, a highly fortified emergency control room that could withstand winds up to two hundred and fifty miles per hour.

He pushed the button to the right side of the door, and within seconds a young man rounded the corner, smiled, and let him in. "Mr. Stewart, I presume," he said pleasantly. "I'm Nathan Goldstein, an intern here at the station. Larry Grimes told me you'd be here about now. Come in. He's expecting you."

Robbie shook his hand, and proceeded through the lobby which contained various large, stand-up placards describing many of the great storms that had struck the Florida Keys, and valuable information on the formation and life of hurricanes. Going through a locked door, he first entered an office area blocked off with partitions, and then into the main room, called the Operations Room, which was now abuzz with activity. Large computer screens sat upon numerous desks of varying sizes. There were at least ten staffers filling almost every seat.

Larry came out of an enclosed area behind Robbie. Robbie turned to an outstretched hand. "Nice to meet you, finally," Larry said. "How was your trip down?"

"It's a beautiful ride, but I wish I could have done it at a more leisurely pace. How's it going here?"

"Well not so good now. Come with me, please."

They entered into the enclosed area from which Grimes had just exited, and then into a doorway that was cut into what looked like a large concrete block tank. Robbie immediately recognized it as the Storm Center.

"What's up?"

"We were just contacted by the plane we sent out of Tampa. We've got a big problem out there."

****

When Ben returned to the table, he said, "Guess what? I just met a weatherman outside the men's room. He's coming from Miami to the station down in Key West. Said there's a large storm heading this way. We should keep a close eye on it."

His three new acquaintances looked at each other with bemused expressions. Samantha said, "Oh Ben, you worry wart. There are storms that pass through here all the time. It's nothing to worry about."

Francois insisted they have another round of Bloodies. By the time they settled the bill, Ben had quite a buzz on. They headed out of Alabama's a half hour after Robbie left.

Samantha wanted to stop next at Lorelei, an outdoor restaurant in Islamorada, just south of Key Largo. Francois always hovered ten to fifteen miles over the speed limit regardless of the traffic. They made it to their next stop in less than a half hour.

Lorelei was beautiful. It consisted of a large outdoor bar at the start of a sandy peninsula jutting out into the Gulf, followed by tables, chairs and a second smaller bar farther out the beach. Two large covered gliders with two opposing bench seats capable of holding four people sat near the water. It was a clear, sunny late morning and the shallow water reflected back azure motifs.

They took seats at one of the beach tables and Francois ordered another round of Bloody Mary's for everyone. Ben thought about protesting, but it was three against one, and he was feeling too passive to voice an objection.

"How long will it take to get to Key West from here," he asked.

"Depends on how many more stops we make," Samantha said with a chuckle. "I've got at least two more on my list. Francois and Katarina, where else do you want to go?"

Katarina answered first. "We've heard there's a cool Tiki Bar just before the Seven Mile Bridge. Beside that, we'll follow your lead."

"As long as we arrive in Key West good and drunk, that's all I care about," Francois piped in. The three younger people in the group laughed openly at this.

Ben was now realizing both of his French companions spoke much better English then they had originally let on. Robbie's warnings began ringing in his ears.

"Shouldn't we appoint a designated driver at this point?" Ben asked. "I mean I'd hate to see anyone get into trouble."

"Aw, c'mon Ben," Samantha said. "Don't be an old stick in the mud. Francois is a professional drunk driver. He knows how not to get caught. Right, Francois?"

"C'est ca," said Francois with a smirk. "And if I drive off one of the bridges, then we'll all just go swimming." Again, another round of guffawing from the three. Ben tried his best to disguise his discomfort.

They finished their drinks, and continued south. Just before the seven mile bridge in southern Marathon, they took a left into the Sunset Tiki Bar. This was again a large, open air restaurant with an oblong bar overlooking a pool and the bridge. Another spectacular setting, Ben thought as they took their seats on the veranda above the light blue pool.

To Ben's chagrin, the Frenchman ordered even more drinks for everyone, this time switching to Mango Margaritas. Ben said nothing. He excused himself to use the bathroom, and looked at himself in the mirror. His face was flushed, and even now he could detect the edges of bloodshot in his eyes. *Okay, Ben me boy,* he said to himself. *Exactly what do you think you're doing? This isn't a second childhood. You're just an old fool.* At that moment Ben decided that, when they got to Key West, he was going to go his own way and get a separate room.

Returning to the table, he disguised his angst as best he could, and joined in the merriment. The Margarita tasted great. As he drank, he felt a sense of euphoria he had never before experienced. The gorgeous day, the palm trees swaying in the wind, even his company seemed especially funny and entertaining. The only unpleasant experience was the slight spinning, or loss of equilibrium he felt. In less than a half hour, Ben would at best be able to recall brief snatches of reality as his brain struggled against the drug poured into his drink by Katarina while he had excused himself.

CHAPTER THIRTY-TWO

Jennifer, after some effort as the champagne had been stored away carefully, found both bottles. Mark uncorked one, shook it slightly, and sprayed her playfully with a little foam. Jennifer took it all in stride, and they made short work of the magnum.

"I don't know if the weather has really cleared, or a weight has been removed from my shoulders," Mark said. "All I know is, that sun feels warmer and looks brighter."

"I think it's shining more brightly. But I feel the same way. A burden has been lifted from my soul," Jennifer replied.

"Of course, the bubbly doesn't hurt either."

"No it doesn't. I think champagne is the best high around," Jennifer said as she took another sip. "Well, except maybe a little pot. The combo isn't that bad either."

"So you've tried pot," Mark said with a smirk on his lips.

"Oh, sometimes. But I've never inhaled." They both laughed.

"I used to smoke a lot," Mark said as he refilled their glasses. "In college. And I do agree it's less detrimental than alcohol. But I've found I don't work as well, or clearly, if I'm hungover on either grass or booze. So I've tended to stay away from both. Except for special occasions like this, of course."

"Well you know I like my splash of wine every so often. A toke every once in a while is not too shabby either."

"No it isn't."

They both drank quietly, enjoying the salt air and breezes. Mark interrupted the silence first. "Jenn, the other day you asked me about why I haven't remarried since my divorce. That also got me thinking. I can't believe you haven't established a permanent relationship since your last break up. Is it the same thing, you just haven't found the right guy?"

Jennifer looked down, and for the first time Mark saw a hint of the same sadness he had detected in the initial photograph included in her letter to him when responding to his ad. This time it did not ease away. "I've got something to tell you, Mark. I feel so bad over not telling you sooner. I just didn't know the right time or place."

"What is it, Jenn? You know you can tell me anything."

"I realize I can. But this is so difficult." She still had trouble looking Mark in the eye as she continued. "I was married once. About five years ago. We had one child, a little boy, Jared. A year ago, when he was three, I was driving him to the park. My husband was at work. Somehow Jared got one of the straps from his car seat undone. To this day I don't know how he did it.

"They say I wasn't at fault. After the accident they checked it and said it was properly latched. But we got broadsided by a large SUV which had run a stop sign. I was saved by the side door air bag, but there weren't any in the back. My son's head smashed into the window."

At this Jennifer had to pause. Tears were dripping from her eyes. "He died four days later in the hospital. Never regained consciousness."

"But it wasn't your fault," Mark pleaded. "You couldn't have done anything about it."

"Well, that's easy to say. I've gone over it in my mind a thousand times . . . ten thousand times . . . how I could have prevented it. In any event, my husband and I couldn't work through it. We separated three months after the accident, and divorced six months after that."

"I'm sorry, Jenn. I had no idea. I don't blame you at all for not telling me about this before now." Mark leaned over and took her in his arms gently and allowed her to work out her grief on his shoulder.

"I didn't realize how guilty I still feel until I heard that storm had turned toward us the other day. I know this is going to sound crazy, but I actually thought that maybe, just maybe, God, or whoever, was directing that storm into my path as retribution for my failure to protect my son. That's why I was doubly relieved when I heard it had changed its path away from us."

"Guilt is a powerful emotion," Mark said. "It's my personal opinion that one of the reasons religion is so important to mankind is that all religions, in one form or another, offer relief from guilt. Atonement. A figure, like Christ, who died so that we can live free from guilt. Someone once pointed out to me that the word atonement could be broken up to spell 'at – one – ment,' which means that we can never feel at one with ourselves, or with God, if we are ridden with guilt, debilitated by it.

"In fact, the word guilt comes from an Old English word meaning 'to pay a debt.' Unless we get to the point where we feel we have satisfied our obligations for something we perceive we did wrong, we will always be anxious. Obsessive compulsive disorder is a major byproduct of guilt."

"You're absolutely right," Jennifer said. "I have suffered from pretty serious depression for many months now. I've made a lot of progress, but have a lot more ahead. Meeting you, Mark, and going on this trip, has done wonders for me, and I really appreciate it."

Jennifer kissed him, first lightly on the lips, then more passionately, as they, for the first time, began to explore each other's mouths, necks and bodies. They ultimately found themselves in Mark's bunk, sweaty and fully sated.

CHAPTER THIRTY-THREE

The plane hurtled through the angry, chaotic morass. Captain Cross used every trick, honed over decades of flying every craft imaginable, to keep it on course and in the air. After what seemed an inestimable time, he shouted into his headset, "I think we're through the worst of it. How's our fuel?"

Bart checked his gauges, and replied, "We're doing well. Plenty enough to get to Cape Verde. We're about seven hundred miles west of Fogo now."

"Okay. We've got a little instability with the rudder, but that's all the damage I can feel right now. I can't believe we made it out of there in one piece."

Jack Porter spoke up: "That's the biggest storm I've ever flown into. Did you see those wind speeds and that barometric pressure? Off the charts!"

"Were you able to get the information back home, Jack?" Jay asked.

"They got it all, even though I bet they won't believe it."

"Well it's not April Fool's yet. They better believe it, and sound the alarm. If this thing ever gets near the coast, it's going to do unbelievable damage."

"It will at that. I'm now recalculating the direction and speed of the storm. I'll shoot that back to them as well."

Bart interrupted. "Wonder what we're going to find when we get to the Islands? We can't get anyone out there: no radio, cell, anything. The coordinates sent by our boys put them right at the Sao Felipe airport."

"I don't know that one at all," the Captain said.

"I've actually been there before. It's tiny, but the runway's in good condition, and is longer than most in that area. We should have no problem landing," Bart interjected.

"That's welcome news. I don't know how many more bumps and jolts Miss Piggy can take. She needs a break."

The crew remained silent for a while, as the Captain listened and watched carefully for any signs of additional damage, and Jack relayed further information to the base.

Bart blurted out, "There's land straight ahead, at about eleven o'clock. That must be one of the westernmost of the islands of Cape Verde."

They began passing more of the chain, but at twelve thousand feet, could not pick out any details below. Soon the Captain announced that they should prepare for landing. He lowered the vessel from twelve, to ten, and then to five thousand feet. Now they could clearly make out the white beaches of the tiny island and volcanic cone of Pico de Fogo.

As they completed their descent, and were at five hundred feet coming over the ocean into the small airport, Bart exclaimed, "What's all that floating in the water, and spread out over the beach? Are they logs, or pieces of driftwood?"

"I can't quite make them out," the Captain answered. Then he hesitated a few seconds. "Wait! Holy crap! Those are bodies. Hundreds.

Thousands of them. What in God's name happened here?"

Bart, looking out over the floating and rotting carnage, and then seeing the total destruction of the buildings and planes around the airport, replied, "Whatever it was, it was not of God."

The plane touched once, then twice, before finally settling into a roll. Jay taxied to the one still standing building, marked Immigration. They remained in their seats for a good five minutes, slowly digesting the magnitude of the disaster that awaited them.

CHAPTER THIRTY-FOUR

Zoe instinctively turned away from the horrific scene. Marcia was already leaning unsteadily on Pedro's arm.

"Let's get out of here," Aaron shouted. "Back to the airport. We've got to start stockpiling food and water. Pretty soon this harbor area is going to be a bed of festering pestilence unless some miracle occurs."

Without another word they turned around and headed back. As they approached the main road connecting the town with the airport, their view of the highlands around the volcano was cleared. It was Zoe who first noticed. "Aren't those people coming down from the mountain?"

Aaron looked, then looked again. All he could see at this point were dots of color – many of them, some reds, blues, whites – moving zigzag across the upper slopes. "It must be, but I can't quite tell."

"I can actually see some horses and donkeys. The colors must be men, women and children. They're streaming toward us. Those must be the ones who evacuated. They've survived."

Emboldened by the fact that there were so many who had lived through the melee, the four quickened their pace to their destination. As they rounded a small copse of trees on a hillock overlooking the airport, Aaron stopped, and pointed: "Look. Another plane. There on the tarmac near our building. It looks like an NOAA Hunter. They must have been sent out to look for us."

Aaron ran up ahead. Just as he was approaching the plane, the lower hatch, located in the belly, opened, and an aluminum ladder descended from the bowels of the vessel. One, then a total of four men emptied out and approached Aaron. By this time Zoe had joined him.

"Major Hotchkiss, we presume," Captain Cross said, extending his hand. "It's great to see that you made it."

Aaron shook the hands of each of the crew, while they introduced themselves. "You guys sure are a sight for sore eyes. But you've come into a difficult situation. Until about a half hour ago, we weren't sure anyone else had survived on this island. Now we can see many coming down the mountain. I fear there will be a lot of injuries."

"Major, where are the rest of your crew?"

"I know Commander Rogerson is dead. The copilot O'Conner disappeared and is presumed dead. The same with the civilian passenger we had on board."

"Well, we need to assess the situation, and then radio back for assistance. But our primary mission is to retrieve you and return to the United States where we'll all be of better service," Cross said. "I just don't think we'll be able to make it in Miss Piggy there. She's pretty beat up."

"I appreciate that, but I couldn't possibly leave if I could be of use here . . . even if we had anything to fly out in. As you can see," Aaron said as he swept his arm around the airport, "there's nothing left. I've taken enough triage and first aid courses to help out, at least."

"And I have as well," piped in Zoe.

"Major, as far as I'm concerned, you're in charge here," Captain Cross said. "Looks like we'll be staying awhile ourselves. What do you suggest we do first?"

"We need to find food and water, foremost," Aaron replied. "After that, we need to set up a triage area for any of the wounded. Only then can we worry about getting help here."

"Sounds good to me," Cross said. "Why don't I and my crew look for supplies, and the four of you attend to the first aid."

"You got it. And then we'll fill in where needed. We're going to set up shop in the immigration building where we spent the night. Good luck."

Aaron, Zoe, Pedro and Maria headed for the building, while Cross and his men spread out to search the airport area. Once inside, the four began arranging the chairs into cots about six feet in length. Pedro tried each interior door, and discovered a supply closet which provided a bundle of clean rags and some rubbing alcohol which could be used as an antiseptic.

They had just organized the chairs when the advance group of those coming down from the side of the volcano arrived. The first two were the apparent police they had encountered earlier. A family of three next came through the door, then a larger unrelated group of four men. All were bedraggled, wet and dirty. None was seriously injured, just dehydrated and hungry. One of the men appeared to be especially distraught, his hair tangled and wild. He muttered incomprehensible words, and would not meet anyone's eyes. Aaron and Zoe began to parcel out their small stock of water and snacks, which were quickly devoured.

Pedro and Marcia spoke to both groups in Portuguese for a few minutes. Pedro then turned to Aaron: "They say they took refuge in some of the small caves that abound in the hills. They also say they have never witnessed a storm like that. One claims he could feel the rocks move around him. Two of the men got separated from their families. Hopefully those will make it down here as well. I also don't think the two we met earlier are really *policia*."

Just then Bart McCollough came through the door alone. He was carrying a large box on his shoulder, which he had to adjust awkwardly to get through the entrance way. Zoe had at first been taken aback by the general scruffiness of the new crew. Bart was especially disconcerting: a large, dark, menacing man whose bushy black eyebrows formed a heavy, solid line above his eyes. She noticed he was also limping. He set the box on one of the seats. "We've got a few things here. Some gallon jugs filled with potable water, and some medical kits I found in one of the outer buildings."

"That's great," Zoe said. "What happened to your leg?"

"I stepped on a nail that was lodged in a board. I'm okay, though," he said roughly.

"Well let me take a look at it. You'll be my first patient."

Zoe sat Bart down and removed his flight boot and sock. The sock was already soaked with blood. It was a bad puncture wound. The nail had pierced through the think rubber sole and into the skin by a half inch.

"I didn't even know the nail was still in there. Guess I should have removed my shoe right away."

"Well, let's see what we can do now. This may hurt for a second."

Zoe squeezed the area around the wound with her thumb and

forefinger, and got it bleeding again. "We need to try to get any poisons out with the blood, and then clean around it." Zoe felt, rather than observed, the intense scrutiny which McCollough directed at her as she worked.

In one of the medical kits she found some bandages, but no antiseptic. "I'm going to use this rubbing alcohol and dilute it with some water. It's not perfect, but it should do the job."

"I appreciate this honey," Bart said. "Wish we could have met under different circumstances. Like a place where we could have a private drink."

Zoe ignored the comment, and turned her face away so he could not see the rising blush on her face.

As Zoe completed the bandaging, Jay Cross and Jack Porter entered the building. They were carrying stacks of clothing under each arm.

"We found a cache of clothes in some suitcases that were left in the baggage claim area," Jay said. "They're dry, miraculously. We need a few extra hands to carry them back."

Aaron turned to Pedro. "Pedro, can you ask some of the men here if they can help?"

Pedro did, and three men volunteered and went out with the NOAA crew to retrieve more clothing. Zoe went around the group to check on their condition. One man sat away from everyone, in the far corner, his eyes fixated on some unseen point in the air. He was the especially filthy one they had first noticed.

Aaron's attention was drawn to that corner. He realized it was

Zoe's stifled cry that caused him to turn rapidly and look. The man was now standing, his arms fully extended in front of him, his hands tightly throttling Zoe's neck. She was literally being forced up in the air, her legs pedaling hopelessly. A demonic look enveloped his face.

It took Aaron less than a second to bound over two rows of chairs and clothesline the guy in the throat with a stiff left arm. The man was thrown backward against the wall, but still somehow maintained his grasp around Zoe's throat. Aaron next threw a straight right hand jab to the assailant's nose, breaking it with a harsh crunch. Still he held his death grip on Zoe, who was now turning blue, her eyes glazed with terror. Aaron began pummeling him with multiple lefts and rights to his body and head, to no avail.

Out of nowhere Pedro appeared with a serrated hunting knife, and in one clean swipe, opened the man's jugular into a gaping second mouth. Only then did he release his grip and put his hands to his own throat, blood spurting between his fingers. He leaned unsteadily against the wall for a few seconds, then slumped slowly to the floor. Zoe also collapsed at his feet.

Aaron picked her up and carried her to one of the previously arranged cots. She was breathing, but barely. Aaron held her closely, telling her everything was going to be okay, that she should try to breath slowly. After a minute or two, her shuddering stopped, her breathing became regular, and she was able to calm herself.

She gasped: "My God, Aaron. He had superhuman strength. What was that?"

"I don't know, Zoe. He was crazed. But he won't be bothering you again, or anyone else for that matter."

As the dead man's blood congealed into a large puddle around his feet, Aaron looked closely at the other newcomers in the room, studying their faces. He saw only worry, surprise, but none of the insanity that had overtaken the attacker.

CHAPTER THIRTY-FIVE

Once back on the highway, the Seven Mile Bridge was directly ahead. Constructed over a four year period from 1978 to 1982 right alongside the decaying buttresses of the old Flagler railroad bridge, it connects Knights Key, the last of the Marathon islands, with Little Duck Key to the south. Part of the steel barriers are made out of the train rails from the old bridge. It is an engineering marvel, dissecting the Atlantic Ocean and the Gulf of Mexico for 35,862 feet over 440 separate spans. Traversing it is like floating above a blue-green carpet at a height of sixty-five feet at its tallest point.

It only made Ben feel slightly ill. He was too giddy to worry about what was happening to him, but the elevation and loss of ground orientation made him feel nauseous. He did remember stopping at a restaurant named Mangrove Mama's, nestled amongst the red mangroves on Sugarloaf Key, just twenty miles outside of Key West.

He also vaguely recalled checking in at a Comfort Inn and being asked for his credit card, and then seeing the bright red and green neon lights illuminating the Sloppy Joe's sign and hearing the ear numbing sounds at Ricks Bar on Duval Street in downtown Key West. His ringing ears also reminded him of the intensity of the live rock and roll music.

He awoke when the early morning sun slanted through the slightly open blinds in the hotel room. It took him a good fifteen minutes just to open his eyes against the crushing headache. His eyes took in the room: the other queen bed unmade and unkempt, two chairs overturned, beer, wine and liquor bottles dotting the floor and bureaus.

Gradually rising just to fall back into the bed again, he emitted a low moan of pain.

Finally Ben was able to make it to his feet. Only then did he realize he was completely naked. He grabbed the sheet and wrapped it around him, suspecting his travel companions were in the bathroom or would be returning shortly. Making it to the bathroom, he threw up some vile bile in the sink. His empty stomach told him he hadn't eaten in some time.

Returning to the main room, he began searching for his clothing. Nothing in the closet, nothing under the bed, finally nothing in any of the bureaus. Now he was panicking. Also no sign of his wallet, holding all of his identification and credit cards, or his cell phone. The enormity of what was happening to him sank in slowly like poison being slowly dripped into his blood stream.

He sat back down on the bed and began to weep. Only then did he see the folded piece of paper on top of the TV. Opening it, he read, "*Good Morning Benny. It was fun. Better learn to pick your friends better.*" At the bottom was a smiley face.

Ben dialed the front desk. "I have an emergency to report. I've been robbed. Can you call the police please?" he said to the young lady who answered.

"Are the robbers still in the room?" she answered.

"No. It appears they've split and taken my wallet and clothes with them."

"Your clothes too?" she said with a barely disguised giggle.

"This is not a laughing matter, Miss. Call the police

immediately."

"Let me call security first so you can make a report."

"You can send security up, but I insist you call the police, or I'll do it."

"Okay sir, I'll call them and notify security."

Ben spent the few minutes before their arrival picking up trash and empty bottles and righting the furniture. He had barely made a dent in the disarray when he hard a knock on the door. With the sheet still wrapped around his lower half, he shuffled to the door and peered through the peephole. There was a younger woman and older man, both with crisp white shirts, black ties and lapel pins identifying them as security.

Ben opened the door, shielding himself partially behind it, and asked them to come in. After a few steps, the female let out a whoop and a loud guffaw. "Whoa! You guys really know how to throw a party!"

"I didn't do this," Ben protested. "The people I came down here with caused this mess, and took all my clothes and wallet in the process. I have nothing!"

"This is like the movie 'Hangover,'" she continued. Leaning over and picking up a frilly red bra which had been partially obscured by the bed spread which lay in lumps on the floor, she shrilled. "Yow! A thirty-Eight D! Joe, when's the last time you had your hands on one . . . ah . . . two of those?!"

"Okay, Gale, that's enough. Let's get his side of the story and see what we can do," the male officer said gruffly.

Ben sat down on the edge of the bed and gave them a shorthand version of the events, starting with his meeting Samantha on the plane, to the point where things starting going really wrong at the Sunset Tiki Bar. Gale took notes, stifling a snicker here and there, while the guy, who identified himself as Joe Anderson, occasionally asked a few questions.

Finally Joe asked, "Do you have anyone you can call? If the hotel took an imprint of your credit card when you checked in, which I'm sure they did, you should be good for last night. But I've got an inkling your *friends* exhausted your limit, plus you've got to cancel the card. So I doubt you're going to be able to pay for subsequent nights with it."

Ben's mind was racing at this point, but at half speed in the breakdown lane. Calling his wife was out of the question, at least for now. Then he thought of Phil. "I'll call a good friend of mine. He'll wire me some money. Do you know the closest place he can send it?"

"There's a Publix supermarket about a half mile down North Roosevelt," he indicated pointing to the sliding glass doors and motioning to his left. "You'll have to go there to make the arrangements."

"But I have no clothes!" Ben nearly shouted. "I can't go anywhere."

"I tell you what Mr. Harris. We look around the same size. I keep an extra uniform – everything, including shoes, socks and underwear – in my locker downstairs. Let me double-check with management, but I'm happy to lend you those until you can buy some new ones. How does that sound?"

Ben thanked him profusely, and they left. Joe soon returned with the apparel. As Joe was leaving, Ben said, "I also asked the operator to call the police. When they arrive, could you send them right up?"

"Mr. Harris. I don't think they'll be here anytime soon. My understanding is they're out flat preparing for the storm."

"I hope they come. If not, I'll go over to the station later."

"Good luck," Joe said, as he closed the door behind him.

Ben made the call to Phil on the hotel phone. Phil picked up, thankfully, on the third ring. "Phil, this is Ben."

"Hey, how's it going, good buddy? Gotten laid yet?" The response was delayed for a few seconds. "Ben? Are ya there?"

"Hey Phil. No, not yet," trying not to think about the incident with Angela. "But I'm in a bit of a predicament here."

"I bet you are," Phil scoffed. "What, you already got the clap? I can direct you to a good doc down there."

"Phil, I need to get serious with you for a minute. Please! The truth is, I got robbed. The three people I drove down here with took off with my wallet, phone and my clothes. I'm in a terrible situation."

The tone of his good friend's voice took the jocularity out of the discourse. "Man, I'm sorry to hear that. I assume you've reported it to the police. What can I do?"

Ben explained he had acquired some temporary clothing, and that Phil could wire money to the store once he set it up. They agreed on a thousand dollars, which Ben told Phil he would repay as soon as he got home.

Phil ended the conversation with yet another admonition. "Ben, my man. Ya know that storm I told ya about a few days ago?" Ben vaguely remembered, primarily because it seemed like months ago. "Well, the weirdest thing has happened. Never seen it before. It was heading straight north for Bermuda, when it unexpectedly took a left and is now heading right for southern Florida and the Keys. It's a monstrosity. We're battening down the hatches here. They're talking about a mandatory evacuation for all the tourists. You better get out of there as soon as you can."

Ben remembered the warning from the weatherman he had met at Alabama Jacks. Now he was concerned. "How long do we have, Phil? When's it expected to hit?"

"In a couple of days, at the latest. You don't have much time."

CHAPTER THIRTY-SIX

Daemon blasted into the Bermuda Triangle, also known as the Devil's Triangle, an area roughly circumscribed by Miami, Florida on the west; Bermuda to the north; and San Juan, Puerto Rico on the east and south. This huge expanse of open sea has been the source of incredible myth, lore, fantasy, and just plain junk science. It is here that numerous ships and planes have vanished without a trace or rational explanation. In this area, Flight 19, a squadron of TBM Avenger torpedo bombers, fell off the radar screens tracking them, only to reappear some thirty years later, disgorged from an alien flying saucer in Spielberg's classic film, "Close Encounters of the Third Kind."

But something even stranger happened to Daemon as it began to near the warm waters of the Gulf Stream. A high pressure system that had barreled up from the steamy jungles of Columbia and northern Brazil intersected with it. The collision caused a massive shearing of Daemon's upper winds, spinning them northeasterly, away from the hurricane's central core.

It had happened before, though rarely. Hurricane Carmen in 1974 spawned other depressions, with destructive lives of their own. Irene, some thirty-seven years later, did likewise, forming, in some satellite observations, a distinct, separate eye, spinning off and beyond its parent.

What happened to Daemon was unprecedented. Possibly it was because of its enormous size, now spanning some 2500 square miles, or as a result of its ferocious winds, screaming at a steady one hundred and sixty miles an hour around its center. Whatever it was, the crash of the powerful South American high with the formidable lows within Daemon blew the top off the hurricane, raking its upper vectors into a frenzy, creating a satanic offspring with its own separate eye, its own distinct personality.

This new storm, already a large tropical depression, cut its umbilical cord and flung loose, on a northeasterly track, toward the jewel of the Atlantic, Bermuda.

CHAPTER THIRTY-SEVEN

Jennifer eased into wakefulness slowly, deliciously, the memories of the prior hours nestled comfortably in her mind. The aroma of freshly brewed coffee stimulated her senses further into consciousness. She felt for Mark, but he was not next to her. Finally opening her eyes, she saw him at the nav station, perusing what she knew to be one of the many charts of the ingress into St. George's harbor, their point of entry to Bermuda. She had come to learn that he loved to pore over his nautical maps, the intricacies of the symbols, depths, and colors hypnotizing him into subconscious states of euphoria. They represented adventure, danger, and the thrill of ultimate destinations.

"You're up! Good morning, sleepy head," Mark chirped. He noticed once again how beautiful she looked despite the remnants of her recent slumber.

"Not quite. But soon," she responded. "This mermaid could sure use a cup of joe."

"Coming right up, my fan-tailed beauty," Mark said, picking up on the analogy.

Mark got up and walked the two steps to the stove, which leaned upright on its gimbals despite the steep angle of the vessel on its port tack. Taking two packets of Equal from the box on the low shelf above the stove, he poured the contents into a cup and added coffee. No milk or cream. He had learned how she liked it. Jennifer reluctantly brought herself up to a sitting position, and accepted the steaming hot liquid.

"Thank you, sweetie," she purred with a soft smile.

"You're welcome, honey pie." Mark leaned over, gave her a gentle kiss on the lips, and returned to the table.

Jennifer sipped her coffee contentedly. She watched Mark out of the corner of her eye so as not to make him uncomfortable. She had grown to love his increasingly shaggy hair and beard. As far as she knew, he had not had a trim of either since they left. Both had traces, but not much more, of gray. The classic salt and pepper touch was very handsome and pleasing to her. His physique, slim and muscular when she first met him, had been further honed by the constant activity required on board and the smaller portions of food necessitated by the cramped quarters for food preparation. She knew she had fallen in love with him, hook, line and sinker.

Mark interrupted Jennifer's comfortable reverie. "The entry through the reef into St. George's Harbor is not easy, but we'll be prepared, and it should be no problem. We'll lower the sails about a kilometer from the pass and motor through. Looks like the winds should be somewhat cooperative, coming behind us from the east."

"When do you think we'll get to the reef?"

"It's 0900 hours now, so I'm estimating, at our present speed, around 1500."

"I'm excited. I love this floating home of ours, but it will be good to get on solid ground and maybe even to a good bar. I'd love to hear some live music for a change."

"Well remember what I told you. It'll feel strange for a while when we get ashore. Your equilibrium will still be rolling with the waves."

"I know, but it'll be nice. We haven't discussed this, but do you think we could spring for an inexpensive hotel room one night? Sure would like to do some rocking and rolling on you in a nice, queen size bed."

"You naughty girl, you," Mark replied with a broad grin. "Look what a little salt air has done to my innocent little angel."

"From an angel to a mermaid, I always say," Jennifer said with a soft chuckle. "A wonderful transformation."

"I'm sure not complaining."

****

While Mark was expertly charting their safe transit into St. George's Harbor, Daemon's progeny was reforming and gaining separate strength. It finally spun loose, hesitated, and then slowly began its own northerly path.

CHAPTER THIRTY-EIGHT

Robbie couldn't believe the beehive of activity in the Operations area. All eight computer screens were being monitored by at least one, and sometimes two, personnel. He knew by experience that the dress code in Key West was perpetually casual, but the degree of informality today clearly suggested that many of those present had been called out of bed, or otherwise, on an emergency basis.

Robbie observed that Grimes was a tall, gaunt man, probably in his early fifties. Because he had to stoop slightly to enter the room, Stewart estimated his height to be over 6'4". His complexion appeared to be eternally ashen, the result, Robbie guessed, of too much time spent within the cloistered confines of the weather station, and not enough in the glorious Key West sun.

On their way in, the Chief said, "I heard you were one of the last out of the building. Was anyone injured?"

"Not that I know of. There were only two of us when the fire broke out. I couldn't believe how fast it spread. Someone suggested it was the hydrogen used to cool the main line computers. It was a total loss."

"Well, what's most important is that everyone got out safely. We're prepared here to take over most of the Miami functions. We can also be assisted by the Jacksonville Office."

"That's great. What's going on now?"

A concerned look hardened Grime's already stern mien. "Well, we finally got some feedback from Miss Piggy. Seems Daemon is off the chart in its strength and intensity. They barely made it out of the center. Winds were cat five plus. It's also one of the largest cyclones size-wise we've seen."

"Yeah, I pretty much learned that from the satellite imagery, and the brief report we got from the first Hunter plane. Is there anything new?"

"There is. Seems Daemon has burst apart at the seams. About twelve hours ago a separate depression spun off and headed northeast. I've never seen that before, even though one of the more seasoned veterans here says it's happened once or twice since we started keeping records. What's most disturbing, however, is the size of the break-off. It's gaining strength quickly – way too quickly for comfort – and headed for a populated area . . . Bermuda."

Robbie's face now shared Larry's intensity. "That's unbelievable. I certainly haven't ever experienced that before. Have we sent out any planes to check it out?"

"Not yet. We just identified the new storm a few hours ago. Wanted to give it some time so we knew what we were up against."

"That makes sense. But if it were me – and I say this respectfully, Larry – I'd get a Hunter out there right away. With strict instructions to use extreme caution."

"You're absolutely right. Let's take a look at the screen first and see where we are."

The two men pulled up castered office chairs to either side of a central computer, manned by a woman. Even though Robbie's attention was immediately drawn to the brightly colored computer data, he could not help but notice that the brunette sitting next to him smelled sweetly of lavender, and was pleasing to the eye.

"What do we have now, Lucy?" Grimes asked their new company.

"More of the same ole, same ole, Larry. As in, something new with this storm every minute. If there's anything predictable about this baby, its the unpredictability. The primary center is still truckin' our way, now at about twelve miles per hour.

"The spin-off has kept a steady track to the north. We may be naming this secondary depression soon, as it continues to grow at an astronomical rate. What's weirdest, though, is we seem to be able to define an eye in the new one. Look at this."

Lucy zoomed in on the mass of yellows, greens, and splotches of red that were now only a few hundred miles from Bermuda. Stewart knew she had it on the "Animated GIF" setting. He couldn't believe the amount of steamy moisture in this new depression, but what most caught his attention was the clear, circular motion around a central core.

"That's unbelievable," Grimes exclaimed. "This storm is no more than twelve hours old, and already it's forming a distinct core. I know I've never seen one come together that quickly."

Robbie remained strangely quiet. His only thoughts were of Val. A storm that could engender a second, in the proportions he now saw for the first time, was something to be reckoned with. He excused himself and called Val on his cell out in the hallway.

She answered on the first ring. "What's up babe?"

"Hey there. Can you talk for a minute?"

"Of course, sweetie."

"I'm here at the shop. Something's happened to raise my concerns about Daemon to a new level. I thought I'd be able to come home after a day or two, but it's clear I'll have to remain here for the foreseeable future. I can't have you in Miami by yourself. You need to get down here pronto."

Val's voice now reflected her husband's concern. "What happened? I'll be okay by myself here. We've made sure of that."

Robbie knew they had spent a great deal of money, and their own time, rendering their home as hurricane proof as was possible given current construction techniques. His profession had taught him a healthy respect for the storms that regularly battered the south Florida coast. They had already successfully weathered some doozies. Not only that, given his position, he didn't know how he could face his neighbors, friends, or colleagues if his own residence was badly damaged or destroyed, or any member of his family was injured.

"Yes we have, honey. But this one is different. I need you here with me. Please start packing – for at least a week or two stay – and drive down here A.S.A.P."

"But Robbie. I had made plans with the girls to go shopping today. Why don't I just drive down in a day or two."

Robbie's tone ended any further discussion. "Val, you know we make almost all of our decisions jointly. But this is one I have to make alone. You must listen to me. Start packing, get the house ready, get on down here."

With that Robbie hung up.

CHAPTER THIRTY-NINE

When Cross and his crew returned to the immigration building, Aaron was still comforting Zoe. Her attacker's body was beginning to stiffen with rigor mortis. Aaron and Zoe filled them in on what had happened. The Captain then also looked around at the others in the room. Most were now sitting in groups against the wall, or standing by the several windows. Bart appeared more upset than anyone. "Those bastards," he said, referring to the entire collection of Cape Verdeans. "Can't trust any of them."

Aaron and the other men wrapped old towels around the body and carried it outdoors. They had no digging tools, so they placed it in the trunk of an abandoned car several hundred yards from the building. When they returned, Zoe and Marcia had placed a piece of carpet over the blood stain.

Jay said, "Come with me Major. Jack and Bart, you guys stay here. Keep a good lookout. Everyone else seems to be okay, but watch any new visitors. Carefully." The men signified their agreement, and the Captain and Major left.

"Where are we going Jay?" Aaron asked.

"I need your help retrieving some items from the plane. I don't want anyone else to see them for the time being."

"What items?"

"You'll see."

They entered the plane via the short stairs hanging from the fuselage. Captain Cross went directly to a locker located in the back right hand side of the plane. Aaron noticed there was a sturdy combination lock guarding its contents. Jay quickly spun the dial back and forth, and the lock disengaged. When he pulled open the door, Aaron saw why the Captain wanted to hasten and secretly retrieve what was inside.

"This one's a Mossberg 12 gauge autoloader," he said as he grabbed one of the long guns. He pulled the bolt to the loading gate back, and a shell ejected from the side. "Holds ten rounds, which can be fired in under six seconds. A lot of fire power here."

Handing the weapon to Aaron, Cross emptied the locker: first a 30-30 Winchester rifle, and finally three handguns, two 9 millimeter Glocks and a Colt Anaconda .44 revolver. "I hope we don't have to use these, but I'm glad we have them. Major, hand me that duffel bag hanging from the hook over there."

Aaron retrieved the bag, and first checking to be sure all the safeties were on, the two men placed the guns in the bag together with enough ammunition to keep them in business for a good while. The Captain also shoved some thick, three ring binders in afterward. "If anyone asks what's in here, just say we had to get some maintenance and navigation manuals. Okay?"

"Roger, Captain. Then we'll both take turns making sure one of us is always within arm's length of the bag."

The two men exited and circled the plane, attempting a first analysis of the damage sustained. "This isn't as bad as I thought," Cross said. "Looks more superficial than structural."

"I agree. I'm a little worried about this hydraulic leak from the port wing flap," Aaron said as he pointed to a puddle of reddish fluid on the ground. "But that can be fixed."

"It's getting late, so why don't you, I and Bart start early in the morning and run all the system diagnoses to see exactly what we've got. Then we can get to fixing any problems."

"Sounds like a plan to me," Aaron replied.

When they re-entered the building they found that several additional people had joined them: two couples and a man. The single individual was arguing with Bart. It had become heated. Pedro was trying to placate the man in his native tongue.

"What's going on here?" Aaron asked, looking first at Pedro, then at Bart.

"Seems this guy doesn't like the way the food is being allocated," Bart answered. "Claims he should get a double portion because he hasn't eaten in so long. I've tried to explain to him that most of the people here are in the same boat. He just doesn't get it."

Pedro had succeeded in quieting him for the time being, and the man turned away, but not without glaring at the three foreigners as he left. "We've got to keep an eye out for that one," Cross said. "I'm afraid that, under the circumstances, we're going to have to maintain watch shifts during the night. Pedro, are there any of your people here you feel you can trust?"

Pedro looked around and approached one of the newly arrived couples. They engaged in a brief conversation, and Pedro returned. "That man and woman over there appear pretty reliable to me. One of them knows a good friend of mine. I think they're alright."

"Great," Aaron said. "Here's what we'll do. There's about twelve hours of darkness, and nine of us. We'll keep watch in groups of two, and then I'll join Jay for the last shift. Each shift will go two and a half hours. Is that okay with everyone?"

They agreed, and Pedro went over and explained the plan to the couple. They distributed more of the remaining food, leaving only enough for a day or two.

The night went smoothly, until around three in the morning, when a young man arrived. Zoe and Aaron were on duty, and let him in. He was in bad shape: shivering, caked in mud, bleeding from numerous cuts and scrapes. They communicated with him as best they could, and gave him some clean, dry clothes and food.

When he saw all the homemade cots were taken up, he became very agitated, and began shaking some of the women, trying to get them off the beds. This rousted some of the men, who began pushing and shoving him. One threw a punch. The crew from Miss Piggy awoke and, with Aaron, order was restored. It took about an hour for everyone to quiet down, the young man sullen and angry, talking to himself, in a corner of the room.

CHAPTER FORTY

Ben had to walk from the hotel to Publix, a distance of about a mile.

"Hello. My name is Ben Harris. There should be a wired cash transfer here for me," he said to the pleasant looking older woman at the counter.

"I'm sorry. The name again?"

"Ben Harris. Or maybe it's under Benjamin Harris."

"Okay. Let me take a look."

She walked over to a computer terminal a few feet away. After several minutes she returned. "Yes, I have it. A thousand dollars, right?"

"Yes. That's it," Ben said excitedly.

"Identification, please."

Ben's mind was now racing. *Why hadn't he thought about that?*

"Ah . . . that's the reason I needed money wired. I was robbed in my hotel. They took my wallet, which had all my identification. You can verify that with the hotel management."

"I understand your predicament, but our rules are very strict here. We'll need some identification, or a copy of a police report verifying your story."

Ben sagged noticeably. His knees almost gave way. He wanted to scream at the lady, but didn't have the energy for a confrontation. He spoke in a low, desperate tone.

"Ma'am. I'm at wit's end. I can call the police, wait for them, make a report. But it could be hours, if not days before I can get an actual written copy of it. I was supposed to go back to the hotel with cash to pay for another night. If I don't, they'll put me out of the room. Even these clothes I'm wearing I borrowed from a security officer at the hotel. Can't you help me? Please!" Ben was almost crying at this point.

The lady's expression softened. "Oh so you did call hotel security? Did they make a report?"

"I'm not sure, but I bet I can get them to. Can I use your phone? They stole my cell as well."

"Of course." She raised a section of the counter and led Ben to a phone on a nearby desk. Using the hotel bill that had been slipped under his door during the night to locate the number, he dialed.

"Security please." Ben heard the line being transferred. It rang and rang. Ben's frustration grew with each irritating *briinggg. God,* Ben thought, *this couldn't get any more difficult.* No answering machine, voice mail, anything. Just incessant ringing.

He hung up and dialed again. "Reception."

"Hi, my name is Benjamin Harris. I stayed with you last night and was robbed. Two of your security officers came up and took a statement from me. I need to get their report so I can access some money I had a friend wire me. They didn't answer their extension the last time I called. Can you find one of them for me? Their names were Joe and Gale."

To his utter dismay, his call was immediately transferred again, and the line rang and rang. "God damn it," Ben yelled into the phone. He noticed some patrons on the other side of the counter flinch.

"Mr. Harris," the woman who had assisted him said sternly. "I must ask you to move to the other side of the counter now."

"Please!" Ben pleaded. "I can't get through to the right people at the hotel. Let me try again."

He called the hotel. Ben noticed the woman push a button mounted inconspicuously under the counter. As soon as the receptionist answered, Ben yelled, "Hold on don't transfer me! I must speak with a security officer immediately!" There was a pause, and the line went dead.

Ben was unable to move. Tension flooded his body. Just then he saw two uniformed men with "Publix Security" stenciled on their shirts. These guys were large and nasty looking, and didn't look like they wanted to chitchat.

"Alright sir, come around the counter now. We don't want any trouble."

Ben stood transfixed. *Was this really happening to him*? The brawnier of the two started to move toward him. Ben simply collapsed, sitting down unceremoniously on the floor.

Both of the guards came up to him, each took one of his arms, and lifting him to an upright position, walked him out the door. He stood out on the sidewalk alone. No way to call anyone. Penniless. No ID. Wearing someone else's clothes. Ben finally let it all out. He blubbered like a baby, the tears landing in puddles on his well polished, borrowed, black shoes.

CHAPTER FORTY-ONE

The Isles of Bermuda started as a gray haze on the horizon, then slowly focused into charcoal hills sitting on the edge of the sea, and finally came to life as green foliage and splashes of pink white beaches. Jennifer gasped with excitement. "Look Mark! Aren't they beautiful!"

"They are. It should get better as we approach the reef."

Mark went below to perform a final check of the wind speed and direction. Out of the corner of his eye he caught the satellite imagery of the south central Atlantic. *What the hey,* he wondered. Something was attacking Daemon. He could now clearly pick out the swirling clouds being ripped away from the heart of the hurricane and forming a distinct depression to the north. Mark was only able to study the phenomenon for a few seconds because they were getting dangerously close to the reef. He went back topside.

In less than a half hour, they could see the tormented sea as it crashed against the outer barrier of the reef which encircled the Isles at a distance averaging four miles. The ocean was now a clear green. Coming from Rhode Island, their approach to Bermuda was from the northwest. St. George's Harbor lay almost directly to the east of the main island.

"Okay, we're going to head southeast from here to circle around to the harbor," Mark advised Jennifer.

"Yes sir, *capitan,*" Jennifer said with a wink. "Am I going to walk the plank now or are we going to lower the sails?"

"No, we'll hold the plank for now and take care of the sails once we get to the east of the island and begin to head in. I'll let you know."

As they rounded the land mass to their starboard side, Mark noticed the swells becoming substantially more pronounced. Jennifer felt it with her legs, as her knees bent and her body rolled with the movement.

"Getting a little rougher, isn't it?" she queried.

"Yeah. I wasn't quite expecting rollers like these. Must be from the storm to the south of us. I thought we'd be well out of their path. Time to don the life jackets."

Jennifer grabbed the jackets from the cabinet and they put them on quickly. She eyed the increasing size of the waves with concern. They hadn't seen anything like this since leaving home, even during the squall. The Beneteau was now bucking like a strapped bronco. They had to hold on for dear life. Frothy spray enveloped them with each downward dip.

"Mark. Maybe we should try a different approach?"

"There really is no other way, babe, unless we retrace our steps for another ten miles or so, directly into the wind. With this opposing current, we might not make any headway at all. We'll be fine as soon as we make it inside the reef."

"It's getting through the reef that has me worried."

Just when Jennifer thought that she couldn't take any more of the constant rearing and plunging of the craft, Mark said. "Okay. I'm going to start the engine. Once she fires up, I'll head her into the wind, and we'll drop the sails."

"Great."

Mark turned the key. The engine sputtered and coughed. Finally she caught. "These rough seas must have churned up some debris from the bottom of the fuel tanks. I'll have to change the filters when we get into port."

They motored with the sails up for about five minutes, when Mark gave the order to turn into the wind and lower them. All the sheets worked their way into the cockpit, making the process facile and fast. Jennifer, holding on carefully to the boom and mainsail, next worked her way to a spot where she could lash down and immobilize the boom. After considerable effort, she accomplished the task.

Mark watched her up ahead as she turned to access the cockpit. Suddenly, behind her, a horrific sight appeared. A rogue wave loomed up out of nowhere just fifty feet in front of the bow. It rose, as if it were born of the deep, and a curl of agitated seawater formed at its top and began descending down on the ship from a height of nearly twenty feet. Mark's mouth opened in a scream, but nothing came out. Jennifer looked at him like he was crazy. A second later it came out: "Jenn. Watch out! Behind you!"

She turned just in time to catch the full force of the wave as it came crashing down on the deck. When the water cleared, Jennifer was nowhere to be seen.

Mark had trained for this eventuality. He knew the drill well. But no amount of advance practice can prepare you for the real thing. Mark did his best to quickly squelch the fast rising panic that wanted to consume him.

He immediately shoved the gear shift into neutral. As he headed for the horseshoe shaped life preserver located just to the side of the wheel, he blew ferociously on the whistle which was attached to each of the jackets. Listening intently for a response, he pulled the preserver from the bracket and tossed it as hard as he could into the ocean to the stern of the vessel. Then he screamed her name at the top of his lungs. His primary concern was that she was injured as she was swept off the deck and might be unconscious . . . or worse.

There it was! The muted shrill of a whistle. Mark strained his eyes to pick her out of the vast sea. He estimated she should be about thirty feet from the boat, but with the huge swells he knew it would be difficult to see her. He caught a quick flash of light. Thank God! She had the wherewithal to activate her strobe, again a vital appurtenance to the life jacket.

Mark next did something he knew was terribly wrong, something against all of the man overboard rules. But now he was reacting from his heart, not from his head. He dove overboard and followed the line connected to the floating preserver some twenty-five feet away. All the while he blew his whistle, and followed the responsive sound. When Jennifer was lifted up by a wave, he could also see the blinking, bright white light. She seemed unfathomably far away.

Going into the freestyle of his life, Mark swam frantically in her direction. When he reached the end of the line, he lifted himself up by pushing down on the horseshoe float. She was still another twenty feet away. He looked back toward the boat, which was rapidly disappearing in the distance. He was now close enough to see Jennifer's forehead gushing a crimson fluid. He had to make a decision. Abandoning the lifeline would probably leave them both floating for eternity on the surface of the water, and then below.

He let go of it and swam with every ounce of his strength. Just when he thought he had failed, when he had traveled the distance he estimated was sufficient to reach her and could not find her, an arm reached around his neck from behind and, for a moment, pulled him under. Mark ducked underneath the crook of her elbow, and slid up at her back. Time was now of the essence. Her eyes were open, but she had no ability to swim on her own. Holding her around the chest with one arm, he stroked with the other and kicked with all his might. "Hang on baby," he said. "Don't panic. I've got you."

Miraculously, his hand struck the preserver. They rested on it for several minutes. He could tell Jenn was incapable of speech. Even though the water was seasonably warm, around seventy-five degrees he figured, it was still cool enough to cause hypothermia after a sufficient period of time. Grabbing the line attached to the ship, Mark slowly pulled them along it. This made the going a little easier.

They finally reached the swim platform at the stern of the boat. It took all of Mark's energy to climb the small set of stairs and pull Jennifer aboard. He then clasped his palm firmly over the gaping gash above her eye, and rested there. Her eyes were fluttering, and her breathing labored. But she was alive and onboard.

CHAPTER FORTY-TWO

Ben had no energy to get up, go anywhere. He was done. Out of the corner of his eye he saw an elderly black woman standing about five feet to his right. She hadn't been there when he first sat down. He figured her age to be around seventy, even though he sensed it could have been much more. An out of style, rather dowdy faded print dress was draped over her substantial figure. A very large cloth handbag hung from her left shoulder, and she clasped a tattered black leather Bible in her right hand.

Apparently seeing him looking at her, she said, "Sir. I don't mean to pry. But is there anything I can do for you?"

Ben looked at her as if she were a mirage. He briefly explained his predicament.

"Isn't there anyone you can call? I've got a cell phone I'll let you use." She pulled an antiquated phone from her purse.

"That's the problem. I don't know anyone down here. I . . ." Ben suddenly remembered Robbie's card in his pocket. "Wait. There is someone. I just met him, but I don't have any other options."

The lady handed him her phone. Ben dialed the number, which went into Robbie's voice mail. Ben began to leave a message, then realized he had no call back number to give him. "He's not answering. Do you mind if I leave your number? Maybe he'll be able to call right back."

"Of course," the woman said. "And I'm not leaving you until you find someone to help you."

Ben rang up Robbie again and left the number given him.

"Okay, why don't we start walking back to my house," she said. "It's not far. Maybe he'll return your call soon. Otherwise you'll stay with me."

Ben felt like crying again. He could not believe the largesse in spirit of this person. "Thank you so much. You are truly my guardian angel."

"Well praise the Lord. It's Jesus who sent me to you."

****

Robbie stepped out of the Storm Center to grab a drink of water. As he was walking to the cooler, his cell vibrated. He checked the number, and not recognizing it, ignored it to see if the caller would leave a message. Larry and Lucy were still at the computer when he returned.

"I did some research on this break away storm," Larry announced. "I know that Irene, in August, 2011, appeared to split off into two separate storms, but later examination proved that to be false. However, Hurricane Carmen, in 1974, which also originated over Africa, clearly divided and spawned two distinct storms. But this occurred as it passed through the Intertropical Convergence Zone."

The inter what?" Lucy asked.

Larry uttered the term again, and added, "It's known by sailors as the doldrums. It's an area encircling the earth near the equator where the northeast and southeast trade winds come together. It appears as a band of clouds, usually thunderstorms."

"Is that what happened to Daemon?" Lucy inquired.

Robbie cut in: "It could be. The zone at this time of year is usually much closer to the Equator. But look at this line of cloudiness here," he said, pointing to a swath of white extending across the screen. "It's right up in the path of the hurricane. Because it's a zone of wind change and speed, it can create tremendous forces of wind shear. I think that's what happened here. The powerful shear ripped off the top of Daemon, spinning those upper winds to the north. Daemon was so huge that this break-off formed into a storm of its own."

"That's amazing," Lucy said. "But did it diminish Daemon's size? I mean you'd think that if a portion was torn off, the primary storm would be reduced."

"You would think that," Larry answered. "But it didn't happen here. If anything, Daemon has strengthened. Very weird."

"Yes, very weird," Robbie agreed.

Robbie remembered the phone call, and decided to check his voice mail. He also needed some fresh air. He went outside in the back, where a huge satellite dish hovered next to the parking lot. Punching the number "1" to speed dial his voice mail, he heard a voice that was somewhat familiar, but not quite placeable until he listened further into the message:

"Hi Robbie. I don't know if you will remember me or not. This is Ben. We met outside the men's room at Alabama Jacks yesterday. I hate to bother you but I'm in such a terrible situation that I'm turning to anyone who might help me."

The caller then gave a brief history of what had transpired, and ended with, "If you can help me, I will repay you ten times over. I need some cash, not much, and a place to stay tonight. I also need a ride to the police station so I can file a report and access the cash wired to me. I can walk to wherever you are. Please!"

Robbie was immediately touched by the tone of desperation in Ben's voice. He paced outside for several minutes, trying to decide what to do. *Is this a setup?* he thought. *I barely know this guy.*

Finally he made a decision. He would help. He was a pretty good study of human nature. If this was a hoax, then he knew nothing about people. He was sure Ben was sincere. He called him back at the number left in the message.

Ben arrived by cab at the station, and per their agreement, Robbie met him outside and paid the bill. Robbie placed his hand on Ben's shoulder and said, "Let me show you inside and give you the special tour before we head over to the police station. I think you'll want to see what we've got coming at us."

"A good friend told me it was a big one," Ben replied. "And by the way, Robbie, I really appreciate this. I know we just met, and I think you're an incredible person to help me out like this."

"Don't worry about it Ben – there's that old expression – there but for the grace of God go I."

"Well thank you again. I really mean it."

Robbie took him inside and showed him the large standing placards describing the destructive forces of some of the great hurricanes that have struck the Florida Keys: Wilma and Katrina in 2005; Charley in 2004. Then onto the displays of radiosondes, the counterpart to dropsondes, which are released by helium balloon from the ground to determine the internal dimensions of a storm. Finally inside to the Operations Center, where Ben saw the urgency surrounding the tracking of the storm. As he passed through a short corridor, he noticed some striking, colorful sculptures to the left.

"Robbie, what are those?"

"The artwork is by a local artist. Bill Harrison. We try to support the local arts as best we can. You'll see some paintings on the walls, again all by locals. That's the thing about Key West. People really get behind each other. It's one of the most philanthropic places I've ever been."

"That's fantastic," Ben replied. "I sure have experienced that through you."

They walked to one of the computer stations in the main room. The person sitting at the screen moved aside and allowed Robbie access to the mouse and keyboard. Robbie hit some keys, and a large representation of two huge swirling masses filled the screen. The outline of Bermuda, the southern East Coast, the Bahamas, and most of the northern Caribbean came into view. Each land mass was already being touched by the outer reaches of the storms.

"That looks like a humongous storm," Ben said. "I mean, I'm no expert, but I've looked at some satellite imagery before, and I don't remember seeing one that large before."

"I don't think you have," Robbie said as he continued to zero in on the weather patterns on display. "It's actually two separate systems, even though it looks like one. This one broke off from the primary depression." Robbie pointed to the white circular clouds now fast approaching Bermuda. "Daemon, our hurricane, is marching westward toward Miami and the northern Caribbean."

"How soon before we need to start worrying here in Key West?" Ben asked.

"Ben, we're way past the worry point. It's pure panic at this stage."

CHAPTER FORTY-THREE

The crew of Miss Piggy awoke first. Jay had been sleeping with his arms around the bag of weapons, not making for an easy night's rest. He was still a little out of sorts. "Okay gentlemen. Let's get cleaned up, do our thing. Then it's out to the bird to see if we can make her air worthy. We have no idea how long we'll be here."

"We're with you, Captain," Bart said. "But let's be sure to keep a close eye on these damn natives."

They all used the bathroom, and then headed out. Aaron awoke, and told them to come get him if they needed an extra hand. If not, Aaron would organize teams to clean up and search for food.

Captain Cross, Jack Porter, and Bart McCullough walked around Miss Piggy slowly, with Bart taking notes on a pad of paper recording damaged areas and their thoughts on what could be done. Over all, it wasn't as bad as they had anticipated. There were some loose panels on the fuselage where the catastrophic winds had ripped off some of the rivets. These could be fixed with a pop rivet gun, and if that was not available, then with some sheet metal screws or bolts. There were also some dents where the chunks of ice in the atmosphere had ricocheted off the wing and tail fin. Again, these were not fatal, and would only cause unpleasant vibration at higher speeds.

The next, and more important test was of the engines. After doing a preflight check, Jay fired up the starboard engine. It sputtered and popped, but finally roared to life.

"That's a great sound," Bart ventured. "Let's see what the other one does."

Captain Cross pressed the ignition button on the port side. Again, a lot of noise, but no firing. They kept at it until Cross said, "We'll burn out the starter at this rate. Let's take a look at it now and see if we can find out what the problem is."

After two hours, all three men were sitting on the tarmac amidst a pile of tools, parts, and small puddles of oil, examining, cleaning and tinkering. They were on a tarp under the wing as the September sun had been beating down on them hard.

Inside all were up, and the remaining food was distributed. Aaron, with Zoe, Pedro, and Marcia's assistance, had set up several teams and already the clean up had started on the bathrooms and sleeping area. It was time to head outside and try to scrounge up more food and water, and hopefully, some more bedding. Zoe and Marcia stayed behind to supervise the cleaning, while Aaron and Pedro took two teams and began the slow process of shoving debris around to root for sustenance.

Back at the plane, Jay was working on some fuel injectors. "These are filled with carbon. I've seen it before. The engine must have konked out for a few seconds during our descent and raw fuel was ignited and backed up into the injector. I think if we clean these out well, she might start."

The three men each took two injectors and, using their own tooth brushes and gasoline siphoned from the tank, went to work. As they sat together in the shade of the wing, they began discussing the commotion of the prior night. Jack opened the dialogue. "That was strange last night. The guy was on the verge of hurting someone. We've got to keep a close eye on that one."

"Not just him," Bart offered. "I've been watching some of the others closely. Most of them look . . . well, spooked. That's the best description I can give."

"They did go through a lot, being up in those hills during the chaos. It must have been horrendous," Jay added.

Jack finished one injector and picked up the second. "Yes, it must have been. But this is something different. I believe a lot of the people in there experienced a truly malevolent force of nature, probably for the first time, and certainly more intensely than ever. It brought out something dark in them. I see it on their faces. I hear it in their voices. I felt the same thing when we were going through Daemon. Something other worldly. Something . . . well . . . satanic."

The men remained silent for a while. In another four hours, the engine was put back together, and they tried to start it again. This time it caught immediately, and the crew let out a loud whoop! Everyone inside the building came out to see what all the commotion was about, and clapped at the sight of the plane, both engines now humming, doing slow, confined circles.

Aaron had taken one team into town. The stench of decaying bodies was so overwhelming that they had to tie clothing around their mouths and noses to stifle the smell. Corpses still lined the seashore.

Some of the men, including Pedro, knew where the several markets had been, so they worked those areas. After several hours of lifting timbers, bricks, stucco and roof tile, they came upon a cache of canned goods at one location. There was visible excitement among the group, and they worked harder to clear the area. Ultimately they carried away, in trash bags found nearby, carton after carton of soups, canned meats such as tuna and crab, and vegetables. They walked back to the airport feeling victorious.

As they approached the airport, they were joined by the second outside team. That team had been able to find hundreds of bottles of fluids, not only water, but fruit juices and various kinds of sodas.

Next to a small outbuilding they saw a fuel pump under an overhang. "Let's remember where that is in case we need it to refuel the plane," Aaron told the group.

When they all entered the immigration building, they were astounded to see the improvement. Not only had the floor been scrubbed and the bathrooms made sparkling clean, they had somehow been able to find additional cushions amidst the wreckage of the main terminal. These had been laid out to form extra makeshift beds. All in all, it was a major transformation.

Aaron took Zoe aside to a seat away from the others. "How did it go in here, Zoe? Was everyone cooperative?"

"Yes, up to a point. Funny. The teenagers and younger children were very anxious to help, and worked hard. The adults not so much. In my training I came across a number of ex-military who were suffering from post traumatic stress syndrome . . . in those who had actually seen combat. That's what this reminded me of. The grownups act like they've gone through a war. Some are almost catatonic. I wouldn't have thought surviving a storm of such relatively short duration – regardless of how terrible it was – would cause the apathy, depression . . . the anger that I've witnessed here."

"Well, I guess the younger people are just more resilient. Plus, we've got to realize that many people here have lost their homes, maybe even loved ones. We can't blame them for exhibiting signs of depression."

"I know. You're absolutely right. But I still think this is something different. It's as if they saw something, experienced something, that shocked them so badly they can barely function."

"Well, hopefully we'll get some help over here, including psychological counseling, that will help them. Until then, we're on our own."

"Yes," Zoe said with a frown. "We're on our own."

CHAPTER FORTY-FOUR

"Ben, let's get you over to the police station. It's not far from here. I'll drop you off and come to pick you up in a half hour. I want to get some supplies."

"Thanks Robbie. Again, I really appreciate this."

"Don't mention it."

The station was just off North Roosevelt Boulevard. Ben got out and walked through an open-air atrium, passing by an Italian fountain in the center of a small outdoor piazza, which Ben found incongruous to the purpose for the building. *Oh well, this is Key West,* he thought. He approached a plexiglass partition on the exterior front of the building.

No one seemed to be around. There was an intercom with a button, so after waiting a minute, he pushed it. Still no response. Not anxious to be a bother but wanting to get this over with, he pushed it again . . . and then again. After another minute, a gruff voice came through the speaker, "What do you want?"

Ben hesitated, not knowing exactly how to state it briefly. About ten seconds passed until he could find his voice. The same harsh voice came through: "State your purpose or leave the area"

Ben blurted out, "No. Wait! I need to file a report. I was robbed at my hotel."

I brief pause ensued. Then the speaker said, "Hold your identification up to the camera."

It was only then that Ben noticed the video camera perched seven feet up in the right hand corner by an interior door. Looking up into the camera as he spoke, Ben said in a loud tone, "That's the problem. They stole my wallet, which had all my ID. I need a report so I can access some cash a friend wired down to me. Please! I'm desperate."

Again another pause, this time longer. Then the voice returned, "You'll have to come back in a few days. All of our available officers are out on emergency detail. We've got a hurricane coming, and an evacuation order for all non-residents is about to issue."

"No, I can't do that," Ben pleaded. "Please, it will only take a few minutes. It's the only way I can get some money."

The unseen speaker came back. "Look sir. I'm not going to say this again. You've got to come back in a few days, or whenever the storm passes. Now leave the area. Immediately!"

Ben was flabbergasted. He hadn't predicted this. He thought it would be easy. Just a few minutes to relate the facts and bring a copy of the report back to Publix. The tone of the man's voice made him hesitate to say anything further. But he had no other options. It was against his nature, but he had to be more proactive.

He shouted at the camera, "I'm not leaving until someone takes a report from me. I have no money, no place to stay. I'm in borrowed clothes . . . ."

His words were interrupted when a huge, burly, uniformed officer came banging through the door by the camera. His face was angry red, and he was snorting. Without a word, he grabbed Ben by the back of his collar, dragged him out to the curb, and unceremoniously dumped him on the asphalt parking lot. Ben was so surprised he couldn't utter a word. He stood, shaken, outside, as the officer went back in and locked the door behind him.

Meanwhile, Robbie was roaming from Home Depot to Strunks Hardware and finally to Walgreens, trying to find additional water, batteries and canned food. He knew the station would be well stocked with emergency supplies, but worried about Val, and now his new charge. The shelves were largely bare, yet he was able to locate several gallon jugs of water, a flashlight, and two packs of double "A" batteries.

He returned to the police station to find Ben sitting forlornly on the front curb. "Hey Buddy, how'd it go?"

Ben looked up at him. His face showed deep lines of despair.

"What's the matter?" Robbie said out the front passenger window as he leaned across the console of the car.

"I couldn't get anyone to take a statement from me. The officer said everyone was out getting ready for the storm. He actually escorted me away from the building, even though 'escort' is a nice way of putting it. I'm fucked. That's all there is to it. I guess I deserve this, thinking I could break out of my rut, go to South Beach, then here. What a fool! God is clearly punishing me."

"C'mon Ben. God's not doing anything to you. You've just caught some bad breaks. You can stay at the hotel where I made reservations for my wife. She's supposed to come down, probably tomorrow. If we still can't get you some cash, I'll front you the money for your own room. What d'ya say?"

Ben began weeping again. He was hungover, hungry, and exhausted. He just let it all out. As the tears dripped on the asphalt, he thought, *I haven't cried since the birth of my son and daughter. And here I've done it twice in one day. What has happened to me?*

He felt himself being lifted by a friendly hand under his arm. Robbie helped him over to the front passenger door, and got him in the car.

"Ben, stop worrying. This will all work out. You're with a friend."

Ben looked earnestly at Robbie, and said, "The only reason I don't think God has it in for me, is you. You are heaven sent. You've reinforced by faith in human kind. Thank you. Thank you."

Robbie just put his hand on Ben's shoulder and give it a squeeze. They drove to the hotel.

CHAPTER FORTY-FIVE

It was getting to be late in the day, and Aaron went out to check on the progress of the work on the plane. The three crew members had cleaned off and put away their tools, and were already heading toward the building to wash themselves up.

"Hey gentlemen. I heard you got both engines going. That's great," Aaron said as he approached them.

Captain Cross, who was carrying the bag holding the guns, answered. "Yeah, all we had to do is clean out the injectors on the port engine. They're both purring along just fine. Now we just need to button down the fuselage where she got torn up a bit. I'm guessing she'll be ready to fly within three to four days."

"That's much sooner than I thought," Aaron said, while joining them on their way back to the building. "We should be making a plan on what we do when the plane is ready."

"I've given it a lot of thought, "Cross said. "I think my crew and I should fly to Santiago. It's the largest island in this chain, and we've got the best shot at getting hold of some communications equipment there. We've got to contact the base to check in and see what's going on back home."

"And also get some help over here," Jack said. "I'm hoping some of the European countries have already made plans to fly supplies in."

"Yep, that's a priority, for sure," Jay replied.

As they entered the immigration building, they found that a small squabble was breaking out over by the food stores. Zoe and Pedro were allocating the edibles, and a small group had encircled them, demanding larger portions. One of the most vociferous was the young man who had arrived late and was trying to force women out of their beds. His back was to the front door as he screamed obscenities at Zoe.

It took only four long strides for Aaron to make it across the room and grab the guy by the back of the neck. He in turn twisted around and took a swing at Aaron. Aaron easily blocked it and decked the kid with a hard right to the nose. He went down, screaming in pain, blood flowing down his nostrils.

The four remaining men in the group – there were no women – turned toward Aaron. There was malice in their eyes. They began shouting at him in Portuguese. Bart moved forward with his fists up.

Aaron yelled, "Pedro, tell them to settle down. Everything's okay. We'll work out the food situation."

Pedro spoke in staccato fashion to the men. They still glowered at Aaron, and one of them spoke back to Pedro.

"He says they all think that the gringos are taking more than their fair share. They just want to make sure they get what they deserve."

"That's crazy," Bart said. "These Verdeans are just plain stupid."

This last word was close enough to its Spanish counterpart to make the locals visibly angry and take a step toward them.

From behind them, Captain Cross wordlessly and deftly pulled the shotgun out of the bag, racked it, and laid it across his arms. The men swirled around at the sound. It took only seconds for them to walk slowly back to their beds.

"That was scary," Zoe whispered to Aaron. "I hope that's the end of that."

"I hope so too, even though I think that's doubtful."

"I tell you what," Zoe said, "Let's get out of here and take a walk together."

"Great idea. But are you going to be able to walk very far on that ankle?" Aaron said, pointing to Zoe's wrapped foot.

"I think it will be okay," Zoe said. I've got it bandaged up pretty good."

"You are one tough lady."

They decided to head up into the hills surrounding the base of Pico do Fogo. The evening was hot and dry. A light ocean wind blew up dust from the rocky path. It also carried the vague hint of the stench of death from the corpses that still lay scattered on the beach.

They crossed back and forth along the way. The sun was just setting and cast a purple and orange pall against the mountain side. After about fifteen minutes, they decided to stop, rest, and watch the sun slip beneath the watery horizon. They took seats on a large, flat rock that was at chair height.

"It's been so crazy over the past two days, we haven't really had a chance to talk and get to know each other," Aaron said.

"You're right. I've wanted to get you alone so we could do that, but it seems something has always interrupted us. Why don't you tell me about where you come from, about your parents," Zoe responded.

"Okay, but I'd rather you start. Please."

"Alright," Zoe continued, "but it's not that long or interesting. I was raised in Evanston Illinois, just north of Chicago. My dad was a professor at Northwestern University, my mom a homemaker. My older brother and I attended public schools, and then we both got scholarships to Northwestern. I majored in Aviation Sciences. I graduated last year, and shortly afterward I got the internship to come here."

"Sounds somewhat similar to mine. I was a military brat. My father was a colonel in the air force. We moved a lot, so I attended a bunch of different schools. I have a younger sister who now lives in Birmingham, Alabama. She was married three years ago, and already has two children. Unfortunately my dad died of a heart attack last year. It was the toughest day of my life."

"I'm sorry to hear that, Aaron. I feel blessed that both my parents are alive and happy."

"So are you married Zoe? A boyfriend back home?"

"No to marriage. It's an ex back home. We were together for our last two years of college. I broke it off. Just wasn't going anywhere. Part of the reason I accepted this job was to get away from all of that. How about you . . . on the marriage, girlfriend end?"

"Same on the marriage. Not yet. I broke up with a girlfriend of five years just about a year ago. Have dated off and on. Nothing serious. I believe you have to be careful when on the rebound. Sometimes you tend to grab anything just to ease the hurt. Then you get into worse trouble."

"Hey I know that one," Zoe said with pursed lips. "Been there, done that."

"We all have."

The two sat in silence while the last rays of the sun created glorious havoc with the sky – bursts of pink, violet, dark blue striated the dome above them.

Zoe broke the silence. Looking up at the sky, she said, "Isn't it amazing that nature can display such beauty, while also causing death and destruction? The weather here has been fantastic over the past several months. Nothing more than a few showers, the rest clear skies and cool breezes. Then this horrible storm. Does God have two faces? One of love, one of hate? How else can you explain this incredible dichotomy?"

"I don't profess to understand it. I think it's mostly incomprehensible to us humans. All we can do is try to promote the positive, the good, and combat the evil. Why it all happens is a mystery. I don't mean to be harsh, but anyone who says otherwise is a charlatan, or a simpleton. I had to weather years at our Baptist church where everyone had the answer. The problem was, they didn't have a clue what the question was."

"I hear you," Zoe said. "Funny, I had the opposite. Both my parents were agnostics, if not outright atheists. I knew nothing about religion growing up. Since then I've taken some comparative religion courses, and found them fascinating. I don't know what's worse – being drowned in religious jargon, or being stranded in an unbelieving desert devoid of any reference to God."

"Both are the extremes, to be sure. I guess I like where I am now. I've got a foundation in Christianity, but feel free to practice it the way I want. My mom and I don't discuss it anymore. It's too painful. She's still conservative Baptist."

"I like where I am now too. Except for . . . ," and here Zoe looked down at the ground.

"Except for what, Zoe? What's the matter?"

"Well, I wasn't going to tell you. But I like you too much to keep secrets."

"You can tell me anything. I'm not judgmental."

"Okay, but please don't think the worst of me. I've never done anything like this before . . . in my entire life."

"I won't Zoe."

"I was here around three months when I met a geologist from the States. He was studying the activity of the volcano. I don't know how it happened, but we had an affair. Only a few times. It wasn't until he abruptly left to go back that I learned he was married with two kids back home. I felt so guilty when I heard that. Of course he told me he was single, but I should have known better. There were a lot of signals I should have seen. I was just too infatuated."

"I don't see how you can blame yourself for that, Zoe. He lied to you. Plus, you were away from home, and probably very lonely."

"I know. I know. But still." Zoe looked up at the sky and the mountain peak, and whispered,"I realize it sounds a little crazy, but when the storm hit when we were up in the tower, I thought it was my punishment for what I did."

"It's not crazy, it's just your feelings of guilt. You've got to let that go. Guilt can really eat away at you."

"You're absolutely right, Aaron. It feels so good being able to talk with someone about it. Especially someone as understanding as you." With that Zoe gave him a light kiss on his cheek. Aaron blushed slightly, but a smile immediately lit up his face.

As darkness descended on the small island, they got up to go back. There was a bright full moon which, despite the scattered clouds, offered an eerie, but sufficient light to make the going relatively easy. Aaron gently took her hand as they navigated the rough path.

When they turned a corner surrounded by some large boulders, Zoe stopped without warning. Aaron looked back quizzically. "Did you hear that Aaron?" she asked.

"No . . . what?"

"Listen." Zoe turned her head toward the direction of the boulders. Now Aaron could hear it. Was it a low growling? The question was answered when the seeming apparition of a large dog slunk out from behind the rocks. It was followed by three more of the same beefy stature. Their snarling could now be heard easily.

Aaron grabbed Zoe and pulled her behind him, placing his body between her and the animals. He then slowly began to shuffle backwards away from the dogs. Zoe stayed behind him, now hugging him around the waist. The canines, teeth bared, edged closer.

Aaron bent down quickly and picked up two large rocks in each hand. Brandishing them with waves of his arms, he emitted a blood curdling, atavistic, terrifying scream. The animals froze momentarily, but bent low, as if to spring.

In a split second, Aaron hurled the first, then the second rock at them, miraculously finding two targets. One dog squealed like a pig and turned and ran. Another backed off. The largest of the dogs, foaming saliva dripping from its mouth and nose, its hair standing preposterously high on its back, kept coming.

Aaron pushed behind him, sending Zoe several steps further back. He then took three quick strides toward the beast and with his military issue combat boot, leveled a powerful kick at its head. It met its target full on, and the dog collapsed in a heap before them. The other two immediately turned tail and scattered out into the fields lining the volcano.

Aaron stood, poised to attack again if the dog got back on its feet, but all it did was quiver. He returned quickly to Zoe, grabbed her hand, and they strode quickly down to the building. It wasn't until they got to within a hundred yards of the structure that they stopped to collect themselves.

Still winded from the confrontation with the dogs and the quick walk down, Zoe gasped, "That was incredible Aaron. I can't thank you enough. We could have been torn to pieces."

"Zoe, honestly, I don't know what happened. Something took me over. In an instant I regressed to a primitive state of kill or be killed. I felt no fear whatsoever . . . only abject rage. I think I got real lucky with those rocks and my kick. It could have gone the other way."

"I'm sure glad it didn't," Zoe said with a shudder.

They entered the building to find things weren't much better inside.

CHAPTER FORTY-SIX

They rested on the swim platform for a few minutes, trying to regain their strength. Jennifer was coming around, slowly. Mark had been hugging her tightly with one arm, while still holding his palm tightly against her forehead to stem the bleeding, which was now just subsiding.

"Jenn, we've got to get into the cockpit to get a bandage for your wound. Do you think you can do that?"

She gave a weak smile and nodded "yes." Mark was able to lift her to a standing position while pulling himself up by the stairway rail into the boat. It was still rocky, but it appeared that the waves had calmed somewhat. As his line of vision came up above the top rail, Mark let out a gasp. "Holy shit, Jenn. We've got to get going. The reef is almost on us!"

Jenn peered out through half-closed eyes. Just fifty yards away, she could make out the froth and spray cascading upward from the force of the sea against the coral. "Mark, leave me here. Get the boat going."

"Okay, hold on tight though." Mark hopped up the stairs and, moving the gear shift into forward, gave it some throttle. The boat lurched ahead, then stalled as the engine coughed, and quit. Mark turned the ignition over and over again, yet it would not catch. The reef was now no more that thirty yards ahead of them.

"Jenn, we've got to abandon ship, or we'll be dashed upon the rocks. Stay right there. I'll get the life raft." Mark moved quickly to the cowling ahead of the mast, opened the container holding the Revere Coastal emergency pod, and threw the raft into the sea to their starboard side. As its tether rope tautened, the pod immediately sprang to life, inflating to full size in only seconds. Holding the line in one hand, he worked his way to the stern. He then pulled the raft up against the swim platform.

"I'll hold it here Jenn. You've got to get in there as best you can. I'll follow."

The lip of the raft was barely over the edge of the platform, and with the swaying of the boat, it was a tricky maneuver, at best, to get inside. Jenn held her breath in case she didn't make it and took a leap of faith. She jumped through the opening and landed safely, squarely in the center of the inflated floor.

"Good job baby! Okay, I'm coming in."

The force of Jennifer's weight against the raft had moved it off the platform, and it was now bobbing erratically some three feet away. Mark stood, timing his leap, when a large wave crashed against them. He missed the raft by a good foot. Jenn immediately scrambled to her knees, reached out and grabbed him by the collar of his jacket as he rose to the surface. With some trouble, considering the extra weight of his clothing, and with Jennifer's assistance, Mark was able to make it into the pod. They zipped it up immediately to make it as waterproof as possible.

"What about the boat?" Jenn said with alarm in her voice.

Mark stared blankly for a moment. "There's nothing we can do now. She's on her own. I'm afraid we may have lost her."

Tears welling in her eyes, Jenn wrapped her arms around his neck. "I know how much Trade Winds meant to you. It meant almost as much to me. I fell in love with her too. She was more than a sailboat. She was our home, our source of adventure."

"Yeah. A lot of work went into her. But it was a labor of love. Strange how a combination of wood, fiberglass, and metal can become so personal."

"Well she's not gone yet. Maybe a miracle will happen."

Mark unzipped the canopy just enough to see outside. The wind had already pushed them many yards from the boat. She was barely distinguishable amidst the crest of the waves and the waning light. The turmoil of the sea about the reef was much closer.

"We're almost on the reef, Jenn. Let's get prepared. There's a patch kit somewhere in here just in case we need it. There's also a very good first aid kit. Let's get started on that."

"Alright. Do you think we'll survive going over the reef? Won't the raft get torn up?"

"With any luck we'll just float right over it. The coral doesn't rise up above the surface except in a few spots. Mostly its at least a few feet below. This thing only has a draft of a foot, if that. We'd have to be real unlucky to hit rock."

"Well, the way things have been going so far, I'm not too optimistic," Jennifer said.

CHAPTER FORTY-SEVEN

On the way to the hotel, Robbie got a call from Val.

"Hi sweetie. I'm on my way down. Just passed Homestead so I should be in KW in about two hours. Looking forward to seeing you, baby."

"That's great honey. I didn't expect you'd be able to break away so fast. Dyin' to see you too." Robbie remembered Ben. "By the bye, I've met a really nice guy who needed our help. He got robbed at his hotel – wallet, credit cards, ID, everything – and can't pick up the money wired to him for various reasons. We're going to front him some money for a couple of days until he can access the bucks. Okay?"

There was a brief pause on the line. "Sweetheart, are you sure it's okay? Can we trust him?"

Robbie looked right at Ben as he spoke. "I'm sure. After you meet him, I know you will be too."

"Okay Honey. I trust your instincts."

Robbie turned toward Ben again. "That was my wife, Val. She got away sooner than I expected. No problemo. I'll get you another room for tonight. We all can have dinner together."

Ben shrugged. "I have no other option than to graciously accept your offer. I've never been a burden on anyone before, and I don't like it. I promise I'll pay you back."

"I know you will. I've got no qualms about that."

They rode in silence for a few minutes when Ben said, "How about this plan. I didn't want to get my wife involved. But now I know

I've got to. She's a real worry wart, and I didn't want her fretting. Why don't I call her on your phone and have her wire money in your name. Then we don't have to hassle with the police."

"You really don't have to do that Ben. I can wait."

"No, I think I should. Marjorie and I haven't been getting along that well recently, but this is something she should know about. We're supposed to be a partnership, right?"

"Yes we are. But it doesn't always work out that way. I'm really lucky to have a great marriage, and we communicate well. I think that's the key – communication. So I applaud your decision to let her in on this."

Robbie handed Ben his phone. Ben dialed, and even though Robbie could only hear Ben's side of the conversation clearly, by the tone and volume of the voice on the other end he knew Ben was in trouble. It made him glad he had the relationship he did.

Ben ended the conversation with, "Marj, I really appreciate this. I know it's all my fault, and I'll make it up to you. I've been fortunate to meet such a nice, generous guy, but I don't want to keep him hanging. Please wire the money as soon as you can and call me at this number when you've done it. Okay?"

Robbie could hear the sudden "click" from where he sat. Ben handed Robbie back his phone, and said, "She wasn't happy about it, but she'll do it. I feel better that I've told her. Thanks."

As they drove by the K-Mart Plaza, Robbie told Ben he was going to stop in and get him an extra change of clothing and toiletries. Ben thanked him profusely again, and they went shopping. On the way out of the store, Robbie took a call. Ben couldn't fully make out the gist of the conversation, but noticed Robbie's voice seemed stressed.

When he hung up, he said, "That was the shop. I've got to go in right after we get you a room. Would you mind going out to dinner just with Val? She's good company and I'd rather her not be alone."

"I'd be glad to. Just ask her to ring my room when she gets in and is ready to go out. Where would you suggest we go?"

"There's a good restaurant right around the corner at the Marriott. It's called Tavern & Town. I've eaten there several times. Good food, pleasant ambiance."

"We'll try that. What's happening at the office?"

Robbie grimaced. "Daemon is heading right for Miami. They think the eye will pass directly over Miami Beach. The coast is going to get socked. It's not just the winds. The storm surge is expected to be horrendous. They're issuing a mandatory evacuation order for everyone except essential personnel. That's going to be a mess."

"Wow, I guess I'm lucky to be down here, then."

"I wouldn't count my blessings yet, Ben. It appears right on track to hit the Keys, including Key West."

"If I didn't know better, I'd say it's following me . . . coming after me for my transgressions."

Robbie noticed Ben said the first part jocularly, but the second in a more serious tone. He let it go. Yet he would remember it later.

CHAPTER FORTY-EIGHT

They walked into the room to find a standoff occurring between most of the Cape Verde men, with a few women, and the crew of Miss Piggy and Pedro and Marcia. Some of the other Cape natives were sitting up against the back wall, looking on with consternation. The Captain had the shotgun across his arms. Pedro was talking heatedly with two of the men.

Aaron grabbed Zoe's hand and led her around to their group.

"Captain, can you tell me what's going on here," Aaron shouted above the arguing.

"This group over there huddled together after you left, and then confronted us about the food and water situation again. The problem is Pedro says they're not making any sense. They can clearly see what we have in terms of stores, yet they still think we're hoarding more someplace else. No amount of explaining helps."

"Let me try," Aaron said as he took up a position next to Pedro. He spoke to Pedro briefly, and Pedro spoke again to the two men, who continued to yell and gesticulate wildly. After Pedro addressed the men, they said some words to each other. In an instant one of them lunged at Aaron, going for his throat with both hands. Aaron sidestepped him easily, and gave him a hard karate chop to the back of his neck, sending him to the floor in a heap.

As if by some silent command, the remainder of the group came at them. There was a deafening blast, as Jay discharged his weapon out one of the windows. He then aimed it directly at the group. They stopped, amidst shouts of fear.

"Pedro, tell them I intend to shoot to kill," Captain Cross yelled above the bedlam.

Pedro looked back at him with a distinct look of alarm.

"Tell them. Now!"

Pedro spoke to the group again, and they began backing away.

Jay turned to his men. "We're going to sleep in the plane tonight, and for the foreseeable future. It'll be tight, but we can manage. Bart, gather up enough food and water for us for three days, and leave the rest behind." He handed the Glock to Aaron and asked Jack Porter to carry the bag with the remainder of the guns.

Zoe and Bart went through the supplies quickly, and tried to estimate what they would need. Zoe didn't want to cause more trouble by taking too much. When Bart kept jamming increasing amounts of food into the trash bag they had procured for the task, Zoe asked him what he was doing, Bart ignored her and filled the bag to the brim. Pedro tried to explain to the Cape Verde people what they were doing. His words were met with a morose silence.

Jay led them to the plane, and the men helped the women up the tiny ladder.

"My God, Aaron, this is cramped," Zoe said as she surveyed her surroundings.

Marcia and Pedro looked at the banks of electronics and tight quarters with worried looks. Cross showed the initiates where they could find the head, and then went about getting his men to make sleeping quarters for everyone. They used some of the life jackets, and inflated the life raft in the back of the plane, which they offered to Pedro and his wife. Its air filled floor allowed for the best sleeping accommodations in the plane. Aaron and Zoe were given two of the four available bunk beds. The Captain would take the pilot's seat.

After they divvied up and ate some of the food and water for dinner, they sat around and talked. Pedro and Marcia had retired to their makeshift bed in the rear of the plane.

"My crew and I will work overtime to get this bird flying again. Aaron, can you help out with that?"

"Of course. I worked in a sheet metal fabrication shop for two summers during college. I don't know if that will help or not."

"It certainly can't hurt," Bart aid.

"Do you think we'll be safe in here?" Zoe said with uncertainty in her voice.

"We will," Jay said. "Nobody can get in here when we've locked the fuselage door from the inside."

"What do you think is the matter with those people?" Bart asked. "I mean, did they really believe we were taking more than our fair share of the provisions. It should have been obvious to anyone that wasn't the case."

Zoe looked at him with apprehension.

"They did go through a terrible experience," Aaron responded. "I don't know exactly how they weathered the storm, but it wouldn't have been pleasant. I know how it was in that tower . . . pure hell. It almost killed all of us."

"That's true. I've been through a lot of hurricanes, but never one like that," the Captain said. "When we were going through the eye, it almost seemed like we wouldn't be able to escape from it. The eye wall was of unbelievable proportions. I got the sense that we were traveling outside of time and space when we were in there. It was eerie."

Bart McCullough cut in. "I got the same feeling. I thought we were going to be torn apart in there. How we made it out, with that level of turbulence, is a mystery to me."

"I, for one, saw something different in the eyes of those people in there," Zoe said. "It was more than surviving a catastrophe. Somehow they were transformed by their experience. And not in a good way. I felt the same when we were attacked by those dogs. Maybe it was starvation or lack of water. I don't know. But there was this primeval aura in their eyes. A fierceness that I can't explain in words."

"Well, we just need to be very careful whenever we venture out of the plane," Cross said. "Why don't we agree no one will leave without being accompanied by one of us with a gun. That's the only way we can assure everyone's safety. Agreed?"

All nodded their assent, and retired for the night. Aaron took the bunk atop of Zoe's. "Good night Zoe. Don't worry. We'll make it out of here and home. That's a promise."

"Thanks Aaron. I appreciate that. I'm optimistic. But we've got to be careful."

"Amen to that, Zoe." They were asleep seconds after their heads hit the pillow.

CHAPTER FORTY-NINE

They quickly surveyed their new, and hopefully temporary home. The pod had a diameter of six feet, which meant, when leaning against the inflated tube around the perimeter, they could extend their legs completely. The floor was also filled with air which was independent of the central tube. The orange canvas roof, which itself was supported by inflated tubes, allowed in a strange iridescent light.

Mark and Jennifer hurriedly went about the process of exploring. They opened each of the five zippered pockets around the edges and emptied them. "Now I wish we had inflated this thing and examined its contents during our preparation time," Mark said as he laid out the contents of the pouches closest to him. "I had a list of what's here, which is probably amongst all the manuals."

"Wait, I think I found the patch kit," Jennifer said excitedly, as she held up a clear plastic envelope.

Mark took it from her hand, opened it, and quickly scanned the instruction sheet. "Hey, this is great. We can apply these patches under water, if we need to."

"I hope we don't need to."

Mark set aside the envelope and opened a first aid kit. Leafing through it, he pulled out some packets. "Here're some butterfly bandages. Move over closer Jenn so I can dress that gash."

The cut on Jennifer's forehead had congealed, but was still nasty looking. Mark first applied an anti-bacterial ointment, and then carefully stretched the bandage across the wound. It was a difficult process because the waves were causing the raft to rear up like a drunken stallion.

They quickly restored the contents: additional life jackets; a flare kit; some charts; two short, collapsible oars; space blankets; and energy bars and food, to their respective storage pouches. The patch kit they left out and ready.

"Now I feel bad that I got you into this Jenn. You'd be safe and sound at home if you hadn't come on this trip. I've done nothing other than expose you to extreme danger."

"Mark, you must be kidding. You've brought me truly alive for the first time in years. I was dead . . . emotionally, I mean. I think I've met the man of my dreams. This trip has been a real awakening for me."

"I feel the same way Jenn. You're the one for me. I know it." They kissed passionately, lingering with their lips together.

Mark again opened the canvas cover at the top and peeked out. "Okay Jenn. Hold on. We're passing over the reef. Let's cross our fingers."

They huddled together. As they hit the edge of the reef, the harsh chop tossed them around inside the tiny craft like marbles in a blender. Several times it almost capsized. After ten minutes, a sudden calm enveloped them.

"Jenn, we've passed over the reef. We're now on the protected side. I think we've made it," Mark exclaimed. He unzipped the cover once again, and standing as best he could, peered around him, covering almost three hundred sixty degrees. Behind them was the agitated water they had just passed over. Ahead was the most magnificent sight he could imagine.

"Jenn, come here. Be careful."

She made it over to the opening slowly, and stood next to Mark. Before her was a broad, restful bay, a cobalt blue blending into a light green. Beyond, at a distance of several miles, were glowing pink beaches in front of palm tree laden hills. The sky was clear blue with puffy white clouds. The only spoiler was a band of large thunderheads to the south.

She turned back to Mark and said, "If the wind keeps blowing the way it is, we should be ashore in a day. What do you think?"

"That sounds about right. That's St. George's ahead of us. But we're also in an area where there's a lot of boat traffic. We'll be okay. Jenn." Mark gave her a tremendous hug. She hugged back.

They settled into a routine. Mark checked outside every thirty minutes to look for other boats, and estimate their progress. They agreed that if they saw anything, they would fire off a flare. Jennifer pulled out some of the bars and wafers and they ate voraciously.

Their mood started to sour a little as the sun set behind the island and they seemed to have made little headway toward land. "I thought we'd be closer than we are now. The wind is about the same, but I'm guessing the current has changed. We seem to be heading more northward now."

"Don't worry Mark. We'll get there. We've got each other, even if we have to spend the night out here alone."

"You got that right, babe. Together we're invincible."

When darkness closed in, Mark suggested they fire off a flare every hour, more so they wouldn't be run over by a larger vessel than for rescue. The night was dark blue, the near perfect circular moon obscured by heavy damp clouds. Mark had sent the third flare streaming into the sky, when he turned to Jenn. "I've got a bad feeling about this. The shore lights seem to be getting farther away. I hope the wind changes direction, or the current shifts."

Jenn looked outside for the first time in hours. "Damn, you're right. The land is definitely farther away. What are we going to do?"

"Not too much we can do. Paddling would be futile. We're way out. We'd just exhaust ourselves."

"Guess we've got to hunker down and roll with the punches . . . or, I mean waves."

Mark grinned at this attempt at humor, and nodded his head. Another half hour passed, and Mark perked up, listening. "Do you hear that, Jenn? Is it getting rougher out there?"

Jenn strained to understand what he meant. She opened the canvas top, and put her head out. She pulled back in. "Shit Mark. Damn if we aren't hitting the reef again. It's right there!"

"We must have been carried north of the island, and now we're into the north end of the reef. Damn! I never thought that would happen. Get the patch kit handy, Jenn."

She pulled it out and they waited. The sound of raging surf got closer and closer. Now they were in the same maelstrom of foam and chop. They held on to each other as they had before. It was pitch black inside the pod. Then the sounds Mark had been praying he would never hear: a loud pop as razor sharp coral punctured the floor of the raft, and a loud hissing and gurgling as the air escaped into the elements. Within seconds they were sitting on no more than a stretched piece of hard rubber, seawater bubbling through a gaping gash in its surface.

CHAPTER FIFTY

After he had made arrangements for a separate room for Ben, and spoken to Val, Robbie left for the station. When he arrived, it was in emergency mode. He received the most recent update on Daemon directly from Larry Grimes: "The storm is now four hundred miles east of Miami. Already they're getting high winds and some storm surge. The city is only half evacuated. It looks doubtful they'll be able to get everyone out in time."

Robbie answered, "That's got the makings of a huge tragedy. But nothing we can do about the evacuation. How are we doing on the storm track. Are the models consistent?"

"Very. We're only a hundred miles apart in the most deviant paths. It's head on to Miami Beach."

"Okay. Let me sit down and keep working on the track and strength analysis."

"Okay, Robbie. We'll all be sharing our information and results."

Robbie went to an unoccupied work station. Everyone was intently working out the formulas and algorithms predicting the future movement of the storm.

Val arrived at the hotel an hour after Robbie had left. She took a shower and changed into white shorts and a pink silk blouse. A little fancy for Key West she thought, but she didn't want to dress too colloquially when first meeting a strange man. She still had her reservations about going out to dinner with Ben, but it was either room service or that. She wouldn't go out by herself. She rang his room on the house phone.

"Hello." With little affect.

"Hi Ben. This is Valerie, Robbie's wife. How are you?"

"As good as I can be under the circumstances. I know Robbie told you what happened to me."

"Yes he did. And I'm sorry. That was a tough break."

"Yes . . . but honestly, I kinda brought it on myself. I was trusting where I shouldn't have been."

"Well, I think it's better to be trusting than paranoid . . . until someone gives you reason to suspect anything."

"That's the way I've been – all my life. Now I'm not so sure. Maybe just being a little more discerning of people is the key."

"Yes, you have to be discerning, and at the same time open to new people, circumstances, opportunities. But in any event, let's go have some dinner and discuss all these things, and also have a good time. Okay?"

"Absolutely. Why don't I meet you downstairs in the lobby in a half hour. Robbie said the restaurant was within walking distance. Does that work for you?"

"A half hour it is."

****

Robbie was studying every tidbit of information available: wind speeds, barometer readings, confluence of other weather patterns. It was a huge database of numbers and equations. This is what he loved. This is what he had studied for. The only countervailing emotion was fear – fear that they would miss something, might make a mistake, anything that could result in an increased loss of property, and possibly of lives.

After an hour, he got up and searched out Larry. He found him on the phone in his office. Robbie sat down respectfully and waited. It appeared that Larry was speaking with a top official in Washington.

"Chet," Larry was saying. "All I can tell you is we've allocated every resource to this thing. We just can't estimate yet what the full impact of Daemon will be. It's too early. There's a total evacuation order for Miami. That's the best we can do right now."

Robbie could hear there was a verbal response on the other end, then Larry continued: "I fully understand the seriousness of the situation. We'll keep you posted every hour. You can tell the President we'll leave no stone unturned in determining the track and strength of this beast."

He hung up and turned to Robbie. "That was Chet Hunter, the President's top aide on emergency responsiveness. It's so difficult dealing with these political types. Their only real concern is, *numero uno,* how the President will look, two, how *they'll* look, and lastly, what the impact on the public will be. It's like talking to a stone wall."

"I hear you. My boss in Miami complained all the time about his difficulties in reporting the status of storms to higher ups. You had to dumb down everything you said to make it comprehensible."

"Exactly. So how are we doing on Daemon?"

"Do you want the bad news first – or the *bad* news first?"

"How about some good news for a change?"

"Don't have any of that for you Larry. In fact, my analysis shows this one getting even more powerful. There's a strong low sweeping down from the northeast and mid-Atlantic states. When it collides with Daemon, the net effect will be a strengthening of the hurricane . . . as if that's possible. It's already off the scale."

"Oh boy. I was hoping for something better. How about its track?"

"I was getting to that. I've got it heading directly for the Keys. In fact, the eye should be right over Key West in about two days. My recommendation is that we advise an immediate evacuation of the Keys. You know how long it takes to accomplish that. One road in, one road out. We need to get those people going – *now.* As it is, they'll still be heading right for the storm, so our advisory should include a strong directive that the evacuation be by air and boat to the fullest extent possible."

"Robbie. Do me a favor, will ya? Send me an e-mail with all the data supporting that recommendation. I'll shoot it up to Chet for his approval."

"I'll do it right away."

****

Ben made it down to the lobby first. He whiled away a few minutes looking through tourist brochures. Every conceivable water sport: snorkeling, parasailing, wave runners – you name it – were available. Ben had just learned from the tourist channel while he was changing upstairs that the Keys were bordered on the south – the Atlantic side – by the only living coral barrier reef in the continental United States. In fact, according to the literature he now held in his hand, it is the third largest coral barrier reef system in the world. He'd like to go out to see it some day.

As he mused about brightly colored angel fish and fan coral, a beautiful young woman exited from the elevator. He knew instantly it had to be Val by the way she surveyed the room with an air of expectation. She was also about the same age as Robbie – early thirties – and carried herself with the same mien of self-confidence, without any hint of superciliousness. Her blonde hair was cut short in a sassy bob, opening her attractive face and green eyes to the world. Ben felt slightly and unpleasantly conspicuous in his cheap department store cargo shorts and too bold tropical shirt.

Sensing she should immediately defuse any awkwardness, Val came right up to him. "Ben, I presume," she whispered in a mock conspiratorial tone.

"Yes," Ben replied, just low enough to mimic her.

Val gave him a quick peck on the cheek, and said with a cute smile,"We have to stop meeting this way. We'll get caught."

Ben loved her right away: pretty, amusing, playful.

"I know. But getting caught is half the fun."

They both laughed.

"Okay, let's go and have a good time. You've been through so much that you deserve a nice night out."

"Thank you Val. I appreciate that."

Their destination was only a four block walk. They crossed North Roosevelt and walked along the sea wall facing the Gulf of Mexico. It was a delightful September evening, mid-eighties and quite humid, but with a moderate tropical breeze that kept them cool even at a decent walking pace. They walked side by side, occasionally having to go single file to allow room for a passing bicyclist. They engaged in small talk: Val's trip down, that she had visited Key West at least a dozen times in the past.

The Marriott Beachside Resort was the first hotel one came upon in passing through what the locals called "the triangle," the entry onto the island and the split into Route One to the north and A-1A to the south – named North and South Roosevelt Boulevards respectively. The northern route led to the business and commercial sector, while the southern to Smathers Beach and luxury hotels and condominiums.

The hotel restaurant, called "Tavern & Town", was a popular watering hole, not just for the hotel guests but for locals as well. The happy hour was notorious for a town well-versed in such things, with a wide assortment of two for one beverages and tasty tapas. Excellent live music was played daily.

When Val and Ben arrived it was quite crowded. A pianist was singing show tunes. The almost circular bar was directly inside. It was all mahogany and brass. They were shown to a table not too far back where they were able to hear the music and still converse easily.

"This is much nicer than I expected," Ben said. "So far I've only seen the dark side of Key West . . . lower Duval. Fun, but not classy. This is classy."

"It is. I mean, I don't mind partying with the best of them on Duval Street, but my preference is for places like this. The three of us should try Michaels in Old Town before we leave. It's the best restaurant in town."

"I just hope I have the money to treat you to Michaels. My wife is supposed to wire the money in Robbie's name tomorrow. That way we'll be able to pick it up without any hassles."

"I'm sure we'll be able to."

The waiter took their drink orders – for Val, a pinot grigio, for Ben, a vodka and tonic – while they perused the menus. "What's good here?" Ben asked.

"Robbie and I go for the tapas. It's just the right amount of food, and all of them are incredibly delicious. We usually order three and split them. I have a bit of a reputation for being able to put together interesting assortments of leftovers, and every time I eat here, I get new, creative ideas."

"That sounds like a great idea. How about this. I'll order one, and you order two. And then we'll share? Does that sound weird with a complete stranger, especially an older guy?"

"Not at all. Robbie says you're alright, and that's good enough for me."

"I'm alright, but pretty naive. Val, I feel I can talk to you. The fact of the matter is, I got myself into a situation I never should have. I'm embarrassed to admit it, but I went to the wine show in Miami Beach to break out of my marriage rut. Things between my wife and I have not been good lately. I thought I could get away from it, experience life more fully.

" Now I realize how much my family means to me . . . including my wife. Thank God my kids are doing so well. I could never call them for assistance. It'd be too embarrassing, and they don't have the money anyway. I also wouldn't want them to worry."

"Sometimes it takes experiences like you had to ground us . . . to get us to realize what's important in life."

"That's so true."

It was time to order, so they followed their agreed upon plan.

"I think, Val, what's bothering me most, is this feeling – a feeling I just can't shake – that I'm going to have to pay for my sins. This huge storm that's bearing down on us, it's like, you know, it's coming after me. Is that crazy?"

"Well, it's not crazy to have strong feelings of guilt. And that's all you're feeling here. I can assure you that the storm is not after you. Otherwise, we'd all have to say it's after us. I don't know if Robbie told you, but my degree is in education, and I work as a guidance counselor in the local high school where we live. I see examples of guilty consciences every day – girls who are having premarital sex, guys who are cheating on their exams it runs the gamut."

"So what do you say to them."

"I tell them, first, focus on what they can control. If I may use your situation as an example, you can't take back your decision to come down here with complete strangers, or undo the fact you were robbed. You certainly can't control a hurricane. But you can control what safety precautions you take to avoid being hurt in the storm, and you can work towards improving your relationship with your wife, which probably got you here in the first place."

"I see what you're saying. Stick with what I can actually do about my predicament, and put aside my paranoid thoughts about some divine retribution for my sins. Is that about it?"

"Yes. And be kind to yourself. Stop dwelling on your past mistakes, and look toward the future, a future that you're now better prepared for as a result of the mistakes you've already made."

"Thank you Val. That's excellent advice."

Their food came, and they whiled away a pleasant dinner with small talk. In the few short hours they had been together, Daemon had traveled another fifty miles closer to the Miami, and the surf bombarding the coast was already causing severe beach erosion.

CHAPTER FIFTY-ONE

Everyone in the plane woke up within five minutes of each other, primarily because of the close quarters. After taking turns in the small bathroom, they sat down and divided part of their food stock. Captain Cross actually made up some scrambled eggs on a one-burner stove plate out of the powdered eggs and milk. To this half-starved band, they tasted delicious.

Cross then went about the process of planning the day's repair work on the plane. Pedro exhibited some knowledge of sheet metal work, so he was included in that crew. Marcia and Zoe were asked to put away the supplies they had brought onboard, and clean up.

When the men exited the fuselage, they saw a few people milling about the immigration building. They gave the plane crew dirty looks. Jay felt more secure with the bag of guns in hand.

Bart was assigned to keep watch. He pulled the shotgun out of the bag and, holding it at cross-arms, stood next to the plane. The others got to work. Fortunately all of the basic tools necessary to do minor repairs were already on board: a pop rivet gun; metal shears; a hand drill; and an assortment of pliers, screw drivers, screws and nuts and bolts.

It was hard going in the scorching September sun. Soon they had to cover the area they were working on with canvas to keep it from getting too hot to touch. Those who were not actually hands on the job sat under the wing for respite.

They made good progress. The high winds had sheared off a line of rivets holding intact a panel of the "skin" of the fuselage. They had to carefully bend the sheet metal back in place, and work the wrinkles out with the hammer to make as smooth a surface as possible. Then the piece was re-riveted back in place. The most time was spent on a small hydraulic line just inside the surface which had been broken in the onslaught.

"I'm amazed we made it down with this line out," Jay said. "It goes directly to the port wing's primary flap. I remember having difficulty lining up with the runway. I thought it was all the wind, but now I see we had a mechanical malfunction as well."

"That just goes to show what a great pilot we had onboard," Jack added.

Except for a few brief breaks, they worked steadily throughout the afternoon. Zoe and Marcia came out regularly to bring water and snacks. Around five o'clock, they decided to wrap up their work.

As Aaron was putting away some of the tools and repositioning the canvas drape over the work area, he heard angry, excited voices to his rear. He whipped around and saw that a group of about ten men from the building had approached within fifty feet of them. They were again arguing with Pedro, who was trying to translate for Bart as quickly as he could.

As Aaron watched – Jay was a little way out on the wing – one of the men pulled out a screwdriver, brandishing it like a weapon. It was only then that Aaron saw two other men holding hammers. Yelling, they slowly inched their way toward the plane.

The scene was shattered by the raucous report of the shotgun. Bart had moved the gun into firing position, and sent a charge into the air. The approaching men stopped, but did not retreat.

"Pedro, tell them the next round will find its mark. Tell them they must back off. Immediately!"

Pedro spoke hurriedly in Portuguese. The men shouted back, but did not retreat.

"They're still claiming we're secreting food on them. This is insane," Pedro said to Bart.

"Well, we're dealing with insanity." He pointed the rifle directly at the chest of the lead man. "Tell them again to back off."

Pedro did so, and after some grumbling, they slowly headed back to the building. The crew quickly packed up their tools, and everyone reboarded the plane.

"This is not going to end well," Aaron said as they settled in. "I saw the same thing in their eyes. Inhuman. Deranged. We'd better get this baby airborne as soon as possible."

"You're right, there," Jay said. "Those guys showed little fear. I'm afraid we're going to have to set up a night watch system by the exit door. We can't afford to have them damage the plane. There are seven of us. We'll take an hour and a half each until morning light."

Hearing no opposition, Jay allocated the times. They then ate, and retired for the evening.

CHAPTER FIFTY-TWO

"Mark, what are we going to do now?" Jennifer said with a hint of panic in her voice. Already the turbulent motion of the sea was tossing them around inside the pod like popping popcorn without the support of an inflated floor.

"Not much we can do until daylight, babe. Let's just try to hang in there 'til then." Mark hugged her tightly to prevent their bodies from bashing into one another.

Several hours passed in extreme discomfort. With every wave they were sent from one end of the pod to the other. Then, and Mark could not figure out why, the tempest subsided. The swells were still large, but the chaotic choppiness was largely gone.

"It's starting to calm a bit. I think maybe the island is running interference for us."

"God, at least something is going right for a change." Jennifer tried to force a thin smile.

"Honey, I still don't think we'll get too far without being seen. Again, this is a very trafficked area."

Mark opened the pod and peered out. The sky was filled with the glow of the full moon. He could see no lights in the one direction they were facing. "Honey, hand me the flare gun, will you please."

Jennifer did so, and Mark fired one into the air. It exploded high above them with a loud bang, and a shower of sparkles. "Anyone within ten miles will see that. I bet ya we get rescued in a few hours."

"I love your optimism, lover. It keeps me going. But however long it takes, we'll make it together."

"That's the spirit, Jenn."

They settled into a routine of firing a flare and peering outside every hour. It was around ten o'clock when Jenn said, "Mark, your several hours have passed, and no rescue. I think you ought to swim back to Bermuda and get us a pizza. I'm hungry."

"How about if I just call room service. That will be faster."

"Okay. That'll work."

A few minutes passed in silence when Jenn said, "Mark I really was serious when I told you I felt something, someone, was punishing me because of Jared. Then when I heard the storm was heading away from us, I thought about how silly that sounded. Now I'm having the same feelings – even stronger. The new storm splitting off and threatening us, our having to bail out of the boat, losing the floor of the raft. It just seems never ending. Tell me I'm just imagining all this."

"You're not imagining the bad things that have happened, but you're imagining there's a reason for it, a consciousness that's behind it. That's your paranoia talking. That's not real. The problem is, when will it stop? Are you going to believe you're being disciplined for the rest of your life because of Jared? Let it stop now. It wasn't your fault. There is simply no unseen force out there that's against you. Get that out of your mind."

Realizing he may have been too stern with her, Mark added, "I'm sorry, Jenn. I didn't mean to be rough on you. I just don't want these emotions of yours to ruin your life. Nothing's worth that."

Jennifer paused, and said softly, "I know you're right, Mark. Thank you. Keep reminding me of that."

****

Daemon's progeny kept up its onslaught toward Bermuda. Its winds howled, scaring the sea into an undulating panic. Huge white caps developed to the south, east and west of the Bermuda Isles. Only to the north could one find temporary respite, the land mass protecting the stranded boaters. Its counterclockwise winds also swept from east to west at its northern point, driving any flotsam and jetsam in that direction.

****

At two in the morning, after they had shot off half their supply of flares, the couple was too exhausted to stay awake any longer. They collapsed against each other and huddled in a corner of the raft. Mark remembered awaking several times, but was in no condition to send a signal or even survey the world around them. Hours passed.

Jennifer was awakened by a bump, and the increasing glow within the pod. The canvas roof was dispersing the early morning light around the interior. She became concerned as the sound of surf against sand became more pronounced. She shook Mark hard. "Mark! Mark! Wake up. Something's happening. I think we may be on the reef again!"

Mark jumped when she touched him, and again at the insistence in her voice. "What is it, honey? Where are we?" He tried to shake the night's unpleasant dreams out of his conscious mind, and focus.

"I think we've hit something."

Mark sat up and listened intently. Then both became aware that they were no longer rising and falling with the waves, but seemed to have stabilized, only being occasionally jarred by a small wave.

"Let's take a look." Mark unzipped the pod cover, and sticking his head out the opening, immediately pulled it back in. "You're not going to believe this, Jenn. I don't know how this happened, or where we are, but we're washed up on some deserted beach. Those are palm trees out there!"

"That's not even funny, Mark," Jenn scolded. "Don't try to fool me like that. We're on the reef again, aren't we?"

Mark silently pulled the zipper to its full open position, and spread the canvas wide so Jenn could see outside. What she saw was the most beautiful sight she had ever seen. As Mark had described, they were washed up on a gorgeous sandy beach, surrounded by a long row of palm trees as far as the eye could see.

"How could this be," she said, already at the point of being giddy. "This is a miracle."

"So now is someone still punishing you?"

"No! Mark if I ever start talking like that again, please dope slap me."

"I'll never do that. But let's get out there and see if we can tell where we are."

Mark grabbed the charts stored on the raft, and they exited their temporary abode. Stepping out onto the soft sand of the beach, they looked around. To the south, their little island, assuming that's what it was, protruded as far as the eye could see. Also, out on the southern and eastern horizons, they could discern the tiny, hazy bumps of other islands.

"Jenn, there's simply no land to the north of Bermuda. We were headed out to Nova Scotia, or Greenland. Somehow I think we've been blown east to what I think is part of Sandy's Parrish. Exactly where, I'm not sure right now. But we're still in Bermuda!" Mark opened the chart and pointed to a small spit of land which curled northwesterly off the western end of the island chain.

"So civilization couldn't be too far off, right?"

"That's right. Let's grab some provisions and trek south down the beach and see if we can find anything."

They gathered some food, medical supplies, and water, and dragged the raft past the high water line. Then they headed down the beach. After a half mile, they rounded a bend, and Mark yelled, "Look Jenn. A sailboat."

Jenn looked up and saw the vessel, listing to one side, its sailless mast tilting toward them. "That's strange. Why would they leave their boat like that?" she questioned.

Mark broke into a mad dash, grinning from ear to ear. "Jenn, can't you see?" he yelled behind him between strides. "It's Trade Winds!"

They made it up to the vessel, and sure enough, it was their boat.

"It must have followed the same current we did," Mark gasped excitedly. "I hope it's not severely damaged."

Their sailboat was resting slightly askew, hard aground in four feet of water. Mark waded out and circled the craft, feeling along its hull with his hand. "As far as I can tell, honey, there's no structural damage. Somehow it made it through the reef – I don't know how many times – and came to a stop here, in the sand. Unbelievable."

Mark and Jenn hugged ecstatically, then sat down together on the beach and bawled their eyes out.

CHAPTER FIFTY-THREE

When Ben got back to the hotel, he decided to try Phil to see how he was going to deal with the storm.

"Hello good buddy."

"Oh. Hey Ben. How are you?"

"Pretty well, actually. I wasn't able to pick up the money. It's a long story. But this new friend I made bought me some clothes and got me a hotel room, so I'm doing okay. Marjorie is going to wire some money tomorrow in my friend's name so there won't be any hassles. I'll make sure your money is returned to you. And once again, I really appreciate it."

"That's good. Ya sure she'll send it?"

"Yeah, she will. Things aren't that bad."

"Well, I hope so, 'cause I won't be able to send any more. I flew out of Savannah yesterday, and am now in the Chicago area with my daughter. They don't have my bank up here."

"I'm glad you got out while you could, my man, but I'll be okay. Marj will come through."

Phil cleared his throat. "I hope so, Ben. By the way, this is the first storm I've ever evacuated for. My condo building is built like a brick shit house, but I'm still worried. I won't get any water damage 'cause I'm too far back, but the wind damage concerns me. I've got my hurricane shutters all set up, but the building has never gone through a category five hurricane before, so no one knows what's goin' to happen."

"I wish you the best, man."

"You be careful too, Benny. It's headin' right for you. Hope you batten down the hatches. You're on a tiny island, with no high ground."

"We're in a pretty solid hotel, so I'll be fine."

"This baby is living up to the origins of the word 'hurricane' – from 'Hurican', the Carib god of evil."

"Jesus, the god of evil?"

"Yeah, also derived from the Mayan god 'Hurakan,' one of their creator gods, who blew his breath across the chaotic water and brought forth dry land and later destroyed the men of wood with a great storm and flood."

"Well, I certainly don't want to be one of the 'men of wood.'"

"None of us do. Good luck, Ben."

Ben next tried calling his wife on the hotel phone. She answered on the fifth ring.

"Hey Marj. How are you?"

Silence on the other end. "Marj, are you there?"

"Yeah. What do you want?"

"Well, I just want to say hi, and tell you I love you."

"You must really want something bad, huh?"

"C'mon Marj. Let's not make this any more difficult than it has to be, okay?"

Again, another pause. This time Ben waited.

"What'd you do for dinner last night, without any money?"

The non sequitur put Ben on high alert. "Well honey, as I told you, I met this guy who works for the weather service. He's really helping me out. His wife came down here to get away from the storm that's bearing down on Miami. Robbie had to go into work, so . . . uh . . . Val and I had dinner together." He only realized how bad that sounded, for someone who didn't know Val and Robbie, after he had said it. He braced for the tempest to follow. He could feel the rising rage in her timbre.

"Oh, so you had dinner with another woman? You just don't learn, do you? I'm up here by myself, and you're partying with floozies. You can forget about the money, you bastard."

The phone went dead. Ben tried to call back five times, and gave up after letting it ring into their home voice mail five times. In each of his messages, he pleaded with his wife to understand, that it was a friend's wife, it was purely platonic. When he went to bed at midnight, he still hadn't received a return call.

****

Back at the NWS Key West station, the first reports of wind damage and storm surge were coming in from Miami. The full moon was creating high tides of astronomical proportions, and the winds were already clocking at eighty plus miles per hour. Many boats were reported off their moorings, and were now crashing into docks, seawalls, and other vessels. Numerous electrical lines had whipped themselves into oblivion. Power was out all the way from Eighth Street and south in SoBe.

Robbie was busy e-mailing summaries of the alerts to Larry. He was very apprehensive. At four A.M. he couldn't wait any longer. He called Val.

She answered sleepily. "Hey there."

"Hey babe. I'm so sorry to wake you at this hour. The info from Miami is not good. We're looking at a catastrophic hurricane here. You know that we can hole up here until it passes by Key West, but space is at a premium. It's first come, first served. I've got to ask you to shower and pack up, and get over here so we can secure you a bunk."

Val paused a moment. "But what about Ben?"

"Honey, I'm afraid Ben's on his own. He can't stay here. No way. It's only employees and immediate family. He'll get his money today and be able to stay at the hotel. I'm not saying that's one hundred per cent safe, but it'll have to do."

"I hate leaving him in the lurch like that."

"I do too. But we have to."

"Okay sweetie, I'll get ready and come on over."

Val placed a call to Ben's room. It went unanswered, so she left a voice mail, apologizing profusely for abandoning him.

CHAPTER FIFTY-FOUR

Zoe had always been a light sleeper. In fact, it was a rare night that she did not wake up and read for a while before falling back to sleep. Most of the women she knew didn't sleep well. *A genetic trait,* she thought, *for the protection of new borns.* Some of her married girl friends with children told her they would awaken at the slightest gurgling of their babies, while the father would snore contentedly nearby.

This night was no different, maybe exacerbated by the prior day's events and the need for a watch. She looked over from her bunk to see who was the lookout for the night. It would be the one sitting by the exit hatch. To her utter dismay, not only was Pedro curled into a fetal sleeping position, but a very light shuffling noise could be barely discerned outside directly beneath them.

She listened intently for a few more seconds, trying to determine if it was just her overactive imagination or reality. The question was answered when she first smelled, then saw, smoke wafting up through the tiny cracks in the door.

"Aaron!" she shouted, while reaching up and trying to stir him in the bunk above. The verbal cry was sufficient to wake him, plus everyone else in the plane, to immediate alertness.

Aaron started, sat up and quickly climbed down from his upper perch. "Zoe. What is it?"

"I smell smoke. In fact, I see smoke," she yelled, pointing in the direction of the hatch.

Aaron stood up and walked quickly over to Pedro, who was now just stirring to wakefulness. Jay and Bart were also beginning to leave their bunks. Jack was further down the fuselage and was only now awaking.

"Pedro, get out of the way. Something's going on outside."

Pedro obliged, and Aaron grabbed the hatch lever and pulled. The door released downward, both sending the ladder to the ground and allowing plumes of acrid smoke to fill the cabin.

"Everybody out! Now!" Aaron screamed. His eyes burning, he could barely make out the source of the smoke, what now looked like a large pile of garbage that had been stacked up under the plane and was on fire. "Jay, grab a gun."

Aaron was the first down, and he began kicking at the pile as best he could to disperse it. Gasping and coughing, the rest of the group made it down the stairs and out onto the tarmac. Jay joined Aaron's efforts, using the butt end of the shotgun to knock the stack of refuse askew. Soon those who had managed to grab their shoes on the way out joined in, stomping and cursing. Jack Porter, the last out, had managed to locate one of the small fire extinguishers. Within minutes they managed to put the flames out.

Aaron noticed Pedro was now skulking about over by the door to the immigration building. He had taken Marcia's hand and led her over there. "Hey Pedro. What are you doing? Where are you going?"

Pedro only looked sideways at him with a glare. He then rapped on the door three times. It opened, and Pedro and Marcia slipped inside without a word.

The group on the runway could only look at each other in

disbelief. "I guess blood is thicker than water," Bart said.

"Or thicker than thieves," Zoe added. She picked up a small duffel bag lying on the ground and poured the contents on the asphalt. Cans of foodstuffs rolled lazily and finally settled. "I noticed Marcia was carrying this as she was going down the stairs. She dropped it when I knocked into her to help put out the fire."

They stood silently, trying to grasp the degree of the duplicity, when Jay said, "We've got our work cut out for us. Let's get something to eat, and start on the plane. I'll need all the men up on the wing with me today. Zoe, can you man the shotgun? If the worst happens, shoot one time in the air, then aim and shoot to kill. Can you do that?"

Zoe looked grimly at Aaron, and said simply, "Yes. I can do that."

Aaron came over and gave her a warm hug. They ate on the tarmac to keep an eye on the building. They saw only a few people occasionally come out and mill around the door. None took a step toward the plane.

They worked on the plane all morning and into the early afternoon. Fortunately the fire had caused minimal damage to the under belly of the plane – some blistered paint and slight wrinkling of the sheet metal skin. Zoe not only carried the shotgun, but handed up water when necessary. The late summer sun was hot by the early afternoon.

At two o'clock they took a break. They sat under the wing and snacked on some chips. Captain Jay Cross spoke first. "We're making great progress. At this rate I think we may be able to do a test run in the air for a few minutes tomorrow afternoon. When we finish today, I want

Aaron and Bart to accompany me over to the fuel depot. We've got to see if the pumps are working, and if so, how much fuel is available. We've got enough to island hop to find more if we need to, but I sure would like to fill 'er up and make it to Bermuda, if not farther. That would be ideal."

"What would you like me to do?" Jack asked.

"Stay here with Zoe and guard the plane. If we hear a gun shot, we'll come running. We'll take two of the other weapons. If you hear one on our end, stay with the plane. We'll be on our own."

They stopped work around five. As planned, Zoe and Jack stayed with the plane, while the other men made a large circle around the terminal to the other side to access the depot. A half hour later, Jack noticed about ten men slip out of the door and congregate to one side of the building. He saw that the crazed young man was talking in an agitated way to the others.

"Zoe, why don't you give me the gun."

"Why, Jack?"

"I just have an uneasy feeling."

She handed him the shotgun. They were still sitting under the wing.

Jay, Aaron and Bart rounded the terminal and approached the depot. It was surrounded by piles of debris – splintered wood, seaweed, stones. After a half hour of clearing, they were able to isolate one of the pumps.

Bart turned it to the "on" position, removed the nozzle, and pulled the trigger. Nothing. "This thing is electrically operated, so without power, we'll get nowhere this way. But most of these have a manual back up."

He took a small pen knife out of his pocket and undid the several screws that held the front panel to the pump. "Here we go. Aaron, hold the nozzle down toward the ground for a second." Bart grabbed a lever located inside the pump and began working it in an up and down motion. Petrol began pouring out of the nozzle.

"Look at that!" Jay exclaimed excitedly. "Is there any way to figure out how much we've got available?"

Bart stopped pumping. "We'll have to locate the covers to the tanks and push a stick down."

They looked around but the ground about them was still mostly covered with palm fronds, leaves and sand. No access covers could be found.

Just then a gun shot echoed around them.

CHAPTER FIFTY-FIVE

They had needed a good cry. It helped relieve the incredible tension that had built up from the prior day's events. Mark and Jenn looked at each other sheepishly.

"I feel better now. How about you," Mark ventured.

"Much better. I thought we'd lost everything, and were going to lose our lives as well."

"I certainly had my doubts."

"You sure hid them well. Whenever I felt I was going to lose it, I gained strength from you."

"I'm pretty good at disguising my emotions sometimes. Especially fear. And so are you. I never suspected you were at the end of your rope at any point."

"I guess we can both be good fakers, huh?"

"I hope not where it counts the most," Mark said with a wink.

Jennifer blushed lightly. "No, not then, for sure."

Mark got up. "I'm guessing it's about midway between low and high tide. It's waxing so I'm hopeful we'll be able to get Trade Winds afloat without outside help. I'm going on board to get my tide charts. Let's load these provisions on together."

They lowered the swim platform ladder. Mark boarded first, and Jenn handed up the bag of provisions they had taken off the raft. The interior was remarkably unscathed. A few items they had not had time to put away– a hand held GPS unit, some cups, a water bottle – were strewn about. There didn't appear to be any damage.

"Babe, we sure got lucky. Just to get her back at all is a miracle. That she's not badly damaged is a double miracle, if that's possible."

"It's also a miracle we're alive."

"Amen to that. Tell you what. Since we have time, let's walk back, deflate the raft, and bring it back. We might be able to patch it back to life."

"Let's do it."

Mark first tossed a small anchor seaward and fastened it to a stern cleat. He also checked the main sail for any rips or tears. Then they walked the approximate half mile down the beach and retrieved the emergency pod. It was heavy enough that each had to take an end. The whole process took over an hour, and they were pleasantly surprised to see the stern of their boat bobbing gently upon their arrival.

"She's already shifted off the ground a little," Mark said as they waded out. "I think we're going to be okay."

In another hour, having boarded and stowed the raft, Mark tried the engine. Once again it coughed and sputtered, but finally lit. He let it idle for a few minutes, and while Jenn pulled the line toward the anchor, he put it in reverse. The engine strained to disengage the keel from the sandy bottom. With a suctioning sound, it was released, and Trade Winds headed backward until they reached deeper water.

"Jenn, take the helm please. I'm putting it in forward. Head southeast while I try to find a safe harbor for us."

Mark looked at his charts. "I'm now sure we're in Black Bay, just off of Ireland Island North. It's all part of Sandy's Parrish. If we head south, we'll run right into Mangrove Bay. It's a very protected area with a couple of marinas. We'll motor the whole way."

"So looks like we made it, huh lover? Welcome to Bermuda!"

Jenn disappeared below, and came up with their last bottle of champagne. She popped the cork, and the foamy liquid poured onto the deck. She then shook it and sprayed them both.

"Hey. Cut that out," Mark yelled, smiling. It was warm and tasty.

They entered into Mangrove Bay in an hour and tied up to the main wharf. Mark went to the harbor master's office and got permission to stay for several nights. "Guess we're going to get a bit of a blow," Mark said as he was leaving the office.

He got a cold stare in return from the wizened, older black man across from the counter. He was dressed in a torn, stained uniform of questionable origin. "Guess you could call 'er that."

"What's the latest on her?" Mark asked pleasantly.

"I'd git 'er outta the water, if I were you."

"What's the chance of getting that done today or tomorrow?"

"Worse than none."

Jennifer noticed the harbor was abuzz with activity. Boats of all kinds were lined up to be taken out by the huge belt lift on the other side of the pier. Others were maneuvering their vessels around to find a good spot with solid anchoring and enough swing room so as not to collide with their neighbors.

She wondered what arrangements Mark would choose to make, or that they'd have to make for the approaching storm. The frenzied activity she observed around her only served to increase her anxiety. When Mark returned, she could tell he was perturbed. "What's wrong, honey?"

"I was hoping we could get hauled out before the storm, but that looks unlikely now. I'm going to study the charts, and ask around a little. See if I can find a decent hurricane hole. This harbor's a little too crowded for my tastes."

"But we could stay here if we needed to, right?"

"Yes, but it's not as protected as I thought it would be. Let's see if we can find somewhere else."

They sat in silence as Mark studied the nautical maps. Finally Mark said excitedly, "I've found it. This is perfect." He called Jenn over. "It's here. 'Ely's Harbour.' It's got plenty of little coves where we can hole up."

"I don't see any towns around there," Jenn said hesitantly.

"That's why it's so good. We can probably find a spot with no one else around. That's how boats get damaged in a storm – banging against one another."

"Okay honey. If you say so."

CHAPTER FIFTY-SIX

Ben awoke early, without the aid of an alarm. His conversation with Marjorie still burned in his ears. *She wouldn't refuse to send the money,* he thought.

He turned on the news and went in to take a shower. When he returned to the room, he saw the tail end of a weather report. The day in Key West was going to be warm – around ninety – but the edge of the ominous cone of Daemon 's path was now directly against the Miami coast. Newsreels showed monstrous waves crashing on the dunes on Miami Beach, against the backdrop of a deserted city.

Just then Ben noticed the flashing red light on the phone, signifying a pending voice message. He picked up the receiver, hit the mail button, and listened. It was Val's voice.

"Hi Ben. I hope you get this message sooner than later. I'm getting ready to leave the hotel and go to the station. Robbie insisted I come over because of Daemon. I wish you could join us but only employees and family are allowed. I'm sure you'll get your money today and will be fine. It was nice meeting you, and be safe."

A momentary sense of panic rose in Ben's throat like a poisonous bile. He decided to try his wife again. Three attempts brought no more than their home voice mail greeting. Each time he begged her to call him back, and wire the money.

Ben went down and had a simple courtesy breakfast. The room was almost empty, except for an older couple. The house television was tuned to the storm. Ben figured every station would have the same.

As he ate, he could overhear the couple talking.

"I told you we should have left this morning," the woman complained. "Now it looks like we won't be able to drive out. Route One is bumper to bumper. What do we do now? We've been ordered to evacuate."

"Well, if we can't leave, we can't leave," the man said gruffly. "We'll be fine here."

Ben couldn't help but inquire. "Excuse me, I don't mean to eavesdrop, but did you say we're supposed to leave Key West?"

"Where have you been all morning?" the man asked tersely. "It's all over the news. The order issued last night . . . late. We're supposed to be out of here by the end of today."

"I don't know how I'll manage that," Ben said.

"Well, that's the order."

Ben returned to his room. He was beyond worried. He tried Robbie's cell several times, and got no answer. He hung out for a while watching the tube. At eleven thirty, there was a loud knock on the door. "Security," a strong male voice said.

Ben opened the door part way with the security latch hooked.

"Can I help you?" Ben said meekly.

"Mr. Harris? I'm officer Weeks, hotel security. Everyone has to evacuate the hotel by noon today. You're also only paid up for last night, and checkout is eleven. Please pack your things and vacate this room within the half hour."

Before Ben could utter a word, Weeks was off down the hallway knocking on the other doors. *What am I going to do now?* Ben asked himself.

CHAPTER FIFTY-SEVEN

The three men, without any communication between them, immediately began dashing at full tilt back to the plane. Aaron, being the youngest, led the pack and separated himself well ahead of the older men. Just before he came around the terminal building, he heard another loud report. He somehow increased his speed.

He first saw a body lying under the wing of the plane and a person standing, holding a rifle at firing position. Selfishly, he thought, I hope it's Zoe who's upright. He next saw a prostrate body closer to the immigration building and a group of about ten people standing around it. They were gesticulating wildly toward the plane.

Aaron approached the plane. It was only then, with great relief, he saw that it was Zoe with the gun. Behind him he heard another shot. He turned to see the Captain, at least fifty yards away, with a pistol held in the air.

"Aaron. Come this way. Keep your eye on them," Zoe shouted, pointing toward the group.

He came right up to Zoe. Jack was lying on the ground with a bloody gash on his forehead. He was struggling to get to his knees. "What happened?" Aaron asked.

"That group started to come toward us. A large rock came out of the pack and hit Jack in the head. When he went down, I grabbed the shotgun and fired into the air. They stopped, then began coming at us again. That's when I shot the lead man."

Zoe was visibly shaking, but kept a firm eye and the gun trained on the Cape Verdeans. Jay and Bart caught up with them.

"Zoe, you've done your job. Good work. Why don't you let Aaron take over now," Jay said, pointing to the weapon.

She clicked the safety to the "on" position and handed the shotgun to Aaron. Zoe then knelt down beside Jack. "How are you doing?"

"I'll be okay. Probably just a bad headache for a while."

Zoe walked over and grabbed a clean rag from the stack the men had been using while they worked on the plane. She then held it against the wound just above Jack's left eye. It was no longer actively bleeding.

The Captain yelled over to the group. Several had already carried the body of the man shot by Zoe into the building. "Do any of you speak English?"

They just stared sullenly at him.

"Where is Pedro? Let me speak to him," Jay continued.

One of the men shouted into the open door of the immigration building. Within a minute, Pedro slowly walked out.

"Pedro," Jay shouted. "Please! Let's all talk. We don't want any more bloodshed."

Pedro glanced at his cohorts. "There's nothing to talk about. Our women and children are starving in there, and you have all the food. Give us your food and then we'll talk."

"You know that isn't true, Pedro," Jay responded angrily. "You've been with us. You know we were fair when we divided the food and water. Tell your people that."

Pedro turned and spoke quietly and briefly with those around him. He then turned to the Captain. "No one believes that. I don't believe that. Give us what you've got and then we'll talk."

Zoe walked up to Jay. "Captain Cross. I know enough Portuguese to understand what Pedro said to them. He said that we have all the food and water, and refuse to give up any. He's actually instigating them against us."

Dusk was beginning to envelope them. Deep shadows were forming around the buildings and higher up on the volcano.

Cross said, "Alright. I guess this is the way this has to be. We've only got five of us now. We'll need two at a time to keep watch, with two of the guns, outside of the plane. Aaron and Zoe, you take the first shift, from eight to midnight. Jack, if you're okay to do it, take the midnight to four shift with Bart. I'll do the four to dawn shift by myself."

Jack was on his feet. "I'm alright now. I can do that shift."

Jay continued. "Good Jack. Thanks. No matter what happens, try to fire one shot in the air first. That will alert the rest of us to come out. Shoot to kill on the second. Agreed?"

"Agreed," they all said in unison.

CHAPTER FIFTY-EIGHT

Jennifer had her reservations about anchoring so far from civilization, but kept her thoughts to herself. Mark had brought them safely to this point, albeit with some squiggles, she reasoned. She would stick with his plans.

They motored the entire way, a distance of about twenty nautical miles. They had to round King's Point out of Mangrove Harbor, and then Danel's Island as they headed south. At Danel's they began to encounter heavy seas as they lost the lee of the Island. It was mostly large swells at this point, primarily in the six to nine foot category,

The small boat rose up and rocked as it hit each one, and spray enveloped the cockpit. They donned all weather gear at the first onslaught. Jenn looked apprehensively at Mark, who was engrossed in keeping the craft on point. They could only do five knots under power in these conditions.

Once past Danel's Island, Mark was able to bring Trade Winds closer to the coast, and the seas calmed a notch. At the mouth of Ely's Harbor at Palm Island, it became downright placid.

"Okay Jenn, we're headed into the Harbor, and already I like what I see. It provides quite a protected area, and there are only a few other boats. We're going to tuck ourselves into this little cove off Wrecks Hill. We'll be good there."

Mark continued deep into the harbor until they entered a small cove. It was only fifty yards wide and completely surrounded by dense woods, with an occasional palm tree at the forefront. No houses could be seen.

"This is really out there alright," Jenn said surveying their surroundings. "How deep is it here?"

Checking his depth sounder, Mark said, "We've only got eight feet at high tide. It could go down to five at low, which will have us scraping the bottom with the keel. I'd rather have that additional support under us than be in deeper water. Babe, go up front and get ready to lower the anchor."

Mark put it in neutral and gave the signal to Jenn to activate the windlass. The chain rode made its way noisily out of the anchor compartment. "Okay, it's hit the bottom," Jenn yelled back to the helm.

Mark shifted the gearbox into reverse and Jenn shouted out the footage of the rope. Every ten feet was marked with a splash of red paint. When she had let out fifty feet, he signaled to Jenn, who locked the windlass.

"We've got a pretty good bottom here. A combination of mud and sand. I think she'll hold well," Mark said.

He readied the dinghy while Jenn retrieved their two longest lines – heavy hemp especially made for this application. Affixing the lines to the two stern cleats, Mark took the loose ends and rowed the inflatable ashore. There he found a sturdy oak, about two feet in diameter. After first pulling the lines as taut as he could, he tied both ends around the tree with a bowline knot.

Trade Winds was now firmly secured: from the stern by the two lines around a tree, and from the bow by the main anchor. Mark felt confident she could weather any storm that might come their way.

Back on board they made a simple dinner: the remainder of some vegetable soup Jenn had made from scratch and the last of their loaf of whole wheat bread. After eating, Mark checked the weather on the laptop. Jenn looked over his shoulder. The depression had grown to tropical storm size during the day, with average sustained winds of over sixty miles per hour. He learned it was given a female name, "Eepa," the next in line.

He turned to Jenn: "Eepa? What kind of name is that?"

"You got me. Never heard of it before. Let's Google it."

Mark typed in the necessary search words. "It's of Hawaiian origin. It means a person with extraordinary, or supernatural powers. Interesting."

"Let's hope this storm doesn't have those powers."

CHAPTER FIFTY-NINE

Ben gathered the few personal items Robbie had bought for him, and tried Marjorie again. Same thing. It went directly into voice mail. His message this time was even more urgent.

He walked the mile to the Publix and checked in at the counter. His money from the prior day was still there, but no new money had been wired to Robbie. He decided to wait several hours to see if Marjorie would come through for him before bothering Robbie.

By late afternoon and no money, he talked the lady behind the counter into letting him use the store phone to call him. This call went directly into Robbie's voice mail as well. When it came time to leave a call back number, Ben asked the gal what it was, and she said it was impossible to reach this particular extension from outside the store. Ben ended the message by asking Robbie if he could pick him up and try the police station once more. He also tried his best to get the woman to release the funds to him without any ID, and he received the same response as before.

Two hours later Ben decided to walk another mile to the police station to try once again to obtain a police report. He was met by the same recalcitrant officer who said they had even less time this day to sit down with Ben than the day before. No pleading by Ben could persuade the officer otherwise. The officer directed him to the homeless shelter on Stock Island for a bed for the night.

The Key West homeless shelter, called KOTS, was located on Stock Island off of College Road. It consisted of several bunker like

Quonset huts, one for women, two to house the males. It was a two and a half mile walk for Ben. By the time he got there, the sun was going down. He was sweaty and tired.

As he turned onto College Road, he caught up with a bedraggled line of pathetic looking men heading for the same place. Some just shuffled along, their faces cast upon the way before them, never looking up. Others looked around belligerently, almost as if they were asking for a fight.

At the shelter, he was logged in and given clean sheets and a towel. No pillow or pillow case. He entered a single large room, about twenty by forty feet. The beds were thin, vinyl covered mattresses laid on top of wooden platforms, providing sleeping space for fifty men. Weeds randomly found their way up through the planked floor. It smelled strongly of cleaning fluid.

He picked a mattress, made it up, and lay down. He had never been more depressed in his entire life. *How long would he have to live in this god forsaken place? Who would come and rescue him?*

Ben wanted to break down and cry, but he feared showing such weakness in front of these men. As he lay there, he noticed an older black man take up residence on the bed next to him, just two feet away. The guy could have been a hundred. His face was deeply furrowed and his long hair, braided into dreads, and beard were mostly salt, some pepper. He was mumbling words that Ben could not at first understand.

The man laboriously removed his outer clothing of bib overalls and a ratty, plaid flannel shirt. Everything was sweat stained, and he reeked of cigars and body odor. Ben almost gagged.

As he listened, he finally made out the words: "Bad juju. Bad juju." Over and over again, like an incantation.

Ben turned to him and said, "What are you saying? What does juju mean?"

The man, who was seated on the edge of the bed, turned toward the sound of Ben's voice. It was then that Ben saw he had no eyes – or what were once his eyes were now only white splotches of sclera. He repeated, "Bad juju," and pointed up to the sky with a quivering finger.

Ben was so unnerved he slid out of his bed, quickly pulled the sheets off, and escaped to another bed on the other side of the room. Still, all night, he could hear the man's intonation of the same words, repeatedly, incessantly. At six in the morning, after a night with no sleep, Ben left the shelter, vowing never to return again.

CHAPTER SIXTY

Aaron and Zoe sat uncomfortably on the tarmac, using one of the rear landing gears as a back rest. The sun was now fully set, and they were cast into abject darkness except for some small illumination coming through the cracks in the fuselage around the exit hatch from the battery powered lights inside the plane.

"Zoe, I just need to tell you, in case the worst happens. This has been one of the most memorable times in my life. Tough, but bearable because of you. You are a fantastic person: caring, loving, and fearless. I don't know how this will end up, but we've got to find a way to stay in touch, and hopefully see each other."

"I feel the same way Aaron. You're strong, intelligent, and good looking as hell."

Aaron blushed. "Well I forgot to say how cute you are. I guess I feel it's so obvious, it didn't need saying."

Zoe leaned toward him and gave him a light kiss on the cheek. It felt altogether amazing. Aaron reciprocated by wrapping his arms around her, as they were seated, and hugging her for what seemed like hours. She hugged back. Tightly.

"Aaron, I'd be less than honest if I didn't admit I still feel I'm being punished for my former transgressions. Too many bad things have happened to us for it to be just a coincidence. I don't believe in a traditional Christian God, but I do believe there's a kind of cosmic justice out there. What goes around comes around. You play, you pay. I think I'm paying for my sins."

"Well, then why is this happening to all of us? I can't say I feel excessive guilt over any one, or several mistakes in my life. I'm no saint, but I can't put my finger on any particular event and say I'm being punished for it. I don't think there's any rhyme or reason for any of this. It's all random. We just happen to have been caught in the storm of the century, and we've got to work our way out of it. If we start feeling forces greater than ours are ganging up on us, then we're making an excuse for not being able to overcome our circumstances."

"That's a good point. I've just got to fight these dark thoughts when they come over me. It's like I think this storm came for *me*. To get *me*. Aaron, if I start talking like this – ever again – whack me hard."

"I won't do that, but I'll sure try to convince you it's just not true."

"I've also wanted to talk to you about something," Zoe said as she slowly stood and stretched. "I'm a little worried about Bart. He's been acting pretty strange. And very aggressive. I don't know if it has anything to do with the wound he received to his foot. I saw him looking at it the other day. Seemed really bad. I think it's infected."

"He is a strange one," Aaron said, as he too assumed a standing position next to Zoe. "I think . . . or hope . . . Jay and Jack will keep a close eye on him."

Just as he finished his sentence, the door to the immigration building blew open. At least five men came rushing toward them, brandishing knives and metal pipes. By the time Aaron got the shotgun in his hands with the safety off, they were almost upon them. He reacted instinctively and fired directly into the pack. Three of the five went down, screaming. The other two headed right for Zoe. She had the Glock, and fired at them. One was blown backward, but the other jumped on her. He raised a huge carving knife above his head with his right hand, and started to come down hard with it. Zoe heard a deafening blast, and saw the man's hand and the knife go flying in the air and land with a thump and a clatter ten feet from her. Blood spurting from his wrist gushed on her shirt.

Two of the first men shot by Aaron got up, apparently having only received superficial wounds. They came directly for Aaron, who was desperately trying to unjam the shotgun. As they came upon him, ready to swing two steel pipes into his skull, five shots rattled off in quick succession, and they both dropped just inches from him. Aaron looked back from where the sounds had emanated, and saw Captain Cross halfway down the ladder from the plane hatch, a smoking pistol in his hand.

The Captain came the rest of the way down, followed by Bart and Jack. They couldn't believe the carnage on the runway. Five men lay in grotesque positions, sprawled on the tarmac. Zoe was covered in blood.

"Mary, mother of God," Jay proclaimed. They leveled their weapons at the door to the building just in case another onslaught ensued. Nothing happened.

"We've got to get farther away from that building," Zoe said to no one in particular. "We're just too close. Captain Cross, how can we do that?"

"I agree with you Zoe. I wanted to wait one more day, but I don't think we have that luxury any more. Men, let's commence the start up procedure for the engines, and see if we can get them going. If we can, we'll taxi as far out on the runway as possible."

"Great idea," Bart said. "If we don't leave soon, I'm going to personally kill each one of those bastards."

Aaron shot a quick glance at Zoe. "Why don't Zoe and I remain outside while you gentlemen do what you need to do," Aaron interjected. "I'm not that familiar with this plane. If I can help, let me know. But right now I think our major concern is protecting the plane and moving the hell out of here."

"Okay," the Captain said. "But Zoe, don't you want to get out of those clothes?"

"Thanks Captain, but I'm alright. Let's just try to get this thing moving."

The three men reentered the plane, leaving Aaron and Zoe outside. Soon they heard the sounds of fuel pumps being activated, and saw the prop on the left wing slowly begin to turn as the engine spewed black, sooty smoke.

It stuttered, stopped, then stuttered again. The starter motor whirred, but began to lose power after several minutes. The battery was running down. Then it was only a clicking sound as the charge completely ebbed from the battery. Aaron looked disconsolately at Zoe. "I think we're screwed."

They heard the sound of the cockpit window – just a small aperture near the pilot's head – open. Jay leaned out and shouted,

"Aaron, I know this is pretty primitive. But would you be willing to take a shot at that prop? When I say when, take it in both hands and heave it clockwise as hard as you can."

"I'll give it my best, sir."

Aaron positioned himself in front of the prop and grabbed the blade, which was at the two o'clock position, with his hands. Zoe shouted, "Be careful."

Jay yelled for him to go ahead, and Aaron pulled down as hard as he could. The prop kicked a half rotation as the engine gasped. He repeated this process three more times.

"It looks like a no go," he shouted up to Jay.

"Just give it a couple more tries."

Aaron pulled again, and this time the prop did two full turns before stopping. "I think it may be catching," Aaron said.

On the sixth attempt, the prop began turning on its own. The engine coughed and expelled more black smoke, but ultimately fired up and the Captain gave it some juice. The engine cleaned itself of the accumulated oil and carbon and smoothed out to a beautiful purr. Aaron looked at Zoe and gave a thumbs up.

Aaron saw the door to the building open out of the corner of his eye. Several people stepped out and stood watching the plane. The Captain brought it down in rpm's and shouted to Aaron and Zoe to get back into the plane. As they climbed up on board, the Captain said, "I can get us out of here on the ground with this one engine."

He increased the rpm's and released the foot brake on the right wheel. The craft slowly began to turn to the right, and then as Jay released the brakes entirely, the plane moved straight forward. They taxied slowly down the runway and came to a stop near the end, about a half mile from the building.

"This will be good enough," Jay said. "We've put some room between us and them. We're still going to keep watch, but we'll have a lot more time to respond now. Is that alright with everyone?"

Receiving no objection, he continued: "Bart and Jack. Zoe and Aaron have seen enough excitement for the night. Why don't you guys take the next shift. I'll relieve you in four hours."

The men exited the plane with two of the guns, and the rest prepared to catch some sleep.

CHAPTER SIXTY-ONE

"Jenn, tell you what. The storm isn't supposed to hit until tomorrow. Let's take the dinghy across the bay. I've found a marina on the chart that has a small supply store. We can always use more batteries and water."

They had spent a comfortable night on Trade Winds, snuggled against each other with the temperatures lowering to the mid-sixties. The water around them was as smooth as a mirror, reflecting the deciduous trees around them. One lone palm jutted from an outcropping just to their right. It was perfectly formed, almost as if it had been trimmed. The sun was now well above the horizon.

"Let's do it. Maybe we could grab a little chocolate at the same time?" Jenn said hopefully.

Mark had grown used to Jenn's addiction to chocolate. At least it wasn't an expensive habit, he thought. She strongly favored the cheaper Hershey's to the more exotic brands. Up until yesterday, there had always been a bowl of candy kisses lying around.

"I know better than to say no to that. A happy wife is a happy home."

"Yeah, but we're not married, so that doesn't apply."

"Same theory, my darling."

They got in the inflatable and begin heading out of the cove to the east. They crossed Pritchard Bay to Robinsons Marina. The Bay opened up to a two mile diameter at its widest point, allowing them to feel the increasing winds from the northeast.

"Looks like the blow is just starting, honey," Mark said. "Let's not spend too much time there."

Looking at the southern sky, the dark clouds now fully exposed to their view, Jenn replied, winking at him as she did so, "Absolutely. In and out as quickly as we can."

The marine store was sold out of double "A" batteries, the only size they needed, but was able to part with several large plastic jugs of fresh water. Most importantly, Jenn walked away with a package of six Hershey bars with almonds. That put her in better spirits.

"Let the storm come," she crowed. "I'm all set."

On the way back the wind had picked up appreciably. Even though they were only a mile from the southern edge of the bay, sharp, ragged waves were pummeling them from the side. Occasionally cold spray wetted their clothing.

"This is getting pretty bad," Mark said above the howl of the wind. "Are you okay?"

Jennifer was holding on to the bow line for dear life. She turned to him and said, "Maybe you could lower the speed a little, sweetheart."

Mark complied. It kept the small craft from slamming up and down, but did nothing to prevent the sea from breaking over the edge. Jenn started removing the water with the small plastic cup they used just for that purpose. After five minutes of increasingly frenetic bailing, the ocean was gaining on them inside the inflatable.

"Mark, I know this thing can't sink, but if it fills with water, she won't move. What are we going to do?"

Mark immediately put her hand on the throttle of the small outboard, took the cup, and moved forward. He hit the water with both the cup and his free bare hand. It seemed to level the odds. The water was no longer rising. But after ten minutes of it, Mark was out of breath. He simply had to take a break.

Jenn, seeing he was spent, grabbed the cup out of his hand, put her arm around his waist and pulled him back toward the engine. She then launched into the same two-handed method, and kept her own. In five minutes they rounded the bend of the cove and the onslaught waned. The sea became placid within a few seconds.

He said, "Jenn, you can ease off now. God, that was incredible. Where'd you get that endurance?"

"Pure fear, Mark, pure fear. We've gone too far to be swamped out in the middle of that little bay."

"Well honey, we couldn't have made it without you. Thank you."

Mark kissed her passionately. She kissed him back, even more so. They almost ran into Trade Winds.

CHAPTER SIXTY-TWO

Ben decided he'd walk to the NOAA station to see if he could speak personally with Robbie. It was a distance of over three miles. He walked along the seawall sidewalk on South Roosevelt Boulevard. The wind had picked up significantly. Fortunately it was at his back. The Atlantic was starting to look like a boiling cauldron.

No one was out on Smathers Beach, a rare occurrence at this time of day. He found out why as he walked by the entry to the beach. Fine pellets of sand blasted his bare skin. He walked faster to the beginning of the dunes and sea wall that offered some protection.

He reached White Street, where he should have headed right to get to the station, but he saw a restaurant a couple of blocks away and decided to stop to get a drink of water. It was Saluté, directly on Higgs Beach. Only a few patrons frequented the bar area at this early hour. The main restaurant area was closed. He sat at the bar and asked for a glass of water. Fans turned lazily from the ceiling. A television was on in the corner.

The news channel was covering the storm in Miami Beach. Ben could not believe the footage. Waves were lapping at the stairs to the Tides Hotel, where only a few days ago he had lounged on the patio in bright sunlight. The palm trees in the ocean park were bent at alarming angles, their fronds actually dipping into the froth of the waves pounding their trunks. The yellowish gray of the sky gave the whole picture a fake, sepia look. The broadcaster was standing in the middle of Ocean Drive, water almost to his knees, barely able to stand in the blasting winds.

The bartender, a young woman in her mid-twenties, stared raptly. She then addressed the television. "My God. I've been right there. I've never seen anything like this. They're saying all of Miami Beach may be inundated. That's never happened before."

A sinking feeling was forming in Ben's gut. "When's it supposed to get down here?" he asked.

The girl, without looking at him, said, "They say sometime tomorrow. It's traveling very fast. Could be here as soon as the early morning . . . around three or four. That's a bad time for it to hit, 'cause it coincides with high tide. It's also almost a full moon, which is compounding the problem."

"Are there any hurricane shelters around town?" Ben asked.

"Yeah, there are," one of the guys sitting at the bar said. Ben now recognized him from the homeless shelter. "I've never been to them, but I also heard that because of the evacuation order they won't be open. None of us are supposed to be here."

"What is everyone here going to do?" Ben asked the small group generally.

The bartender said something about her boyfriend living in a condo that was very sturdy and had survived many hurricanes over the years. The guy said he'd go back to the shelter for the night.

"What about you?" the woman asked.

Ben hesitated. "I don't have a clue. I met a guy who works at the weather station down here. I hope he can help me."

"Good luck," she responded, doubt in her tone.

It was then that the lights in the restaurant flickered and

extinguished, and the TV went black.

"What's going on?" Ben asked.

"I don't know exactly, but all of our electricity comes from Miami. I'm guessing they lost power, so we have too."

Ben left after a few minutes and returned to White Street. He decided to walk to the end of the pier which afforded an expansive view of the ocean. The White Street Pier jutted some three hundred feet into the Atlantic. Passing by the Aids Memorial at the foot of the pier, he wondered for a moment if there was going to be a similar monument to the survivors of Daemon – if there were any.

He couldn't approach closer than thirty feet from the end of the pier. Waves were already crashing into the bulwarks, and spray was fanning out across the concrete deck. He noticed a section of the wall, rust stained from the exposed and protruding rebar, was beginning to crumble into the sea.

The National Weather Station was about five blocks up. The traffic light at Flagler was dead. The streets were eerily empty. As Ben approached the station, he could not see any lights on in the vestibule that housed the exhibits describing the famous hurricanes that had struck Key West. The neon sign that announced information about tours of the facility was also out.

At the top of the stairs, to his right, he saw a black button under an intercom box. Ben pressed it once for a couple of seconds. No response. Not wanting to aggravate those inside, he waited a minute and pressed it once more. Again nothing. Ben became increasingly anxious. Robbie was his last resort.

He leaned on the button. After an hour of hitting the intercom and pounding on the glass of the main doors, Ben decided to circle the building to see if he could see any signs of life. His access was restricted by a tall chain link fence with concertina barbed wire which circumscribed a large area at the rear. There was simply no other way to attract the attention of those inside, so he went back to the front door and tried over and over again. His fingers and hands became sore from striking the button and the door.

Inside the Storm Center, they were setting up cots for the seven staff members and several of their spouses and children. There was barely enough room for the beds, four computers, and tiny kitchenette. Separate half bathrooms were accessed through a door to the right. Val and the other wives made up the beds as the forecasters manned the stations or lounged around the single coffee pot.

After finishing with the beds, Val walked over to Robbie, who was now getting some coffee. "I'm worried about Ben," Val said. "What if he couldn't get his money? What would he do?"

"I'm a little concerned too. I wish there was some way to reach him other than the hotel. I tried it several hours ago, and they told me he had checked out. I don't know what that means."

"Well he knows where to find us if the worst happens," Val replied.

At that moment the lights and computer screens in the small room flickered. Then a clunking sound as the backup generators kicked in.

Larry Grimes, who was sitting at one of the screens, yelled out,

"We're on auxiliary power everyone. Let's turn off a couple of these lights to conserve electricity."

"Larry. How long will the generator run without refueling," Robbie inquired.

"We've got at least three days, if not more."

"What happens after that?" Val asked.

"I don't know. It's never happened before."

The tempest attacking the island gradually grew into a wailing banshee. Darkness descended on the land. Ben realized the large, slanted roof covering the landing at the top of the stairs afforded him some shelter. Exhausted, he curled into a fetal position in a corner to gain warmth. He fell asleep, despairing of surviving the night.

At a little before midnight, most of the men had retired. Val, Robbie and Larry were the only ones up, the two men taking a break from studying the data on the storm.

"Why don't you two get some shuteye," Larry suggested. "I've set up a schedule for all of us during the night." He handed Robbie a piece of paper which contained a grid showing four hour segments and the two personnel who would track the storm at those times.

"Okay Larry. Val, let's get ready for bed. I'll have to get up in four hours to take the next shift."

"Get me up too, baby, and I'll make some fresh coffee for us."

"We'll see about that. If you're snoring contentedly, I probably won't disturb you."

"I'll be glad to get up honey, so wake me. But before we retire, can we step out into the lobby to see what's going on outside? I feel like

I'm in a bubble in here."

"Sure, let's go."

They walked through the Operations Room to the door leading to the lobby. The lights were very dim. When they opened the door, it was pitch black in the lobby.

"What's going on here?" Robbie asked no one in particular. "Stay here, Val. Let me ask Larry why there are no lights out there."

He did, and Larry answered, "For efficiency purposes, the auxiliary power doesn't extend that far. The only thing hard-wired into the generator is the fire alarm. We wouldn't know what was happening out there. The buzzer is also inoperable."

"What! You mean if someone is out there trying to get our attention, we wouldn't hear it?" Robbie shouted.

"That's right. Are you expecting someone?"

"I don't know for sure, but possibly."

Robbie grabbed a flashlight off of one of the shelves and returned to Val. He explained what Larry had told him.

"I didn't realize that," Val said. "So if Ben came to find us, we probably wouldn't know anything about it."

"That's right. Let's go out and look around."

They started with the interior of the lobby first in the event someone had been able to gain entrance. When the beam of light happened to hit an outside window, it illuminated just enough of the frenzy outside to scare the wits out of them. Debris of every kind flew by with tremendous velocity, occasionally striking the thick glass panels with a scrape or a thud.

The last area to search was the exterior deck leading to the front door. Robbie swept the area with the flashlight, but all they could see were leaves, dirt and branches covering the concrete floor.

"Well I feel a little better. Ben's not here. He must have made it to safety somewhere."

"My God, Robbie. What is that out there? Past the deck?"

He cast the light farther out, a distance of fifteen feet, to where the stairs would reach the deck. Robbie was horrified by what he saw. Water was lapping at the top stair, just six inches from the surface of the deck.

"I can't believe this! The ocean has risen this far? We're at least a half mile from the Atlantic, twice that from the Gulf. We never calculated this degree of storm surge."

They approached the door leading to the outdoors to get a better look. Robbie again swept the area with the light.

"Stop, honey," Val said. "Over there. To the left. In the corner. Is that someone's hand?"

Robbie focused the light on the corner, and there, encased in grime, leaves, and broken palm fronds, they could barely make out the form of a human body, several fingers reflecting the rays from the flashlight.

Robbie handed Val the light, and firmly gripping the panic bar on the door, slowly pushed and opened it a fraction of an inch. The blasting wind began to hurl the door outward, and it took all of Robbie's strength to keep it from flying open and crashing against the glass to its side.

He braced his body against the now fully open door, and Val came out and poked around the mound, scraping leaves away.

"Oh God! It's Ben. Wait. He's alive!"

Ben moaned, turning on his side toward them. Through clenched teeth, he rasped, "Robbie and Val. Thank God."

CHAPTER SIXTY-THREE

Bart and Jack sat with their backs against the front tire, as Aaron and Zoe had done with the rear landing gear just hours before. They were good friends, having flown scores of missions together.

"Hey buddy," Bart said as they both had settled in. "We haven't had a chance to discuss this whole mess yet. Everything's happened so fast. What a debacle."

"Well, at least we landed safely and found the survivors. I have to say, though, passing through the eye of that hurricane was the weirdest experience I've ever had. I swear I heard some kind of music through my head phones. It reminded me of a Wagner piece, the 'Ride of the Valkyries.' But far, far away. I mean, I know there wasn't any music for real. Maybe it was the sound of those colossal winds at that altitude. I don't know."

He looked over at his friend to make sure he hadn't sounded too crazy. What he saw was a look of total astonishment.

"That's impossible," Bart cried out. "I heard the same thing, but inside the plane, without head phones. I didn't mention it because I figured you'd all think I was bonkers. But now that you've brought it up, that's exactly the piece I heard. I'm very familiar with it. Is it possible the Captain was playing it on a CD player of some kind?"

"I don't think so. I've never seen anything like that on board. Let's ask him if he heard anything when we get a chance. By the way, I've forgotten. What is a Valkyrie?"

"They're from Norse mythology," Bart continued. "A Valkyrie is a female figure – a so-called 'chooser of the slain' – who decides which soldiers die in battle and which live. The dead go to the afterlife hall of Valhalla, presided over by the god Odin."

"What do you think happened to those people in there," Jack asked as he pointed in the direction of the immigration building. "Especially Pedro and Marcia. Some of the others were acting weird from the get-go, but those two were normal until just a few hours ago. It's almost like some mass psychosis, with all the elements of paranoia."

"We don't know exactly what they went through up in those hills. It must have been pretty rough. I'll rack it up to that."

"I guess so. It sure is pretty strange."

"I just hope we're the ones who are chosen to live," Bart said without much humor.

Inside the plane the three took turns brushing their teeth, and then settled down for the night in their respective bunks. They were exhausted, but still wired from the events of the night.

"Captain, things have been so crazy, we've never had a chance to learn more about you," Aaron said. "Are you married? Any kids?"

"Yes to both. It'll be twenty years this March. A boy and a girl. Craig will be eighteen next month. He just started his freshman year at Villanova. Julie is sixteen and a junior in high school. I've been lucky. They're great kids, and haven't given us any trouble – no alcohol, drugs, driving violations. Knock on wood."

"That's great," Zoe said. "Sometimes you hear such terrible stories about young people these days, it makes you not want to have children. I've always thought I wanted them, but lately I've been questioning that. I think it's just a matter of meeting the right guy."

"Yes it is. Or the right gal, huh Aaron? I don't mean to embarrass you two, but from what I've seen so far, it appears to me you're a good match. Funny how circumstances can bring people together. You've seen each other in ways you probably never would have in a lifetime. Tells a lot about a person, how they handle stress, difficulties."

"Yes it does. And from what I've seen so far, Zoe's got more . . . uh . . . guts than any woman I've ever met. I like that."

"And ditto to you, Aaron," Zoe said. "And the other things too. Good night, y'all."

It was around three in the morning. Try as they could to stay awake, both Jack and Bart fell asleep. The exhaustion of the day was just too much for them. So they didn't hear the stealthy footsteps of the three men approaching the plane from behind.

Pedro and another, each armed with recently sharpened carving knifes, carefully made their way toward the sleeping men. At a prearranged signal, they took one final stride and slit the throats of the dozing figures from ear to ear in a single, swiping gesture. The two crew members' eyes opened wide in an instant, never to close again, while they made forced gurgling sounds from their torn throats. Deep burgundy blood flowed across the runway. The attackers seized their weapons and returned to the building, awaiting their next opportunity to attack en masse.

CHAPTER SIXTY-FOUR

Mark and Jenn loaded their few provisions onto Trade Winds, and Jenn spent some time putting them away, making sure to pack them carefully in case things got hairy outside. Mark got the dinghy up on its davits, and the outboard carefully affixed to the mounting board at the stern of the boat. Both of them then lashed the cover to the tender so it would not fill with water.

"Hey baby, let's do one more walk through topside to make sure everything is ready. Then let's do the same below, and eat."

"Okay."

They took opposite sides and pulled and shook hatches, sail covers, anything that might go flying. When they met at the bow, they stood transfixed at the reflection in the water. They could see a hazy version of themselves and the boat from a frontal perspective, framed in the pinkish hue of the setting sun. Just beyond, the trees and dark green leaves flowed from the surface of the water to their real counterparts above the shoreline.

Mark broke the silence. "A beautiful time of the evening, huh baby? Wish someone was on shore to take a picture of us."

"Well, let's capture this for eternity in our imaginations, okay?"

"Alright by me. But how about we go below and snuggle for a while. I'm getting horny."

"Yeah. Let's get a good one in before the blow starts." Jenn blushed slightly as she realized how that sounded.

"A blow outside, a blow inside. Sounds good to me."

They went below, shed their wet clothing, and made good on their recent promises.

Around midnight Jenn was awakened by the sound of a freight train right outside the portal to their stateroom. As she lay listening, her stomach tightening, the roar grew to a wailing shriek. The stays vibrated like violin strings, and the lines, even though strung tautly, clanged against the metal mast. She turned to Mark, who somehow was sleeping soundly through the melee.

After a few hours wondering if their small boat could withstand the onslaught, Jenn noticed the winds gradually calm, and the noise abate. Naked, she slid silently out of the berth, and carefully unlatched the double, bar style doors leading to the outside deck. Stepping out into the cool night air, she was amazed to see a full moon unsheathed above, the only clouds vaguely circling on the horizon. A gentle breeze caressed her bare body and hair. *Is the storm over?* she asked herself. *That wasn't as bad as I thought it'd be.*

She lay on a cushion with her head propped so she could study the sky. The moonlight formed a diamond strewn path in the water flowing directly toward her. *What is that?* She remained totally still, not even taking a breath. *A sound. A song? Was someone playing music on another unseen vessel? Or somewhere on shore?*

She craned her ears to the left, then to the right. Yet the sound seemed to be coming from everywhere. She even got up and turned around to see from where it might be originating. Again, only an amorphous combination of notes emerged from the darkness.

Mark's head appeared in the entry way. "Hey. What's going on babe?"

"It's so beautiful out here Mark. I can't believe the storm's over so quickly. But come on up. I want to see if you can hear what I'm hearing."

"The storm's over? Already? That's impossible. It was too large for it to be over." Mark came all the way out on deck and listened. "What is that? Is it music?"

"Sure sounds like it to me. I can't quite make out what it is, or where it's coming from."

"Funny. It reminds me of the beginning of an opera by the composer, Wagner. I can't remember the name of it. Someone must be playing it on shore, or on a boat. Sound travels so far and is so deceiving on the water."

They lay down together on the slim cushion and listened in silence for a few minutes.

The first indication of it was a slight rustling of the leaves onshore, and rattling of the halyards on board. "Seems the wind is picking back up, honey. Was there supposed to be another front after the first?" Jenn asked.

"I didn't see one on the radar earlier today."

Within minutes the air became horribly disturbed, blasting them from every conceivable angle and growing in intensity with every passing second. "This is not good. The wind is coming from the opposite direction than before. Let me check below."

Mark went back down and fired up the computer. It took a few minutes for it to acquire a signal. What he saw on the NOAA site frightened him to his core. Somehow Eepa had grown into a full-fledged hurricane, recently upgraded to a category two. The animated reds, greens and yellows spiraled crazily in a counter clockwise direction on the screen.

He yelled up to Jennifer. "Jenn, please come down here immediately." Mark helped her down the companion way stairs and securely locked up the doors.

"Honey. What's going on? You're scaring me."

"Jenn. Eepa has become a hurricane. A cat two. Almost a three. In just the past seven hours. I don't know how, but it did. The lull out there is just that – the lull as the eye passes over us and we get the back end of the storm – the worst part."

"Oh my God, Mark. The fucking thing is following me. It's here for me. To get *me*. I *know* it."

Mark had no adequate response this time.

CHAPTER SIXTY-FIVE

"Let's get him up and inside." Robbie grabbed Ben's arm and helped him to his feet while Val brushed him off. Together they were able to walk him into the lobby. When his legs suddenly went out from underneath him, they had to sit him down and lean him against one of the exhibit counters.

"I'll be okay," Ben whispered. "Just need to get my bearings. How long was I lying out there?"

"We don't know. We came out to see the storm in real life, rather than on the computer screen. We almost missed seeing you entirely," Robbie said.

"What time is it now?"

Val checked her watch and told him it was just after two in the morning.

"As best I can figure, I must have been lying there for over six hours. I don't know how I slept through that mayhem," Ben said pointing to the rage outside the glass walls.

"You must have been exhausted," Val said.

"We're going to take you inside, Ben. Ordinarily, only employees and family are allowed, but we're going to make an exception here. We've also got to get you out of those wet clothes."

As they opened the door to the Operations Room, Robbie looked back and saw seawater flowing under the lobby doors leading to the outside. "My God, Val. Look at that! The water has risen to record highs. As far as I know, it's never made it above the stairs before."

Robbie went into the Storm Center, had a brief discussion with Larry, and came out with a change of his own clothing . "Honestly, Larry doesn't like it, but he knows we don't have a choice. Ben, we're about the same size. Try these on in the men's room over there and then knock on that door. We'll let you in."

Ben changed. The pants were too tight so he left the top clasp undone and kept them up with the belt provided by Robbie. He hung his wet clothes over the door leading to the enclosed toilet, and, walking over to the Storm Center, knocked and was let in.

He was amazed at the close quarters. At least twenty cots were arranged end to end against the walls, leaving a bank of computers and monitors in the center. All but three of the beds were occupied, mostly by men, but some by women and children.

"Ben, take this one, next to us," Robbie said as he walked over to a cot in the corner. "Then come over here and let me show you something."

Ben turned down the blanket and sheet to show the bed was taken, and came over to one of the computers where Robbie had taken a seat. Val lay down on her bunk.

"I can access the several video cameras located outside. These are identical to the ones in Miami," he explained to Ben. "Let's take a look."

Robbie expertly used a joy stick to adjust the cameras to sweep the outside area. Ben couldn't believe his eyes. It was as if they were sitting in the middle of the ocean, with the tops of fences and nearby houses peeking up out of the depths. The water was being whipped into a frenzy by the catastrophic winds. Floating cars, boats and pieces of homes were blown by them at an uncanny speed.

"Jesus, Robbie. If you hadn't found me when you did, I would have been swept out into that mess. I owe you my life."

"Take a look at this as well."

Robbie hit several keys and now a satellite image of Daemon appeared on the screen. Ben could see the outline of the surrounding land masses superimposed in the background.

"Is that right?" Ben gasped. "Is this hurricane covering all of southern Florida and the Keys?"

"That's right, Ben. The eye will be passing directly over Key West in about twenty minutes. At the rate it's traveling, we'll have a lull of about forty-five minutes. Then we'll get our asses kicked."

"Why is that?"

"Because the strongest winds in a hurricane are found on the right side of the storm. That's as a result of the counterclockwise motion of the hurricane contributing to its swirling winds. This baby is moving westward, so we got hit by the left side first."

The two men stood there transfixed by the images broadcast before them. Robbie toggled between the various outside video feeds and NOAA images of the storm. Larry Grimes sat two stations down from them, his ear pressed to the emergency phone tying them to the first responders on the outside.

Ben turned to Robbie. "Robbie, I've got a good friend who believes the earth's storms are intensifying because of global warming. You're an expert. What's your take on it?"

"Well, I've really studied the issue," Robbie replied. "There's no question that since the early 20th century, the Earth's mean temperature has increased by around a degree and a half Fahrenheit, with about two-thirds of that increase occurring since 1980. Therefore I have to conclude that the warming of the climate systems is unequivocal. And I think the vast majority of scientists attribute it to increasing concentrations of greenhouse gasses produced by human activity such as the burning of fossil fuels and deforestation. These findings are recognized by the national science academies and all major industrialized nations."

"And here I always thought my friend was blowing hot air, if you'll pardon the pun. Do you think the size of this hurricane is an indication of bad things to come as a result of the warming?"

"Hard to say," Robbie answered. "Clearly we've had an increase in the number of, and more destructive, hurricanes over the past twenty or thirty years. But in climatological terms, that's a very short period of time."

"Maybe I should have listened more carefully to Phil's warnings," Ben said.

As Robbie had predicted, in almost exactly forty minutes, the external monitors revealed a gradual decrease in the winds. Soon the sea settled, appearing almost calm except for the currents bringing the water farther and farther inland. Ben started for the door. "That's amazing. Let's just check outside."

Robbie leaped from his seat and grabbed Ben's arm just as he was about to pull the heavy handle to the door. "No! Ben. Don't open that. Come here and take a look at this."

Ben sheepishly accompanied Robbie back to the computer. Robbie pulled up a feed Ben had not seen before. It was a shot of the interior of Operations just on the other side of the door Ben was about to access. Every window had been blown out. The winds screamed about the interior. Water, about two feet deep, sloshed around the room. Although all the work stations were bolted to the floor, everything else – chairs, trashcans, loose papers and supplies – flew around the room or floated willy-nilly in front of the camera.

"Ben, if you had opened that door, even an inch, the force of all that water would have prevented us from closing it. We'd have spent a pretty wet night in here."

"Gosh, Robbie. I'm sorry. I had no idea."

"No harm, no foul, Ben. I know you had no conception of what was happening out there. Those windows are rated to withstand winds up to 165 miles per hour. That gives you a clear indication of the magnitude of the storm. We should have put the lock on the handle to that door earlier. I'm going to do that now to prevent any mistakes."

Robbie got up, reached onto a shelf by the door and placed a large, thick lock through the holes in the handle. "That'll prevent anyone from opening it by mistake. And keep us dry."

Robbie and Ben went to bed. One weather specialist stayed up to keep tracking the storm. At five thirty, Robbie awoke, really needing to use the bathroom. As he came to consciousness, he saw his arm was draped over the edge of the cot, with his hand hanging down. He pulled his hand up and looked at it. *What was that? It was wet. What the heck,* he thought. He turned his head to see the one analyst at the computers sound asleep, his head resting on his chest. Robbie swung his legs around, and planted his feet firmly on the concrete floor. They splashed.

He jumped up, now fully awake. The entire floor was covered in three inches of salt water. He ran around to each of his co-employees, including the one seated at the station, and shook them to wakefulness. Their cries of astonishment awoke everyone. "Okay," Robbie yelled. "We've got a serious problem, but we're going to figure it out. Everyone stay in bed except the NWS boys. "

They met at the computer stations. One asked, "Is it coming from the door?"

They all looked carefully around the perimeter of the door, and even though they couldn't see the base, there were no air bubbles or flows of water signifying a leak. They looked carefully with a flashlight around the edges of the room, and found nothing.

Finally one of the specialists, named Eddie, said, "I do remember hearing, several years back, one concern about this building. That it was conceivable – albeit highly unlikely – in a catastrophic storm surge, the hydrostatic pressure of the water against the concrete floor might allow water to integrate through into the interior. I fear that's what's happening here."

"Well, how high could it go?" Larry asked.

"No higher than the water you see outside. Water rises to its own level."

Larry went to the computer and brought up one of the video feeds. They saw the water lapping against the side of the building some three feet higher than their level.

Robbie said, "The good news is, as long as the water doesn't rise any farther, we won't drown. The bad news . . . we could be required to tread water forever."

CHAPTER SIXTY-SIX

Captain Jay Cross awoke and put on a pot of coffee. He wanted to surprise the watch keepers with some hot java. The small drip coffee maker took five minutes to produce its first yield. Jay poured two cups, adding cream in Bart's and sugar only in Jack's, as he knew they liked it. He pulled the handle to release the hatch, and descended the short stairs carefully so as not to spill a drop. His back was to the front wheel as be stepped onto the tarmac.

When he turned toward the front, the two ceramic cups dropped and shattered into small shards on the asphalt. Jay fell to one knee, his breath being knocked out of him by the visual before him. Both men lay on their sides, their heads at impossible angles. Coagulated blood formed a fly infested carpet in front of them.

Jay stood up and shakily approached the bodies, doing a quick but careful scan of the surroundings to detect any threat. Not seeing any, he put his index and fore fingers to each of their necks and waited for a pulse. There was none. He looked around again, and saw that the men's guns were gone.

He ran up the stairs in two quick bounds and closed the hatch, locking it firmly. He next went to Aaron's berth and shook him firmly. Aaron raised his hands in defense, crying out in shock.

"Aaron. Sorry to wake you like this, but something's happened. I need your help."

Aaron slipped to a seated position and shook his head to clear the cobwebs. Zoe had so far slept through the exchange.

"Captain, what is it?"

The look of fear on Jay's face spoke a thousand words. "They've killed Bart and Jack, the fuckin' bastards. We've got to get out of here, 'cause they've got the guns. Help me get the engines going."

Aaron still couldn't comprehend the full enormity of what the Captain was saying. "Dead? Dead? Are you sure Jay?"

"Yeah I'm sure. Their throats are cut. Let's get the engines fired up and then we'll go out and get their bodies. We've got no choice but to try the starboard engine now. The port ran fine yesterday."

Aaron didn't have a lot of hands-on experience with the start up protocol, but he had some. He sat in the copilot's seat and took instructions from Jay. Battery level. Check. Fuel pump. Check. And so on. Finally Jay pushed the ignition to the port engine, the one that had lain dormant for over a week now. "If I need you to go out and pull the prop again, can you do it?"

"Of course. Just let me know when."

The engine wheezed and coughed, blasting out oily black smoke, which because of the direction of the outside breeze, filled the inside of the plane. Zoe awoke in a fit of coughing. "What's going on?" she yelled while trying to get out of the narrow berth. "God! What's all that smoke? Is there a fire?"

Aaron turned to address the cabin behind him. He had to shout above the sputtering of the gasping engine. "No fire, Zoe. We've got to start the engines. When you can, I need you up front in the cockpit."

"I think it's catching." Jay grabbed Aaron's arm as the prop began cranking faster, faster and then spinning as the smoke cleared and the sound became a healthy whine.

After a minute of warm up, the Captain signaled Aaron that they were commencing the start-up procedure for the other engine. This time the starboard engine fired up immediately, and was purring after a few seconds.

Zoe joined them in the cockpit. Her breath, like theirs in the close cockpit, was early morning without the benefit of a brushing. "Okay gentlemen. Tell me what's going on. Why are we starting the engines so early?"

"Honey," Aaron answered. "There's been a tragedy. Bart and Jack were killed last night . . . most likely by the Cape Verdeans. They also took their weapons. The Captain figured we needed to get out of here, if we were able, as soon as possible. Now that we have the engines running, we'll go down and retrieve the bodies. The least they deserve is a proper burial."

"The very least," Zoe responded sadly. "I can help with the bodies."

"It's a pretty gruesome scene out there, Zoe," Jay said.

"I can take it. My mom was an emergency room nurse when I was in high school and they let me watch her. Nothing can shock me any more."

"Well, this may," Jay said.

Zoe walked back to the cabin to put on some shoes. As she passed by one of the portholes in the fuselage, something by the immigration building caught her attention. *What was that glint by the door?* She stopped and looked more carefully. "Aaron, Jay. Can you make out what's going on over at the building? I see something, but don't know what it is."

Jay, whose cockpit window was facing in that direction, peered out for a few seconds and then opened a compartment above his head and removed a small set of binoculars. Gazing through them, he remained silent for a half minute. "My God. We've got to move now! They're assembling outside of the building. I can see the guns. Everyone's very agitated, jumping up and down. Many of them are holding large sticks. I think they're coming this way."

"But what about Bart and Jack?" Aaron protested.

"Unless we want to join them out there, we've got to hope we, or someone, can come back at a later time and retrieve their bodies. We've got no choice but to boogie outta here."

Jay jacked the throttle all the way on the right engine, and the plane slowly began to turn around to face the full length of the runway. Even though the maneuver only took less than a minute, Aaron, whose window was now facing the trouble, saw that the assembly had broken into a mad dash toward them, strange shrieking emanating from the group. They had already lessened the distance between them by half.

Aaron turned to Jay. "Gun it Captain. They're almost on us."

Without even fastening their seat belts, Jay pushed both engines to three quarters throttle, saying a silent prayer that the left engine would hold together. The plane started to roll ahead slowly, and bounced as it ran over the bodies on the tarmac.

"Jesus Christ," the Captain said. "We're going to get those

bastards, if it's the last thing I ever do."

The craft began to pick up speed. The sound of a gun blast came from their right, the direction of the mob, and they heard the sound of myriad pellets bouncing off the sheet metal skin.

"God, they're shooting at us," Zoe screamed.

"We need to get out out of range. Hold on. Here we go!" Jay pushed the throttles to the max, and the plane leaped forward, sending Zoe backward until she was able to catch herself on the edge of a seat.

Now a full volley of gunshots rang out. A bullet whistled past, just over the craft's nose. Another punctured the fuselage and came out the other side just inches from Aaron's head. "Everyone down," he shouted.

Zoe dropped to a sitting position on the floor and the men hunched in their seats. Outside, she could now see several of the men, their faces contorted in anger, running at full speed just beyond the wing, One was waving a rifle wildly, firing randomly.

The men slowly fell back as the plane picked up speed. More shots ensued, but the marksmanship was bad. The craft shuddered, then began to lift off the ground. "We're airborne," Aaron shouted joyfully back to Zoe. "Get yourself buckled in now."

CHAPTER SIXTY-SEVEN

Jennifer sat down on the settee where she could still see the computer screen. Mark remained at the computer. He toggled back and forth between various weather sites. They tried to ignore the scream of the winds outside and the groaning of the boat as it pulled and strained against the land lines and its anchor. There was nothing more they could do to secure the craft. The couple remained silent for almost an hour.

Finally Mark said, "We should be out of the thick of things in around three or four hours. Eepa is moving very fast. Why don't you try to get some sleep. I'm going to stay here and monitor her progress."

"Thanks honey, but I couldn't sleep through this. I'm not that tired anyway. We got a good night's sleep last night."

"Yeah we did. I understand. I wouldn't be able to sleep either. Why don't I make some tea. We haven't done that in a while."

"I'll make it. You stay right there."

Jenn went to the stove, refilled the tea pot with water, and turned on the heat. She pulled out their favorite brand – Celestial Seasonings Mandarin Orange. Soon two steaming cups of the tangy liquid had been placed side by side on the navigation table, in easy reach of them both.

"I know this is going to sound corny Mark, but those cups remind me of us. Just a little while ago they were separate, standing on a shelf or a corner somewhere, no communion between them. Now here they are, together, filled with warmth and good things.

"We've been through so much together in just this short period of time. I feel I know you inside and out. I would trust you with anything."

"That's really sweet Jenn. And very poetic. You know I feel the same. I wish there was more I could do to lessen the burden you feel about your son. Maybe I'll find better ways as time goes on."

"Mark, you already do that. Every single day. You can't replace Jared, but you've slowly filled the void that was left in my heart. I'm finding I dwell less and less on him each day. Not that I'll ever forget. I just don't want it to be the ruling force in my life. I want you to be that."

Mark got up from his chair and sat next to her on the bench seat. Placing his arm around her shoulders, he looked deeply into her eyes. "Baby, I'll be there for you. Forever. I've never met a woman like you, nor will I ever again. You're stuck with me, for better or for worse."

"It's for better, honey. Always." Jenn snuggled her head into the crook of his neck.

The moment was broken when a particularly strong gust slammed into Trade Winds. She reared against her restraints and slammed down in the sea. Both cups of tea flew in the air and crashed against the wooden floor, splintering into tiny shards.

"Damn," Jenn yelled. "I shouldn't have put them there." She got down on the floor and began picking up the mess. Mark immediately did the same, the two of them side by side, carefully removing the sharp pieces of ceramic from the floor.

"This storm may try to destroy what we've got, but it's not going to," Mark said as they worked together. "We'll always be able to pick up the pieces of our relationship, right sweetheart?"

"Absolutely."

They finished cleaning up the spilled tea and broken cups. Mark went to the stove, and in a few minutes had two more cups of tea ready and steaming on the galley counter, this time in plastic and contained by the small railing around the counter. "Let's hold these and drink them now. No telling what this storm is going to do." They sipped the delightful fluid happily.

"Mark, I promise not to keep dwelling on the storm coming to get me, or anything like that. In my heart I know it's silly. It's just the first reaction I get when I see it increasing in intensity, and bearing down on us."

"I know. Frankly, when I saw that Eepa had grown to hurricane force after spinning off from Daemon, I had the same negative thoughts. But of course it's all nonsense. Storms don't have a will, an intellect, even though we try to anthropomorphize them with human names and characteristics."

"It's easy to do," Jenn said as she finished off her tea. "They're such powerful forces of nature. Far more powerful than us puny humans, whether singly, or as a group, society, or nation. It's just like when the ancient Greeks, or Romans, or whoever, put human names and personalities to the gods. It was their way of making the unknown and the all powerful more approachable and knowable."

"That's exactly right. But now I suggest we try to get some sleep. It could be a long night. First, though, I think I'll go above to fasten down the main halyard a little better. It's starting to clang."

It was only after Mark said those words that the sound of the errant line crept into Jennifer's consciousness. Now that she heard it she knew it would be difficult to sleep with it. "Okay, honey, but be careful. It's really blowing out there."

Mark took some time to don his all weather gear – rubber boots, pants, and Gill jacket. Taking the flashlight, he exited through to the upper deck. As he pulled back the hatch and swung open the doors, a torrent of rain swept into the cabin. He made his way quickly and closed everything up tight.

Jenn could hear the soft thud of his footsteps above as he made his way toward the mast. The sound of the halyard banging against the metal mast slowly subsided. Then silence, except for the wind. That was harshly broken by Mark's cry, the crash of what must have been a large branch against the deck, and a loud splash as something hit the water right next to the boat.

"God!" Jenn let out a scream.

Barefoot and only clad in a t-shirt and sweatpants, she grabbed the extra flashlight and clamored out onto the deck. The rain, now combined with tiny pellets of hail, pierced her bare arms and face like ice picks. Momentarily she thought of going back down to get a jacket or some form of protection, but that notion was quickly dispelled when her flashlight caught a body, floating face down in the water, being swept away from the boat by the wind.

This was Jenn's worst nightmare – visited upon her in the worst possible circumstances – the thought of jumping into a black sea with no life jacket or other safety apparatus. She froze for what seemed like an interminable five seconds.

Then some internal force carried her over to the railing and propelled her into the unfathomable deep. She swam quickly to the body, which was now a good twenty feet away. Coming from underneath, she turned it over. Holding the head above the waterline, she swam with all of her might to the shore, which her failing light showed her was the closest refuge.

Mark was sputtering and coughing up seawater as she dragged him partway up the rocky embankment. Jenn turned him with his face down and heaved on his back. He vomited, gasped, and finally inhaled on his own. It was only then that she noticed the large contusion on the back of his head, the beaded blood being diluted by the seawater retained in his hair.

"Mark. Can you hear me? Mark!" Turning him over once again on his back, she slapped him gently across the face. "Mark. Baby. Stay with me. It's me."

His eyes fluttered open, once, twice, and then for good. "Jenn. What happened? Where are we?"

"You got hit in the head baby. And knocked in the water. We're up on the shore now."

Mark looked around. They were somewhat protected by the large palm tree they had marveled at earlier. "Where's Trade Winds?"

"She's still there. About twenty yards away. I can barely make her out. We'll rest here for a while and then figure out what to do. How do you feel now?"

"Like a truck just ran over me." He pulled himself, with Jenn's assistance, to a sitting position. "I'm pretty dizzy."

They sat on the embankment, huddled together against the elements. Both were caked with mud and leaves. Twenty minutes passed.

"Baby. Do you think you can swim to Trade Winds?" Jenn asked softly.

"I'm not sure. Let's see what happens when I try to stand." Mark slowly stood, wobbled for an instant, and immediately sat back down again. "I don't think we ought to chance it. Let's move deeper into the woods and try to find more protection and give it some time."

They crawled on all fours into the dense underbrush and up a fairly steep hill. That put them at least twenty feet above the water below. Finding a natural depression in the soil, they pressed against the warmer earth on one side. Mark removed his waterproof jacket and covered them both. They remained that way seemingly forever as the hurricane wrecked its havoc around them.

CHAPTER SIXTY-EIGHT

Ben had stayed on his cot like everyone else except the weather men. The children remained fast asleep, but most of the adults were awake. He listened intently to the conversation.

"I just spoke with Chet," Larry Grimes was saying. "There's no way they can get any emergency assistance to us in the next twelve hours. They can't even get the chopper up in these winds. We're on our own."

"I thought that would be the case," Robbie replied. "Okay, let's make preparations for the worst case scenario in here without causing a panic. This place isn't equipped with any life jackets or rafts because it was never contemplated they'd be needed."

Robbie looked around for anything that would float. The low illumination from the emergency lights afforded some visibility. The mattresses were fabric, not foam, so they wouldn't help.

Ben spoke up. "I took life saving many years ago. I saw a way to turn regular long pants into life preservers. You tie knots at the ends of the legs, then pull the waist through the air and into the water. The air gets trapped and the pants become buoyant."

"Excellent, Ben," Robbie said. "Everyone out and about the room and find every pair of long pants in the room. Tie knots as Ben suggested and let's have them ready."

All of the men searched the room. The ladies looked through the duffel bags and small suitcases they had brought with their few belongings. There were a lot of shorts but only a few long pants.

Somehow they were able to collect a sufficient number of pairs so there was at least one for each man and woman in the room. The parents would take care of their children.

After the legs had been knotted and the pants distributed, Robbie said to all the adults, "We won't be able to practice this until the water gets to at least three feet. Ben, why don't you at least show everyone what the basic idea is."

Ben, still seated on his cot, picked up the pair allocated to him. "I've never done this before, but here's what I've seen. You take the pants by the waist band, and swoop them through the air and down into the water." With that, he performed the maneuver. The pants easily filled with air, but lost it because there wasn't enough water to trap the air.

Ben continued, "So that's what you do, basically. Worked real well on the video I saw."

"Okay. Everyone. Give it a try. At least get the basic premise down." Robbie took his pair and mimicked Ben's example. Same result.

"I know this will work if the water gets deep enough. Dads and moms, you'll be responsible for inflating your pants and keeping your children afloat as well."

One woman in the corner asked, "But what's our escape route from this room? What if the entire room fills with water? At least outside we have a chance. There's no ceiling."

"I'm sure that's never going to happen. The water can't get that deep. It's way beyond the record book already," Robbie assured her. "However, to answer the question, we can go right out the door here. The ceiling is higher by about two feet in the Operations Room so we'd have even more of an air pocket in there. Then, worst case scenario, it's outside."

Larry ordered the computers to be shut down because of the rising water level. Everyone then retired to their beds to wait out the storm. Val turned to Ben. "Ben, that was a great idea about the pants. Way to go. I'd never heard of that before."

"I don't know how I remembered it. It has to have been thirty, maybe forty years since I heard about that. Amazing what's stored in here that you don't even know about," he said pointing to his head.

"That's true, until you really need it. By the way, what happened to the money that was supposed to be wired to you?"

"It never came, and I couldn't get my wife to take any of my calls. I had to spend the prior night at the homeless shelter. It was terrible. Smelly. Noisy. I'll never go back there."

"I'm sorry to hear that Ben. I thought she'd come through for you regardless of the problems you two were having. Frankly, I think that's terrible."

"It is. She had to sense how desperate I was. I guess the one good thing to come out of this, if you can call it good, is the realization that my marriage is over, and I've got to do something about it. I've been avoiding the obvious for at least several years now."

"I've never encouraged a divorce in my life," Valerie said. "But in this case I've got to make an exception. Maybe one alternative would be to separate and see how that goes. Maybe it will shock her into an understanding of what she'll be missing."

"Possibly. I don't see that happening though. I think the water is too far over the dam at this point. Frankly, Val, I have more clarity on this issue than I could imagine. Going through all this . . . seeing my wife's response . . . also experiencing your and Robbie's relationship.

"It's shown me what I want out of life in the future. And it's not grinding numbers every day at a desk and commuting to work in horrendous traffic just to support a woman who wouldn't come to my aid in a time of crisis. I don't care what it costs me. I've got to change the course of my life."

"Well, whatever happens, I wish you the best. You're a good man."

"Thank you Val. And you know how I feel about you and Robbie. That you would come through for a total stranger like you did speaks volumes about your character and integrity. Thank you. Again."

Just then Val flinched involuntarily. She looked down and saw that the water had risen over the lip of the edge of her mattress, and was now filling the surface of her cot. "Oh God," she whispered to Robbie. "It's higher than my cot. This is bad."

Robbie marveled that there wasn't even a hint of panic in her voice. Within a few minutes there was general alarm around the room as everyone, one by one, experienced the same thing. Robbie stood up in the water that was now two feet deep. "No need for concern, everyone. We'll be just fine. The water's warm in here, so we have no fear of hypothermia. It's just going to be a little uncomfortable for a while."

"How long?" someone from the back of the room asked.

"I can't say for sure," Robbie answered. "I guess the short answer is, as long as it takes. We *will* survive this . . . *if* we stay strong."

Two hours passed, mostly in silence. There were some low, scattered conversations here and there. At one point a couple tried to stack their cots, but the top one just slid off into the water. One by one they stood up on the beds to get most of their bodies out of the seawater. Fathers held whimpering children in their arms.

Robbie walked over to Larry. "Larry, I think it's time we got ready to open the door . . . or at least make sure it will open. Give me a hand, will you please?"

They took the few steps together over to the door. Larry reached onto the shelf where Robbie had originally located the lock. "The key is somewhere up here. Ah, got it."

Larry turned toward the door just as Robbie lifted his arm to help him locate the key. Larry's hand struck Robbie's arm and the key went flying in the air and landed with a *kaplunk* just under the computer desk behind them.

"God damn it! Where'd that go!" Larry yelled.

A few people close by asked what had happened. Robbie grabbed Larry's arm to quiet him and said to them, "Nothing. I just dropped my cash clip. It's okay. I don't need it now."

Larry looked at him strangely. Robbie whispered in his ear, "Larry, if anyone thinks we've lost the key to this lock, then you're really going to see some hysteria. We're essentially locked in here with no means of escape."

Ben walked over to the two men and said in a low tone, "Guys, I saw where it fell. Let me take a look."

Ben went to the desk, and bent down and tried to feel around on the floor. His hand would not reach if he stayed above the surface of the water.

"Hang on guys." He ducked his head under the water and began moving about, scouring the concrete below for the key. His hands hit something, but it wasn't the key. He felt carefully around the object again, then popped to the surface, his head dripping water. He went over closer to the two men. "Robbie and Larry. I didn't find the key, but damned if I didn't feel the edge and top of a grate of some kind. It feels like a drainage grate."

"I don't know of any drainage under there," Larry said. "Let me look." He dove under water as well, and came up thirty seconds later. "You're right. There is a drain cover there. Never knew about it."

"Is that where the water could be coming from?" Robbie asked.

"I don't think so," Larry answered. "But could be. I didn't feel any flow, in or out of it. Let's try to cover it as tightly as we can and see what happens."

The three men looked around, and Ben located several heavy, hard bound manuals on a shelf under the computers. They weighed over ten pounds each. "Let's try these. Then we can take turns standing on them and see what happens."

He placed them over the grate, and was just able to put one foot on top of them under the desk. He couldn't put much weight on it. "Robbie, take that marker," Ben said, pointing to the top of the desk, "and mark the water level on the wall."

They each took a shift of doing their best to stand on the books. A half hour went by and the water rose at the same unrelenting pace. "This isn't doing any good," Ben said. "Either the books aren't blocking the drain well enough, or that's not where the water's coming from. Let's re-think this."

The men went over to a corner of the room. Ben continued to take the initiative. "I worked as a plumber's apprentice for three summers during college," he explained. "There's one thing I learned about drains in the floor. They're there to get water out, not let it in. Now either it's a passive drain, which means water is just supposed to flow naturally down through it, which of course isn't happening now. Or it's active, meaning there's got to be a pumping system somewhere to get rid of excess water. With a place this sophisticated, I'd really be surprised if there isn't an active system somewhere."

"But how do we access it? Where is it?" Larry asked.

"I worked mostly in commercial buildings," Ben continued. "The pumping apparatus was always tied into the electrical system. In this room, it'd be the emergency back up system. Does anyone know where that is?"

"There's got to be an electrical panel somewhere in here," Robbie said. The men walked around the perimeter of the room, sloshing their way through. On the walls were several clocks and charts of the Keys.

Ben went to one of the charts, lifted it away from the wall, and said, "Lookee here. Amazing what you can find behind one of these things."

Behind the chart was a metal panel door, twelve by eighteen inches. "Sure looks like a circuit breaker box to me. Let's see what we've got." Ben opened the door. It was a typical circuit box, with various black switches, all pulled to the "on" position. Except one. It stood by itself, and was red. It was off.

"I wonder what this here thing is for," Ben said with amusement in his voice.

"Wait, are you sure you should touch that?" Larry protested.

"Larry, what's the worst that's going to happen?" Robbie asked. "We'll all get electrocuted? That's better than drowning . . . in my book."

Ben smiled as he pulled the red switch. Nothing. The men looked at each other. A gurgling sound could be heard, emanating from the drain area where they had put the books. "Help me get those off of there!" Ben yelled.

Robbie ducked under and shoved the books off the drain. Now they could clearly hear the sucking sound as the water directly above the grate began spiraling down. As they watched, astounded, the water level dropped an inch every minute, until, within a half hour, the floor was free of water except for small damp spots around the perimeter. Ben turned the switch to the "off" position as soon as a loud slurping noise came from the grate area, signifying no more water was flowing out. The key to the lock to the exit door was lying on top of the grate.

Everyone clapped in unison, and the adults got up and slapped Ben on the back, congratulating him as they did so. Val came up and gave him a kiss on his cheek. "Ben, that was amazing. You saved us. Thank you."

CHAPTER SIXTY-NINE

The big Orion aircraft rose in the air to five thousand feet.

"Okay Aaron." Jay said. "This is as high and fast as we go without any radio contact. Now we have to decide where we're heading. We've got about five hundred miles of fuel left. She's flying pretty good, but even if she was full of gas, I wouldn't chance it all the way back to the good ole U S of A. Any ideas?"

"I was thinking about it last night when I realized we weren't going to be able to refuel in Fogo. I've been studying the maps over the past few days, and I think our best course is to Sao Vicente to the north. It's around two hundred miles away, and the airport has been recently rebuilt. We should be able to fuel up there. Then it's only another thousand miles to Bermuda. We'll basically hopscotch across to the mainland."

"I'm onboard with that plan. Can you get me a compass bearing to Sao Vicente?"

Zoe, who had gotten up and was now standing in the doorway to the cockpit, added, "I've been there. Last year. The airport is brand new. They built a huge new terminal with a bright, lemon green roof that ripples and waves like the wings of a large manta ray. Don't know why they picked that color. Kinda stands out like a sore thumb, if you ask me."

Aaron pulled out his navigational maps and mulled them over for a few minutes. "Captain, head 'er at three hundred and forty degrees north by northwest. That should get us there in about an hour at our present speed."

"Got it. Three forty it is."

Zoe went back to make coffee on the stove. The two men spoke.

"I don't know what we're going to find in Vicente," the Captain said. "The cone of Daemon covered a diameter of over five hundred miles. That would include our current destination."

"Not only that, but according to these topographical maps, Vicente is flatter and lower than Fogo," Aaron said. "We already know that everything on the coast of Fogo was totally wiped out. The only survivors came from high up on the volcano. There's no such refuge in Vicente."

"Well, I hope we're wrong, and some on the island survived. Or, at the very least – and I don't want to sound selfish – they've got enough gas to get us to our next stop."

Zoe appeared with two cups of steaming hot coffee.

"Hey look at this," Aaron said as he took one of the cups from her. "Thanks honey. You're the best."

"I'll second that. Thanks Zoe. I really need this," Jay said as he took his cup.

"I think we all do. That was really traumatic back there. The worst was having to leave Bart and Jack behind. I just hope they get a decent burial," Zoe said as she went back to get her cup.

Jay said, "I'm going back there. Soon I hope. And I swear to God, if their bodies were desecrated, I'm going to get even. I don't know how, but I will. I've known them and their families for over twenty years. I'm the one who's gonna have to break the news to them."

They were about fifty miles out of Fogo when the first wave of an immense sonic boom picked the plane up and tossed it forward and sideways. Jay struggled to keep it in the air. Zoe was catapulted first into the metal door jamb, and then backward into a seat just behind her. Their coffees flew into the air.

"What the . . . ?" Aaron's cry was obliterated when a sound like five nearby mach two jets roared by them.

Zoe shook her head to clear the cobwebs. Putting her hand to the right side of her head, she felt blood flowing lightly from a gash just above her eye. "What's going on?" she asked toward the cockpit.

When no answer was immediately forthcoming, she peered behind them through the small window. "*Oh God!*" she mouthed. But no sound came out.

Pico Do Fogo was spewing enormous rocks and flames out of its center. Bright orange lava was already flowing down the lip of the crater. Then, within seconds, as she was watching, another enormous eruption blasted out of the now torn crater. The shock waves hit them again like a body blow to the solar plexus.

"I don't know if we can take another one of those," Jay shouted. "I'm increasing our speed to try to get out of the impact zone."

Aaron watched as their air speed climbed from two hundred, to two fifty, and finally three hundred fifty miles an hour. The damaged craft shuddered and moaned as it cut through the air. He looked back and saw Zoe's forehead glistening with blood.

"Sweetheart. You're hurt." Unstrapping himself from the copilot's seat, he quickly grabbed a first aid kit from a compartment above his head, and went back to Zoe. "I bet they've got a couple of antibiotic swabs in here, and some bandages. Let's fix that up right now."

Zoe didn't turn around. "Those poor people. Look Aaron. It's a tremendous explosion. The lava is covering the entire side of the mountain. It's already inundated the upper villages, and will hit Sao Felipe within the hour. I don't see how anything can survive that."

Aaron came to her side and gently turned the affected area of her forehead toward him. "We can look at all that in a few minutes. Let's stop this blood flow and dress the wound."

He carefully touched the cut with a pad. "This may hurt a little." He cleansed and bandaged the wound. He could tell it was not that deep or severe.

After completing the task, Aaron retrieved a pair of binoculars from an overhead bin. He handed them to Zoe. "Let me know what you see."

Zoe focused the lenses and sat transfixed by the scene before her. Five minutes passed. Finally she reported back to Aaron. "I can't see all the details, but it looks to me that this a catastrophic eruption. Huge boulders are cascading over the entire island. The lava has now coated the entire west side and is now hitting the sea. The plumes of steam are simply amazing."

She handed the binoculars to Aaron. He watched intently for several minutes. "That *is* unbelievable. Regardless of what we felt about those people, most of them deserve better than that."

He turned and walked to the edge of the cockpit. "Captain, you're not going to believe what's happening back there. The lava has already obliterated Sao Felipe. I don't mean to sound insensitive, but we won't have to worry about a burial for the men. Nature has taken care of that."

"That actually makes me feel better. Now at least the families will know their bodies are safely entombed, inaccessible to the elements and animals . . . of all species."

They flew in silence toward Sao Vicente. After almost exactly one hour of flying time, Aaron, who had moved back to the copilot's seat, pointed forward and said, "I think I can see the roof of the airport. It's a yellowish green, right Zoe?"

"Yeah. Kinda a puke green."

"That must be it alright. At least you can't miss it."

As they approached closer, Captain Cross said, "There's something wrong here. Aaron, take a look at that again. Tell me what you see."

Aaron held the binoculars, which were still around his neck, to his eyes. "Jesus," he gasped. "That roof is no longer on the terminal. It's lying in sections right across the runway. The middle of the runway, I might add."

"I'm engaging the auto pilot," the Captain replied. "Let me take a look." He took the lenses and studied the terrain in front of and below them. It was a tawny brown, with little vegetation, and windswept. The runway, now about thirty miles ahead, was like a river cut into the adjoining canyons. There was no sign of life. "I'm going to do a flyover to see what we've got."

They descended to fifteen hundred feet. The runway ran east to west. They approached from the west, the Captain and Aaron studying the skies around them for other planes. "I don't see anything around us, Captain," Aaron said. "I think it's a go for a flyover."

As they approached, they could clearly see that the terminal, lying to their left, had no roof. It was crumpled in several sections like huge beached whales along the runway.

"Damn. Our luck today," the Captain said. "It's basically cut the runway in half. This is going to be a very hairy landing. As soon as we touch down, everyone brace themselves. I'll brake as best we can, but we're not going to have much room left. And it looks like it's just mountains at the end. Okay, let's circle back and git 'er done."

They strapped themselves in tightly. The Captain brought them in at a hundred feet. Just as they passed the last section of twisted, contorted sheet metal and steel, he plunged the craft down. It bounced harshly twice before rolling at high speed down the remaining runway. Lowering the flaps and back exhausting the engines at full throttle, the plane lurched and pitched. The mountain at the end loomed ever larger.

"Hold on, guys. I don't think we're going to make it!"

Zoe put her head between her legs, and began uttering quick, silent prayers. Talk about a fox hole conversion, she mocked herself.

The roar of the engines and squealing of brakes and tires was deafening. Aaron looked up and saw they were almost upon the end of the landing strip. He braced. They hit some loose gravel first, then tall rough grasses. The plane bounced even harder. Miraculously it skidded to a halt, the nose only ten feet from the front face of a rocky crag protruding from the hillock. Eleven feet more and they would have been crushed by the stone overhang.

Zoe heard a simultaneous gasp of relief from the men in front of her. Only then did she let the tears flow – tears that had been in storage for too long now – suppressed only to keep her strong in the face of all the adversity they had faced over the past days. She let it all out now.

CHAPTER SEVENTY

Jenn didn't catch a wink of sleep. Strangely, Mark slept like a baby. As she lay awake, snuggled up against him with his rain jacket over them, she thought about the changes in her life since she had met him.

It had been a tremendous leap of faith for her to go on a trip like this with someone she had just met. Combine that with her inchoate fear of the ocean, she marveled that she had gotten this far. Her earlier plunge into the inky blackness of the water to save Mark demonstrated to her most keenly that she was beginning to overcome her trepidations.

More than that, her thoughts were no longer dominated by the sorrow and self-hatred that the death of her son had engendered. It was almost as if their varied experiences with the storm had cleansed her in a way that no analysis or counseling could duplicate.

She had fallen in love with this man. His kindness, the respect with which he treated her, his strength in the face of adversity, had endeared him to her as no other man had in the past. She had even begun to fantasize what the rest of her life with him would be like. It was good.

Mark coughed and turned toward her. The jacket was up over their heads, only leaving their bodies uncovered from the knees down. Jenn was tiny enough that she had been able to pull her legs up under the cover for most of the night. It had been fairly warm, despite the ongoing tempest.

At the first sign of light, Mark opened his eyes. He gazed upon Jenn. "Hey baby. Man, I was totally out." He paused for a moment to listen to what was going on around them, "Sounds like the storm is really winding down. I only feel a little drizzle."

"It's pretty much done. It was a crazy night. I'm amazed you were able to sleep through it all."

"So am I. I was far more exhausted than I realized." He put his hand to the back of his head. "Of course, getting whacked like I did didn't help much."

"That scared the hell out of me," Jenn admitted.

"Did you jump in the water after me?" Mark asked. "And get me to shore?"

"Yeah. That was me." Jenn smiled.

"My God, girl. That's amazing. Now I guess it's my turn to say thank you."

"I just consider us even."

Mark peered into the thick woods. "I can't see more than a couple of feet. I wonder how Trade Winds fared overnight. Frankly, I'll be amazed if she survived. I think I'm ready to stand up and walk."

"Okay. Let's give it a try."

Jenn stood up first and helped Mark get to his feet. They took a few tentative steps. "I think I'm going to be alright," Mark said. "So long as we don't have to run a marathon."

"We'll save that for tomorrow."

"Here, you take the jacket."

"No, you wear it. I'm fine. You're the one with the busted head."

Mark put on the rain coat. Jenn led him in the general direction where she knew the water to be. They had pushed through the thick foliage only a few feet when their feet hit water. "What the heck!" Jenn shouted. "We climbed up a steep hill last night. I'm sure of it!"

"Maybe you got turned around. Could it be back the other way?"

"No, this is the right way." Jenn took another step and pushed a large branch out of their sight line. They were now looking at a broad stretch of sea, studded with trees. "Look, those are tall pines and deciduous trees. The water is almost to their first branches. At least fifteen feet up. No, the ocean has risen to this level overnight."

"That's incredible," Mark said. "I've never heard of a storm surge like that, much less seen one. What do we do now?"

"I don't know, exactly. I guess we have to find out if the boat is still there. If we start swimming, at least we'll have the tree trunks to grab hold of if we get tired. I don't think it could be any more than fifty or sixty feet away. The edge of the forest has to be right in front of us."

"Okay. Let's bite the bullet. Last one in is a monkey's uncle!" Mark lowered himself into the water. It was uncomfortably cool. All the rain, he surmised. He heard Jenn splash in just behind him. Remarkably, the rubberized rain coat, although restricting his movement a little, actually added to his buoyancy.

Doing a breast stroke, they were able to avoid the trees. After twenty feet, Mark said, "I think I see it clearing just ahead!"

They kept stroking. Some tree branches obscured their view of the cove. They swam up to them and pushed them aside. Mark scanned the water in front of them. Trade Winds was nowhere to be seen.

"Damn it. The storm took her. God knows where. We're going to have to head back."

Jenn, who was just behind Mark, said, "Hold on. Let me get up on this branch and see if I can see anything." She lifted herself up on the limb of a large oak, one she estimated must have been a full twenty feet above ground without the water. Standing, she craned to see left and right.

"Wait. Mark. I think I see her. She must have drifted out. She's close to the shore at the mouth of the bay, about two hundred yards away."

"Thank God. Can you see if she's damaged?"

"I can't from here. We're going to have to swim out to her. If we stay close to shore for a while we can hold on to the trees."

"Okay. Let's get going," Mark said as he started the slow process of swimming to Trade Winds.

They had to stop often to rest. Both of them started to get chilled. When Jenn's chattering teeth alerted Ben to the level of her discomfort, he stopped by a tree branch and removed his coat. "Jenn, this makes it a little harder going, but it keeps you warmer."

"No honey. You keep it. I'm okay."

"Jenn. Take it. This is a direct order."

Jenn looked him in the eyes, and immediately saw his seriousness and the futility of resisting. She took it and felt more comfortable instantaneously. "Thank you honey. Let's get going. We're very close now."

Mark could see the vessel was no more than a hundred feet away. They swam with the energy of knowing their goal was within reach. Finally Mark grabbed the edge of the swim platform, and helped Jenn up the ladder. "Get inside and change, baby. I'm going to swim around her and see what damage there is."

Mark went carefully around the hull, on occasion dipping under water and knocking the fiberglass with his fist. When he got back to the ladder, he heaved himself up. Jenn was still waiting in the cockpit.

"I can't believe it. There's not even a scratch on her." Looking toward the bow, and observing tattered pieces of rope hanging from the cleats, Mark continued, "Looks like the two bow lines chafed and broke. But the stern anchor line held. The anchor dragged, but it's holding now. We lucked out again honey."

"I think Trade Winds is trying to tell us something," Jenn said. "We're all together in this, and no one's leaving."

"All together, Jenn. That's for sure."

CHAPTER SEVENTY-ONE

They only had to turn the pump back on twice during the night to rid themselves of the inevitable seepage into the room. It wasn't comfortable because all the bedding and their clothing was soaking wet, but at least they were warm and weren't being pickled in salt water.

Ben, Robbie and Val were lying on their cots. Val spoke up first.

"Ben, I just want to say again how much we appreciate you. We'd be treading water right now if you hadn't figured out that pump thing."

"That was incredible, Ben," Robbie said. "And brave. I don't think I would have stuck my head under that water to find a key, much less locate a grate."

"I see it more as being in the right place at the right time," Ben responded. "Not really brave. I sensed if we couldn't find that key, even if the water didn't rise any higher, there'd be widespread panic in here when people found out there was no easy way out. The rest was just using some old experiences . . . experiences I haven't thought about in many years."

"Well, that's just like you, Ben. Self-effacing. I like your humility, but sometimes I think you ought to be more assertive, just as you were when figuring out the pump," Val said.

"To be honest, guys, I feel a huge burden has been lifted from my shoulders. I've been existing in a marriage that had no love, with a very negative woman. I've played my part in it all, but the past several days have shown me I can't just drift through life accepting whatever comes my way.

"It was a step out of my comfort zone to come down to Miami in the first place," Ben continued. "Of course, I had no idea how far out it would become. I feel I can handle adversity and change much better now, with less fear . . . and most importantly, less guilt. If I get out of here alive, I'd like to spend more time with my children. Sure would like to be able to contact them soon to let them know I'm alright."

Val sat up on her bed to change her position and try to dry off a different area of her clothing. "That last point is the thing I noticed first about you Ben. I did sense you were suffering from some very deeply entrenched guilt feelings. Not just the guilt associated with breaking out and coming to Miami. No, more the guilt we all feel about our failures in life . . . maybe not progressing in our careers as we think we should have . . . our tepid marriages . . . that we could have raised our children better. Whatever."

"You're very observant, Val. And sensitive to other people's needs," Ben said as raised himself on one elbow so he could look at her. "That's exactly what I've been suffering through for a long time now. A general sense of failure. And remorse over having failed. The trials and tribulations I've gone through recently have started the process of absolving me of that guilt. It's like I've paid the price . . . suffered enough . . . and now I can move on."

"That's great, Ben," Robbie piped in. "How about the fears you expressed earlier that this hurricane was following you, was after you to punish you. Do you still feel that?"

"Robbie, it just doesn't make any difference any more whether I feel that or not. The fact is this storm has punished me, has put me through the fire, so to speak. But because of that I've been cleansed, and become a new person. That's what's important now."

"Yes it is," Robbie agreed.

They were able to turn on the computers. That provided them the video feeds to the outside world. They were not uplifting. The screens still portrayed a ghastly scene outside. Now the winds and surge had taken away huge portions of the homes in the area around the station. Several could no longer be seen at all. The massive satellite dish mounted to a tower in back had been ripped off and was of parts unknown. The sea was still at least fifteen feet deep just outside the Storm Center. Not only that, the satellite views showed Daemon stalled over the Florida Keys.

Larry, Robbie, and the other weather specialists huddled around the computer desk. Larry said, "It doesn't look like we're going to be out of this for some time. Seems the storm is going to hang with us for at least another twenty-four hours, if not more. God knows how long it will take for the water level to go down. Then I'm not sure what we're going to find once it does subside. It could be that most of the island has been destroyed."

"That's what I see as well," Robbie said. "Let's assume we'll be in here for a week, maybe longer. We'll need to allocate the food and water, establish a clean-up schedule, especially for the bathroom, and find ways to amuse the children."

"He's right," Larry spoke to the other men. "Sam and Tom, you guys take a look at our food and water supplies, and work out an apportionment that will last for at least two weeks. There should be enough for that long. I'll do a cleaning schedule with Robbie. Robbie, let's ask Val to get the ladies together to find ways to keep the kids occupied. Okay?"

They all agreed, and went to work.

****

Daemon finally released its death grip on the Keys, and vented its rage up the west coast of Florida through Tampa, then Pensacola. The juggernaut smashed the southeast, causing unparalleled destruction in Alabama, Georgia and the Carolina's. It quickened its pace and strength as it flew up the southern coast into Virginia and Maryland, almost as if it were hurrying to a secret rendezvous with a lover.

That illicit meeting occurred. Eepa was just roaring in from Bermuda to the mid-Atlantic states. There, in an incestuous union, it combined with its progenitor and formed a super storm of heretofore unknown dimensions and fury. It descended upon New England like a giant arachnid, devouring its prey in a web of tornadoes, howling winds, and giant waves. New York City, Boston, and Portland Maine were reduced to pre-nineteenth century remnants. Hundreds of thousands of people suffered the terrible death of drowning in the surging seas.

CHAPTER SEVENTY-TWO

Aaron unstrapped himself and came quickly to Zoe. Sitting next to her, he pulled her to him and let her tears soak his shirt. They didn't say anything for about ten minutes. Jay just sat silently in the pilot's chair, not looking back out of respect for his friends.

Zoe looked up and wiped her eyes. "I'm alright now. I needed that."

"We all need a good cry now and then," Aaron said as he lifted her chin up and kissed her wet lips tenderly.

"Roger that," the Captain added, his own eyes moist.

He came back, knelt by Aaron and Zoe, and they gave each other a group hug. "We can relax here for a while before exploring around for fuel if you want," Jay said.

"No, I think we should get right to it," Zoe said as she stood with some determination in her eyes.

"Okay then," Aaron replied, with similar resolve in his voice.

Jay lowered the center hatch, grabbed the canvas bag with the remaining guns, and the three climbed down. They could see right away that the ground around them had been underwater for some time. The grass was yellow from the seasoning of the sea, and ocean detritus – seaweed, bits of coral, occasional bottles and cans – were strewn everywhere.

"Well, the water certainly got up this high," Jay said. "I can't tell if it rose above those hills. I doubt it. But I don't see any houses or other structures up there, so I assume it's just too rocky to build on."

"Or they got blown or washed off," Zoe said.

"I'm going to bet on blown," Aaron cut in. "Let's walk over to the terminal and look around."

They covered the quarter mile to the terminal at a fast clip. As they approached, they could see that it had been wrent into a jumbled erector set. Giant steel girders lay across each other at odd angles. They couldn't get through the main entrance door, which itself was crushed by a colossal beam.

"Nothing here," Aaron commented. "Let's walk over to those buildings there," he continued, pointing to a collection of three attached structures two hundred yards away. There appeared to be several large trucks parked nearby.

Zoe was the first to see the lettering on the side of one of the vehicles. "Wait! I think it says 'FUEL' on that truck. We may have lucked out here."

"If we can get the damn thing started," Aaron said.

"I'll get it started. Don't worry about that," the Captain said with a wink. Aaron knew he could do it.

Sure enough, as they got closer, a medium sized fuel truck was pulled up to the edge of a small parking lot adjacent to the structures, which appeared to be offices for maintenance and repair. Aaron climbed the one metal step to the cab and looked in. "No sign of keys in here. Let's take a look inside the buildings."

Surprisingly they found that the primary door to the maintenance building was unlocked. When they entered, the furniture was tossed around inside, and the floor was covered in sand. They looked in every room, and at one point found a key rack containing several sets of keys. They tried each one, and none worked.

"Okay, on to plan B," Jay said. Searching around inside, he found a large and small screwdriver, and hammer. Lifting himself up into the cab, he popped the ignition switch with a deft crack of the hammer on the larger screwdriver, He stuck the smaller one in the open hole. Aaron had climbed into the passenger side.

"Aaron, when I tell you, turn the screwdriver clockwise, and give 'er some gas." Jay exited, opened the hood to the truck, and put the blade of the large screwdriver across a lead to the solenoid switch and the starter motor. "Okay Aaron, give 'er a rip." The engine kicked and fired up.

"We have ignition, Captain," Aaron yelled with a grin above the roar of the motor.

""Roger that," Jay responded.

Just then Zoe came from the back of the truck. "Not so fast, gentlemen. As far as I can tell, the tank on this truck is as dry as a bone. That gauge back there doesn't even register."

The men went back and sheepishly admitted there wasn't a drop of fuel in the tank. "Damn it," Jay cursed. "I thought this was getting too easy."

"Is there a plan C?" Aaron looked at Jay.

"We keep on looking. There's got to be a pump or two around here."

They left the engine running and spread out to keep checking out the area. Zoe went behind a large, seven foot high hedgerow. Her scream caused Jay and Aaron to come running toward the sound. Aaron flew around the corner first.

"Holy Jesus!" he shouted.

Jay arrived just after him. He saw the other two staring in horror at a pile of dead, decomposing bodies. There must have been twenty or thirty stacked one atop the other. Human limbs stuck out like bristles. The entire mound was covered with a white powder that looked like lime and which partially, but not adequately disguised the smell. Zoe held her arm and sleeve against her nose. "God it stinks."

"Let's get out of here," Aaron said as he grabbed Zoe by the sleeve of her shirt and began pulling her away. "These bodies were placed here by someone, or something. I just don't like the look of this whole thing."

Jay led the way back to where they had just split up. "I saw something over by that water tank before we heard you, Zoe. Let's all explore over there."

"I'm all for sticking together," Zoe responded, still shuddering from the sight they had beheld.

They redirected their search toward a large, metal tank which stood on a concrete pad. When they got close they were delighted to see a gas pump behind it.

"Maybe we're getting luckier," the Captain said. "Let's see if it's got anything in it."

Aaron went over and took the nozzle off the side of the pump. There was a lever on the other side, but it had a small, badly rusted combination lock preventing it from moving to the "on" position.

Aaron picked up a good size rock and struck the lock twice sharply. It gave way easily. "I think we may be in business now."

The Captain took the nozzle and Aaron activated the pump. Gas poured from the hose.

"Halleluiah!" Zoe shouted. "We *are* in business. The only thing is, how are we going to get the gas to the plane?"

"Tell you what," Aaron answered. "I'll drive the tanker truck over here and we'll see if we can't get a few hundred gallons into her. If we can, we'll simply take the truck over to the plane."

"Sounds like a good idea to me," Zoe said.

Aaron left for the truck. Behind them, Zoe and the Captain could not see the two pairs of eyes watching them intently from behind a ridge approximately thirty yards away.

CHAPTER SEVENTY-THREE

They climbed aboard Trade Winds. Mark walked around the entire deck. "Nothing broken up here."

"I'll go below." Jenn went down and shouted back up, "A few dishes and the salt and pepper shaker were thrown around, but that's it. We're good to go."

Standing on the bow, Mark looked around. This vantage point gave him an excellent view of the bay. "Hey baby, can you bring the binoculars up when you come?"

Jenn appeared almost immediately and walked them up to him. Mark swept the expanse of water and the surrounding shoreline. "I can barely make out where the water ends and the shore starts. This surge must be at least twenty feet. That's catastrophic. The only terra firma I can see is on the upper level hills. And I don't see any human activity."

"That's not encouraging," Jenn replied. "Can I take a look?"

Mark handed her the glasses. She looked for less than a minute. "That's scarier than hell. It's like we've first discovered Bermuda . . . in its primitive state. I think I may have seen some shells of homes – they were very hard to make out – but definitely no roofs. The wind must have taken those. So what do we do now?"

"We just hang out for a few days until the ocean subsides a bit. I'd guess she'll go down eight to ten feet in a few days. We've got enough food and water for that time. Then we'll take Trade Winds around and see what we can find."

"Sounds like a plan, Captain. I guess we could stand a little more togetherness, huh?"

"I sure could," Mark said with a wink.

Mark cranked the engine to get some hot water flowing. They took showers on deck using the wash down spigots. The temperature was in the comfortable low seventies. The sky was still overcast from the remnants of the storm.

They crawled into a bunk together, savoring the body warmth. They made love with a compassion born of their many recent dangers. They had survived, each had saved the other, these experiences forming a bond between them which was now expressed beautifully in their sex.

"Wow! That was the best, baby," Jenn cooed.

"About as good as it gets."

Jenn pulled the light blanket closer under her chin. "What do you think we're going to find out there?"

"I really don't know. I've never lived through something like this. We'll spend some time by the radio this evening to learn what we can."

"In a certain way I don't even want to hear it. If it's really bad, I kinda want to stay cut off from all the tragedy, whatever it is. What we've got between us is so good I'd like to rest in the nice little nest we've created here."

"That's sweet, Jenn, but at some point we're gonna need more supplies, and find out for ourselves what's out there."

Mark got up slowly and went to the head. Jenn could not help but notice his cute little ass and bulging biceps.

She said loudly so he could hear her: "Let's just say . . . for the sake of argument . . . that it's a total disaster out there. I mean nothing left. Where do we go from there?"

Mark came out of the bathroom and began making some tea. "It really depends on where Eepa and Daemon ultimately go. If we head west, those storms kinda have the north and south covered. I'm hoping we can continue our trip to the Virgin Islands, which are much further south and east than Miami and the Keys."

"But that depends on whether or not we can stock up on more food and water, right?"

"That's right."

After making the tea, they both got dressed. Jenn began making some dinner: spaghetti bolognese, Mark's favorite. She made it with a barely discernible, but still poignant combination of garlic, onion and nutmeg.

When they had finished their dinners, Mark sat down at the computer and also turned on the radio. Jenn took up a seat on the settee near by. Mark started by pulling up a satellite image of Eepa. It was moving slowly, heading in a westerly direction toward the coast. What was remarkable was its footprint: the spinning turbulence at its outer reaches formed a circle with a diameter of over six hundred miles.

"My God," Mark said. "Eepa has grown. I would have expected that once she started moving into cooler waters, she'd wane. That isn't happening."

He switched to the NOAA website. "It's still only a cat three."

"I didn't think I'd ever hear you say *only* a three," Jenn said with a frown.

"Yeah. Guess that shows what we've gotten used to. I'm reading some preliminary reports on Bermuda. It's bad. Mostly the storm surge. That combo of full moon and high tide at the height of the storm was lethal. They're apparently only getting sporadic radio reports. Massive damage. I can't seem to get any radio reception at all."

Jenn got up and moved closer to the screen to get a better view. "At least there are those. Someone besides us is still alive. That's encouraging."

"Sarcasm? From my Jenn? I've rarely heard that."

"I'm not so sure I was being sarcastic. I can only imagine what it would be like to be all alone, bobbing around the sea in this little boat, no port to call home."

"That's pretty scary, Jenn."

CHAPTER SEVENTY-FOUR

It was the wetness that got to them the most. It never seemed to dry out. The mattresses were still fully soaked after five days. Everyone began developing nasty sores that never healed.

Ben organized a system where they would rotate each mattress, hang it up and take turns fanning it with file folders stapled to a broom stick. They also took turns hanging them next to the one ventilation duct with a fan that operated continuously. It helped a little, but mostly sent the moisture to one end of the bedding.

They also rationed the food and water to last fifteen days, the maximum allowed by their inventory. By the end of the first week, the water level outside had subsided to about three feet, still making navigation impossible.

Tempers flared up now and then. One man got into a heated argument with his wife and demanded to be let out. He was large, about 6' 2", and over two hundred pounds. The other men tried to get him to settle down, but he just became more agitated and belligerent. Finally, after a few busted lips, they managed to get him down on the floor and restrain him with zip ties. Except for infrequent bathroom trips, that's where he stayed, on the floor, leaning against the wall, muttering to himself. His wife helped him into bed at night.

Robbie called a meeting of all the men. He spoke quietly in a corner of the room. "Guys, pretty soon some of us are going to have to venture out to look for some supplies. Hell, we're about to run out of toilet paper in a few days. The tempest we just survived will be nothing like the storm created when the ladies hear about that. We also need to see if we can make contact with the outside world."

Ben piped in, "We might consider getting two or three of the strongest swimmers and make an attempt to find a boat. Anything that will float will do. We might be able to get around even if we have to paddle it."

"We're not quite there yet," Larry Grimes said. "We'll be good for a few more days. Let's assess the situation in three or four days."

Four days came and went. The conditions did not improve outside, and only a little inside. The bedding dried a bit, but the sores worsened. When the toilet paper ran out, as the men had anticipated, the ladies implored them to do something.

Ben offered to join a team that would forage outside for provisions. Robbie and Larry agreed to be the leaders. All three had been strong swimmers in their day.

They were able to get the door to Operations open without a flood of water engulfing them. They turned on the pump to discharge the little that flowed in. Outside the water was well below the level of the top of the stairs, but still came up to their waists as they carefully lowered themselves into the sea. They stayed to the easterly side of White Street where the current carrying the seawater back to the ocean was not so strong. The going was slow up to Truman Avenue.

Truman had normally been the business boulevard on the island. Now it was as quiet and vacant as a bombed out war zone. Most of the wooden structures, comprising the majority of the homes and businesses on the street, had collapsed at the onslaught of the water. The few brick and stone buildings were filled with water. No windows remained intact.

The men plowed through the water yelling at regular intervals to see if they could elicit any response. They didn't come upon a living soul.

"Let's make our way to Solares Hill and see what we find," Larry suggested.

"What's Solares Hill?" Ben inquired.

"It's the highest point of land in Key West," Larry answered. "It's all of eighteen feet above sea level. Remember, we're just a tiny little piece of coral rock here."

"Well I'll take eighteen feet," Ben said.

As they proceeded west on Truman and took a right on Windsor, the water became shallower as the elevation rose. By the cemetery they were only ankle deep.

"I guess we might see some caskets floating by," Ben said.

"I doubt it," Robbie cut in. "All of these tombs are solid concrete, constructed above ground. The water table is too high, and the coral too hard, to put them below."

"I'm not unhappy about that," Ben said.

Still the men saw no life whatsoever. The devastation was complete. No building was left unscathed. After several minutes at the top of Solares Hill on Angela Street, which only afforded them a very limited view, Larry said, "My last thought is to get over to the Key West lighthouse on Whitehead. That baby has withstood some tempests in its time. If it's still standing we'll be able to view the entire island from the top."

"What about the La Concha Hotel?" Robbie asked. "We can get up eight stories there."

"I'm worried we won't be able to get in. Either the door will be locked or the first level will be too cluttered with debris to afford us access. At the Lighthouse we could climb over the fence if the gate is locked. I know a way to get in from there."

"Okay, the Lighthouse it is," Robbie replied.

It took them over three hours to wade their way over to and down Whitehead. They passed by the Hemingway Home almost directly adjacent to the Lighthouse. Even though all the glass windows were blown out, and there was some slight structural damage to the second floor balcony, amazingly other than that the building seemed to be largely unscathed.

"The house was built in 1851 and has seen some hurricanes in its day," Larry said. "I'm not surprised to see it weathered another one. But I still don't see anyone around."

The Lighthouse was only about fifty feet south of and on the other side of the street from Hemingway's old residence. Here too, the structure showed no damage. The gate was open and swinging in the soft breeze.

"Looks like we lucked out," Ben said. "Let's get up there and take a look."

Ben ran two steps at a time up the circular stairs in the interior of the structure. Half way up he was completely winded and stopped to rest. The other two were still far below.

There was a rectangular opening in the two foot thick wall at this level, one of the few "windows" in the tall structure. Ben was able to peek through. What he saw sucked the wind out of his lungs. Although his perspective was funneled through the small aperture, it covered about a twelve square block area north and east of the Lighthouse. Ben had never witnessed such total devastation. They had only been able to perceive a small fraction of it while walking the streets. Now the full panorama of the hideous destructive forces of Daemon were laid before him. It was as if God, or Her counterpart, had grabbed huge fistfuls of wood, metal and concrete, and flung the mass into lumps around the City.

His attention was interrupted as Larry and Robbie arrived at his level. "I don't know if we really need to go up any higher," Ben said. "Take a look."

Robbie let out a low whistle. "Holy crap. Can you guys believe that?"

"I sure can't," Larry answered. "It's much worse than I imagined."

"I still want to go all the way to the top," Larry said. "It will give us a view of the entire City."

They made it to the black, cast iron catwalk that encircled the upper part of the structure. Their first view at the top was toward Mallory Square and the Key West Harbor.

"Jesus Christ," they said in unison.

A huge cruise ship lay on her side in the middle of the channel, her enormous starboard prop hanging exposed like a windmill from the stern. The shores of Sunset Key and Wisteria Island were littered with beached vessels in various states of ruin. The La Concha Hotel stood as a lone sentry eight stories above the melee, all of its windows blown out.

It looked like a nuclear blast had unleashed its wrath upon Key West.

CHAPTER SEVENTY-FIVE

Aaron negotiated the tanker to within ten feet of the pump. The hose reached easily, but the process of filling the huge thousand gallon tank was painstakingly slow.

They had to take turns holding and pulling the trigger to the nozzle as their hands became numb after only ten minutes. Zoe insisted on taking her turn. As the sun beat down on the reflective aluminum skin of the tank, they had to spread leaves and dirt on the top to deflect the heat.

Finally, after six hours of exhausting, hot work, the truck was filled. They capped it, and Aaron, with Zoe in the middle and Jay riding shotgun, drove it to the plane.

The process of refueling took far less time. The truck was equipped with a powerful pumping mechanism that shot twenty gallons a minute into the plane's empty tank. They were done in less than two hours, and could mostly rest in the shade while the gasoline flowed.

"I can't believe we got Miss Piggy fueled up, start to finish, so quickly," Jay said. "Now we just have to figure a way to pull her away from this cliff so I can turn her around and head out."

"Do we have any cable aboard?" Aaron asked.

"None that is long or strong enough. I should have thought about this when we were looking for the gas."

"Let's go looking now," Zoe said. "Could we use rope?"

"It'd have to be very thick and strong," Jay replied.

They drove the truck back over to the fuel depot and the maintenance room they had previously entered. They searched in vain inside and out. No cable, no rope.

Zoe said, "I hate to mention this, but now that I think about it, I'm almost sure I saw some heavy rope back around where we found the bodies. I think someone had tried to cover them with a tarp. I know the last thing we want to do is go back there again, but I think we've got to at least check it out."

"Good memory, Zoe," Aaron said. "I don't think we have any other option than to take a look see."

"Agreed," Jay said.

The three walked the fifty or so yards around the back of the buildings to the putrid pile. *It stunk far worse than before, if that was even possible,* Zoe thought. She pulled her t-shirt up over her mouth and nose, baring her tight belly and bra by a few inches. Aaron could not help but notice how shapely she was. Uncharacteristically, he visually undressed her, stem to stern, making sure she didn't notice.

Around the back of the stack of corpses they saw what Zoe had seen earlier. A large canvas tarpaulin lay bunched on the ground. A stout length of rope remained over the cover and under the bodies. The ends were in a loose knot on the ground. They would have to pull the rope from under the pile.

"Let's all take one end and pull as if we were in a tug of war," Jay said as he untied the knot and grabbed and lifted up the rope. "I'd pull the truck up here, but there's no way we could maneuver it close enough to tie the rope on."

Aaron placed his hands close to Jay's and Zoe followed suit.

"Okay guys, let's give it all we've got. On the count of three."

On three they heaved with all their might. The rope moved less than six inches.

"What the heck," Aaron said. "What's holding this thing down?"

"Those bodies weigh a lot more than we think, I guess. They're bloated and probably full of fluids," Jay responded.

Jay counted to three again, and once more they put their weight into the rope. It pulled out another six inches.

"This sure is going to be slow going," Aaron said.

"Sure is," Zoe added.

They worked for another ten minutes, extracting the rope a full twelve feet. Now they could see it was saturated with human waste. Unimaginable waste. The stench grew worse as the rope was exposed.

"God, we don't even have any work gloves. This is horrible," Jay said as the line slid through his hands, leaving a dark brown and red stain.

"I'm just shutting it out of my mind," Zoe said. "If I focus on it, I'll get sick as a dog."

After three hours of gruesome labor, they managed to pull the rope all the way out. They decided to take a break, and sat under a small palm tree that afforded them some dappled shade.

Aaron started looking around, and speaking to Jay, said, "Jay. By the way. Where's the bag with the guns?"

The Captain looked around, bewildered. "Yeah. Where is it? I put it down somewhere while we were working."

They got up and searched around the area. Zoe went back to the truck to check inside. She was sitting on the passenger side of the front bench seat when a man, apparently Cape Verdean, his clothes ripped and falling off of him, opened the driver's door and lurched into the cab. His long dark hair was matted down on his scalp, a deep jagged gash still oozed blood just above his hairline.

Zoe emitted a blood curdling scream, and reached for the door handle on her side. As her hand closed on it, it jerked down suddenly, almost breaking her wrist. The door opened and another man, this one more wild and animalistic than the other, pushed her over toward the center of the seat. She was now surrounded.

The man in the driver's seat reached for the ignition to start the engine. Pointing to the ignition cylinder, he began screaming at Zoe, "Chave! Chave!" Zoe, attempting to gather herself and placate the uncontrollable man, gently began explaining in English and gesticulations that the vehicle had to be jump started. The man to her right reached around, grabbed her harshly by the hair, and banged her head against the metal back of the cab.

In an instant both doors to the truck flew open, and Aaron on the passenger side, and Jay Cross on the other, yanked the men off the seat and onto the ground. Aaron gave his guy a sharp kick to the groin, then stomped his head on the hard asphalt. Jay drove his knuckles deep into the other's throat, shattering his larynx and dropping him choking to the ground. Another fist to the nose put the guy out.

Aaron leaped up beside Zoe and hugged her. He was amazed to

see no tears, no shaking. “Are you okay?” he asked.

"I'm better than they're doing," she said with a wry smile, pointing to the two unconscious figures on the tarmac.

“You're a tough lady, you know,” Aaron said. “But also soft in all the right places.”

Jay already had the hood up and was jumping the solenoid. Aaron took the small screwdriver, which he had placed in his pocket, and started the engine. Jay climbed in the driver's side and said, “Okay guys, let's go get the rope, get out of here and get our bird in the air as fast as we can.”

CHAPTER SEVENTY-SIX

They gave it two days. Pure boredom encouraged them out. In their little cove, the sea had receded just a few feet.

After a lot of discussion about what to do next, Mark said on the morning of the third day, "I guess this is the day. I haven't heard any more reports from Bermuda, so we just need to go explore. We'll motor around the bay, and if we can find a place to land, we'll do it and walk around. Sound okay?"

"Yeah. I know we have to do it. It's just that I kinda like the cove, in this protected area we have. I've really enjoyed our time alone here. Somehow the world out there seems more sinister and threatening."

"Let's get ready. Make sure everything is tied down below because it will be rougher out there. I'll get the blower going in the engine area."

It was a gorgeous Bermuda day. Only a few clouds could be seen on the eastern horizon. Otherwise it was nothing but blue skies.

Jenn came back up and told Mark everything was set below. He started the engine and pulled the anchor up with the electric windlass. Before long they were motoring out of their cove and into the main bay.

Mark was surprised by the calmness of the sea. "This is really nice," he told Jenn. "After what we've been through, we deserve a respite."

He set the compass for the marina they had frequented days before. They took turns surveying the land with the binoculars for any signs of life. There was nothing moving. The only houses to be seen were jumbles of wood and glass. The tide was still unimaginably high.

As they neared the place where they knew the marina to have been, Jenn, who was holding the binoculars, said, "Mark. I can't see anything. I think the marina and the small town around it are totally covered with water. Is that possible?"

"It seems we're now in a dimension where anything's possible. I've never seen a storm surge like this. See if you can find someplace we might be able to take the inflatable and get onto terra firma."

Jenn swept the glasses from side to side. "There's not much but I think I see a clearing with some flat rocks in front. We might be able to take the dinghy and step out onto the rocks. What do you think?"

Jenn handed the binoculars to Mark. In a few seconds he said, "Let's give it a try."

They set anchor and and lowered the dinghy. It took but a few minutes to make it to their selected spot. Mark expertly negotiated their small rubber craft against the low boulders. The water lapped gently against a large flat rock that afforded them easy access. Once they were safely on land and had pulled the tender halfway up on the rock, Mark suggested they climb to the top of the hill in front of them. The way was not easy going, as it was very rocky and slippery from the incessant rain of the past days.

Finally they made it to the summit, about a hundred feet in elevation. The scene laid out before them left them speechless. Mark spent five minutes with the glasses, then silently handed them to Jenn. She took the same time and lowered them.

"This is worse than I thought," she said. "I don't see that

anything has survived."

"It doesn't look like it to me. I don't feel we need to explore any farther. It looks all the same in every direction. What do you think Jenn?"

"I'm with you on that babe. I feel safer onboard Trade Winds. You just don't know what you're going to meet up with on land."

"No, you don't. But right now it doesn't seem like anything is alive around here."

They made their way back down the path. The way going down was more difficult than going up. They slid and sidestepped most of the way. As they came around a large stand of mangroves opening out to the rocks where they had left the dinghy, Mark grabbed Jenn's arm to stop her. Someone was standing by the inflatable, inspecting it carefully.

"Don't move," Mark whispered.

At first he couldn't tell if it was a male or female. Long, gray-white hair flowed down its back. The figure was thin enough to cover both genders. But his slightly wider shoulders and larger feet ultimately gave him away as a man.

The figure turned towards them. He had to be at least eighty, even though the attack of the sun on his burnt and wrinkled face certainly could have aged him beyond his actual years. He was wearing tattered jean cutoff shorts and a shirt that had possibly once been white but was now a mosaic of brown spots and tears. Through one hole Mark could see the outline of a rib.

The man spoke first, a raspy guttural sound that they could barely make out. It sounded like, "Dat yo bot?"

Mark, quickly sizing him up as no threat, answered, "Yes, that is our boat. What happened here?"

"Awrible. All deed."

"Everyone's dead, are you saying?" Jenn asked.

"All," he repeated, while sweeping his arms around the island.

"That's terrible," Mark said. "Are you sure?"

"Shure. All deed."

"How did you survive?" Mark asked, trying not to sound too incredulous of the man's claims.

The man motioned for them to follow him, and turned and disappeared in the same direction from whence they had just come.

"Should we go with him, Mark?" Jenn asked.

He paused, then said, "Why not? I want to see what he's got to show us. Maybe it will explain why he's here, and no one else is."

"Okay."

They passed by the same mangroves, but instead of turning up the hill, they circled around it about ten feet above the encroaching sea. They could barely keep up with the old man, who displayed a nimbleness surprising for his age and apparent condition.

After ten minutes, Jenn said, "Shouldn't we ask him where he's going? We don't want to get lost if he loses us."

Before Mark could answer, they saw him stop in front of a small stone hut that was barely visible amidst the deep foliage. There was no roof. Several large timbers and many planks of wood surfaced with ripped tar paper lay scattered around as a testament to the ferocity of the recent winds. The boulders forming the walls of the small structure were impossibly thick, quickly explaining how it had survived.

He motioned for Mark and Jenn to follow him in. A small metal cot with a wire mesh mattress was bolted to the stone wall to the right. A propane stove and ancient battery-powered two way radio sat atop a wooden table with some containers of salt, pepper, coffee and flour. A few pots and pans lay randomly on a lower shelf. A bookcase, consisting of flat stone slabs held up by bricks and packed with hard cover books in every stage of decay, adorned the back wall. Jenn took note of several titles: many Ernest Hemingway's; some Rudyard Kipling's; and Ulysses by James Joyce. *This guy's intellect is decoyed by his appearance and speech,* she thought.

The man motioned for them to sit down on the bed. They looked at each other and nodded their silent agreement to one another.

"What's your name?" Mark offered once they were seated.

"Dey calls me Cap'n Bill," he said with a smile that was more yellow and black teeth than it was mirth. "'Bout you?"

"I'm Mark, and this is Jenn. Have you come across any survivors?"

Bill shook his head slowly. "Nobody. Nuthin'. Dis be wha we git fo foolin' with motha earth. I bin tellin peeples dis fo years."

"How far have you looked around?" Mark asked as he made a circling motion with his arm.

"Ehrey where," the captain replied. "Also bin callin' on dat radio." He pointed to the archaic contraption. "Nobody said nuthin' back."

The three sat in silence for a few moments, contemplating the enormity of the situation.

"How did you make it through?" Jenn interrupted the quiet.

The old man patted the thick stone wall next to him with his palm. "Stood here over fifty year. Not goin' nowhere."

"You have a lot of books here," Jenn said. "Have you read all of them?"

"Ehrey one," he said. "Dis da best."

He pulled out a single volume. Mark and Jenn saw it was "The Old Man and the Sea," by Hemingway.

"That is a classic. And an excellent novel," Mark said.

"Bin fishin' dese waters for ov'r seventy year," Bill said. "Dat da only one dat really tell it like it be."

"Yes, man's competition with nature. Nature usually wins out in the end," Mark said.

"Eet won now," Bill responded.

Mark and Jenn implored Bill to come with them. He would not hear of it. They left with him standing alone at the entrance to his hut. They made their way back to the tender and were soon under way on Trade Winds. To exactly where, they didn't have a clue.

CHAPTER SEVENTY-SEVEN

The three men laboriously made their way back to home base. They decided not to tell anyone the full extent of what they had seen. On the way, they tried to devise a plan.

Robbie opened the conversation: "I was able to see the airport from up there. It looks like the runways have drained nicely. Most of the planes are a jumbled mess, but the tower survived. I'm thinking they might have a backup system like ours for the computers. I think we all ought to try to make our way over there. The tower, at least, should be drier."

"I like that idea," Larry said. "I've seen enough marooned boats around to figure we can use some to help us get over there. I'm guessing that if any rescue attempt is going to come our way, it'll be by plane. At least we'll be ready and waiting."

"Good thinking," Ben said. "Why don't Robbie and I try to find some boats that still float. Larry, you go back, let everyone know what the plan is, and get them ready for the trip. Have them grab as many pairs of trousers as they can . . . for flotation, if we need it."

"Okay," Larry said. "I'll also come back with additional men to help you guys out."

Larry took off for the station, and Robbie and Ben commenced their search. It didn't take them long to locate a partially submerged cuddy cabin twenty-five footer. They inspected the hull, and could not find any cracks or breaks.

They climbed aboard and found a bucket floating in the cabin. They used that to start bailing.

"Note the water mark above that teak strip on the side, Ben. We'll work for a hour and see if it goes down."

After an hour of energetic bailing, they brought the water down four inches.

"We're making progress," Ben shouted across to Robbie, who was using his cupped hands during Ben's turn with the bucket.

"Yeah, we are. At this rate we'll be done in about six hours," Robbie said.

"Larry will be back here shortly with reinforcements," Ben replied.

He was right. In less than an hour, Larry came wading around the corner of a nearby building with three other men.

"Man, you guys are a sight for sore eyes," Ben said to the men. "We were about to give up."

The four replacements got into the boat and took turns removing the water. They found two large storage containers in one of the vessel's cabinets and used them to bail. In two hours they were down to rags and sponges to mop up the residue.

"Looks like she's floating well," one of of the new arrivals said.

"Yeah it is," Ben responded. "But I don't see how we're going to get the engine going. I checked the compartment, and the starter battery has been under water for some time."

"Not only that, we don't have a key," Larry added.

"Let's find some flat boards," Ben said. "We'll use those as paddles. With everyone at it, we should be able to make some headway."

All six men jumped back into the water and searched around. It didn't take long to find a dozen pieces of lumber that would do the trick.

"Okay," Larry said. "You guys," and at that he pointed to two of the other men, "go back and look after all the others. We're going to try to get to the airport in this thing. If we're not back in a day, you've got to fend for yourselves, 'cause that'll mean we're dead."

"Good luck guys," one of the departing men said.

The four remaining men: Robbie, Larry, Ben, and a guy named Sam, got back in the boat, grabbed some planks, and started some semblance of paddling. It was difficult going because the gunwales were so high they had to lean half way out of the boat just to gain traction with the water.

They turned down White Street toward the pier, and then east on Atlantic Boulevard. Amazingly, the pier remained intact with only the front concrete railings broken down. They had made it six blocks when they had to rest.

"This is tough going," Larry said, "but we're making some progress. Let's pull next to this street sign and hold on so we don't go the opposite way in the current."

The flow of water returning to the sea wasn't that powerful, but sufficient to send them back the way they had come if they let it. They held onto the pole for fifteen minutes, then began again. In two hours they had made it to Bertha and South Roosevelt, and in another hour to the entrance to the airport.

"I suggest we tie it up here to the airport sign and walk the rest of the way in," Ben said. "It's not as deep here."

They found a bow rope, tied up and waded toward the terminal. Every window had been blown out, and the arrival area was under a foot of water. They walked the hundred yards up and down the ramp to the departure area over to the tower. They were pleased to find the door unlocked.

They climbed the twenty steps to the top. All the triple pane safety glass windows at the top remained intact. Looking out over the runways, they could not have imagined the chaos they were now witnessing. Several smaller commercial jets had been blown into the terminal. One wing of a plane extended through a bank of windows. Another had been flipped onto its back, the landing gear sticking up in the air as a final act of surrender. All of the smaller private planes, including some Lear jets, were plastered at strange angles against the heavy mangrove stands lining the northern border of the airport. Yet the primary runway, which angled mostly east-west, was almost completely dry.

"I can't believe how well that runway has drained," Robbie said. "I think a plane could easily land on that."

"Easily," Ben agreed.

"Well gentlemen," Larry said. "Why don't I stay here and find out as much as I can. Do you mind going back and getting everyone? This structure is much drier."

"No problem," Ben answered. "We'll go get them. May take

a day, but we'll bring them back."

CHAPTER SEVENTY-EIGHT

They had to drag the bodies out of the way to move the truck in the direction of the plane, even though running over them was not a primary concern. Aaron left to gather the rope they had so painstakingly extracted from under the pile of bodies and returned with it to the truck.

Jay tied it around the back of the truck, and on the way back to the plane, said, "Let's hope whoever found the guns won't use them against us." He backed up to within ten feet of the rear of the plane.

"Okay, let's get this baby pulled away from those rocks," Jay said. "About forty feet will do it. Zoe, Aaron and I will attach the rope. Do you think you can drive this thing when I ask you?"

"No problemo," Zoe answered. "My dad was a truck driver. He let me drive them sometimes. This one's easy."

"Great," Aaron said. "The renaissance woman comes to the rescue again!" he added with a look of loving bemusement.

The men tied the rope to the rear bumper of the truck and then to an eye hook attached to the rear fuselage of the plane. They removed the few larger rocks in the plane's path, then stood by to reorient the plane the best they could if required. Zoe shifted into first gear and moved the truck ahead slowly. Aaron and Jay watched with trepidation to see if the rope would hold. It did.

Zoe expertly navigated the truck and plane about fifty feet until Jay told her it was enough. They untied the rope from both ends, Zoe moved the truck far to the side, and Jay entered the plane, being sure to pull the hatch up so the stair legs would not drag on the tarmac. He fired up the engines.

Jay shouted out to Aaron and Zoe from the small side pilot's window. "Okay guys, I'm going to turn her around. Could you just help me make sure the ends of the wings clear all obstructions?"

They waved their acknowledgment. Jay put the gas to the left engine and stood on the right brake. The plane slowly began to spin clockwise. In two minutes it was positioned for takeoff with just half a runway for their escape.

Jay lowered the hatch from inside, Just as the first leg hit the tarmac, a shot rang out. As Aaron approached the stairs, he heard a bullet whiz right past his left ear and bury itself in the fuselage just ahead of him.

"Jesus Christ!" he yelled. "Where'd that come from?"

Aaron saw Zoe dash from her position at the tip of one wing. He yelled, "Hurry baby. Hurry!" as more bullets ricocheted around them. He heard the engines scream to maximum velocity, and Jay yelling something.

Zoe fell hard to the ground five feet from him. Aaron didn't remember much of what happened next. In one movement he scooped Zoe off the runway, heaved her over his shoulder, and jumped the stairs two at a time into the body of the plane. The aircraft immediately jumped forward as Jay released the brakes. Amidst scattered gunfire, the plane blasted down the runway with its belly hatch open and the stair legs dragging on the asphalt, throwing sparks into the air. It became airborne just before it would have struck the wreckage they had narrowly avoided on their landing.

Aaron, who had ended up lying on top of Zoe, rolled off. "Zoe, were you hit? Are you alright?" It was then he noticed for the first time the expanding circle of blood forming around her right shoulder. Her eyes fluttered to consciousness, a look of pain filling her ashen visage.

"I'm alive, Aaron. That's a step in the right direction, isn't it?" Somehow she managed a wry smile.

Aaron kissed her gently on the lips. "That's the right direction alright."

Aaron first closed the hatch and then carefully removed Zoe's shirt and bra. Neither felt any embarrassment. He carefully explored around the wound. Even though it must have hurt like hell, Zoe didn't let out so much as a whimper.

"Honey, I think we got lucky. The bullet only grazed your upper arm and passed on. We'll clean the wound and bandage it, and I think you'll be good to go."

"As long as we're going, that's all that matters to me."

Aaron retrieved the first aid kit from a locker and dressed the wound. The bleeding had stopped before he applied the bandage.

"As good as gold," he said. "Take these and you'll feel even better." He handed her two high powered Tylenol and a cup of water and she washed them down. He helped her to one of the bunks and settled her in with a light blanket.

"Okay honey. You give a shout if you need anything. *Anything.* I'm going forward to talk to Jay."

Zoe blew him a kiss. *What a woman,* Aaron thought as he moved to the cockpit.

"How's it going back there, buddy," Jay asked as Aaron sat in the copilot's seat.

"We got lucky, Jay. The bullet took a small chunk of flesh out of her shoulder, but it's really just a grazing wound. She'll be fine."

"That's great news. Now I guess we know who found the bag of guns."

"Yes we do. So where to now?" Aaron asked.

"I think we ought to follow our plan and high-tail it to Bermuda. Could you hand me those charts in that sleeve?" Jay asked as he pointed to a pocket next to Aaron's seat. "I think Daemon went south of there. Anything in the Bahamas or Florida will be chancy. They took a direct hit."

"Bermuda it is. How far away is it? Do we have enough fuel?"

"About a thousand miles. And yes we have enough to get there. We'll have to refuel in Bermuda, though."

"Okay. Let's go." Aaron handed Jay the charts. Jay put the plane on automatic pilot and began preparing their itinerary. The two men sat in silence for a while.

Aaron went back to check on Zoe. She was sound asleep. She looked beautiful in repose.

Three and a half hours later Jay announced they had Bermuda in their sights. Aaron returned to his seat next to Jay. "We're closing in," Jay said. "I'm going to do a fly-by to see what we've got. Let's hope we've got enough runway."

They descended to a thousand feet. As they passed over the airfield, Aaron said, "Looks good to me. The main runway is fairly clear.

Looks like all the smaller planes got blown to the side. I don't see any larger commercial ones at all. But the main terminal sure took a hit."

"I think we're good to go," Jay said. "I've got plenty of room."

He brought the plane around again and executed a perfect landing. He taxied to a corner of the terminal and shut down the engines.

"Let's sit here for a few minutes and see what happens. After the Cape Verde islands, I'm a little gun shy."

"Well put," Aaron said.

CHAPTER SEVENTY-NINE

They had just started into the bay when the roar of an overhead prop driven aircraft shocked them into full alert.

"What's that?" Jenn cried out, afraid it might be thunder from a newly formed storm.

"Sounds like a plane to me." Mark pushed the gear lever into neutral and strained his eyes into the cirrus studded sky. Soon he could make out a silver object, reflecting the sun back at him. "It *is* a plane! I wonder if it intends to land?"

They watched as the object, which became more clearly a plane as it grew closer, passed almost directly above them and disappeared into the eastern sky.

"Damn," Jenn said. "I was kind of hoping it would land. Then maybe we could get some information on what's going on."

Mark put the engine back into gear. "I say we go back to the cove and spend one more night. Then we can take a day to plan our next move. We've got sufficient supplies for two to three days. But that won't get us too far."

"Okay. I guess there's nothing more for us to do," Jenn said. "Let's plot our course tonight and get started first thing tomorrow morning."

Mark started back for the cove. Four minutes later, they heard the sound of a plane again. "That's either the same one," Mark said, "or it's an amazing coincidence that two planes would be flying low over us, one after the other."

Jenn quickly procured the binoculars from their holder and watched intently as once again the silver object closed in on them. "I think it's the same one, Mark. I can't be certain, but it's got two props and appears to be the same size."

The plane descended in front of them and disappeared beyond the low hills surrounding Hamilton. "They've got to be landing," Mark said. "The airport is right in that direction, on St. David's Island. I just never thought the runways would be dry enough for a plane to land."

"What are we going to do, Mark? We still don't have internet service and no one responds on the radio."

Mark paused, then responded. "I guess we should head over there and see who landed. They've got to have more information than we do, which is *nada*."

"That's what I suggest too. I'd sure like to know what's going on out there."

Mark started replotting their course to St. David's. It was on the other side of the island. "We can take either a southerly, or northerly route. I vote for northerly because the winds are strong from the south. The land will shelter us from the larger waves. Either way it's about six nautical miles. We should be there in an hour and a half."

"You're the *capitan*. You decide."

"Northerly it is," Mark said. "We'll motor the whole way to make better time."

They traveled in relative silence. Mark was right. As soon as they rounded Somerset Villages the sea became comfortably calm. In almost exactly the predicted time, they were through the pass into St.

David's north of Coney Island.

"I think we'll anchor right off Kindley Field Park. It looks very sheltered there. We'll take the tender to shore. It's only a short walk . . . maybe a half mile to the terminal. Hopefully they'll still be there."

In another half hour the inflatable pushed up on a small beach. When they walked up a small rise , they could see the absolute devastation even more clearly. The tower was non-existent, the terminal only a series of shattered metal girders.

"Holy cow, Mark," Jenn said. "Look at that!"

"Yeah. Look at that. Worse as you get up closer. But I see the plane. It taxied to within a few hundred yards of the terminal, or what's left of it. Let's head directly for it."

As they approached, Mark said, "Wow. That's a Hurricane Hunter Aircraft. I've see lots of them on TV."

They saw a hatch lower from the fuselage and some stairs descend to the ground. Three figures climbed down and stood outside looking around. They apparently saw Mark and Jenn because they began waving and shouting in their direction. The two returned the greetings.

Mark and Jenn walked up and introductions were made all around. Mark gave the NOAA group a short version of their travels and experience with the storm, including their current situation and low supplies. Jay, Aaron and Zoe did likewise.

"Frankly, I'm amazed you two made it through Eepa," Jay said as he pointed to the terminal. "I've never seen destruction like that."

"It was a miracle," Jenn replied. "We both know that."

"Have you been able to determine if anyone survived on the

Island," Aaron asked. "When we did the fly over, we didn't see any signs of life."

"We ran into one old man," Mark said. "He lives in the hills about a mile from here. I'm convinced there's no way he's going to leave."

"So you won't be able to get any more supplies . . . any more food and water? What's your plan?" Jay asked.

"We were just trying to figure that out when we saw you. Any suggestions?" Mark asked.

"We do have room on board," Jay said pointing back to the plane. "Our next destination is Key West Florida. We've got some people to rescue there. I don't know how long it will take to get reinforcements out here."

"I think you ought to come with us," Aaron said.

Jenn looked forlornly at Mark. Quietly she said, "Baby, what about Trade Winds? We'd have to leave her here?"

Mark looked at her lovingly. "Jenn. There are other Trade Winds out there. There's only one of each of us. I can't say with any certainty how well we'll manage around here. We've got a ride back to the U.S. with these guys. I think we have to grab it."

"I understand," she murmured.

"We'll give you time to make whatever arrangements you want to make with the boat," Aaron said. "We've got to refuel. That'll take a while. Why don't you meet us back here in around three hours?"

"We'll be here," Mark responded.

Mark and Jenn went back to their tender and then to Trade Winds. They threw a few personal items and some changes of clothing into a knapsack and secured the boat as best they could: stem and stern anchors and battened-down hatches all around.

They stood silently for a few minutes looking at the craft that had been their home for the past several weeks. Then just as silently they loaded the knapsack into the dinghy and motored back to the shore. Pulling the inflatable as far up on land as they could, they made their way back to the plane. They noticed a fuel truck pulled up next to the plane and a hose protruding from the side of the fuselage.

"Guess they found their fuel," Jenn said. "That's good news."

"Looks like we're good to go," Mark said with little enthusiasm.

Zoe helped them load their gear on board, and explained their luck in finding a nearly full tanker that still had the keys in it. She showed Mark and Jenn where to stow their few personal items. "Why don't you take Jack and Bart's old lockers," she said. "Unfortunately they were killed in Cape Verde."

"Killed?" Jenn asked.

"Yes. It's a long story which we'll be glad to fill you in on. We want to preserve their personal effects for their families, so why don't we empty each separately. You hand me the items and I'll put them in these two duffel bags."

Mark and Jenn began emptying the lockers. Mark removed several hanging shirts, jackets and pants from Bart's locker and handed them to Zoe. At the bottom he came across a large canvas bag which was zipped shut. He pulled it out. It was very heavy, about fifty pounds, he estimated.

"What's in here? Should we open it?" Mark asked.

"I guess so. It's not locked," Zoe responded.

Mark unzipped the bag. It was full to the brim with canned goods, all with Portuguese labels and clearly from Cape Verde. "Extra food stores?" he asked.

Zoe stood there dumbfounded. The realization came slowly, but when it sunk in fully her knees almost gave way. She steadied herself on a hand grip hanging from the ceiling. "Oh God," she said hoarsely.

"What's the matter? Are you okay?" Jenn asked.

"I'm okay. It's part of the same long story. But this time the joke's on us."

Aaron returned to the cockpit while Jay finished pumping the last of the two thousand gallons into the plane. Zoe yelled to Aaron: "Aaron, could you come back here for a second?"

Aaron spoke back into the cabin. "What's up babe?"

"I just want you to take a look at this."

Aaron unbuckled himself and came back to her. He saw the open bag and said, "What in the heck is that?"

"We found this in Bart's locker," Zoe said.

Aaron bent down and began sorting through some of the canned goods, then looked up at Zoe with a bewildered look. "Is this possible, honey? Was Bart actually hoarding food on all of us? My God."

"'My God is right,'" Zoe replied. "He sure caused a lot of trouble by doing this. And he paid for it in the end."

"He paid for it alright. As did Jack," Aaron said.

Mark and Jenn looked at each other with confused expressions.

"You guys can tell us all about this later if you want. Sure sounds like it's a serious matter," Mark said.

"It was, and it caused the death of two of our people, and almost killed us all," Aaron said. "Not to mention a number of the native Cape Verdeans."

Jay had finished fueling the plane and returned to the cockpit. Aaron resumed his seat next to Jay. Zoe moved up close to them.

Aaron said, "You're not going to believe this Jay. We just found a large bag full of canned goods in Bart's locker. All Cape Verde stuff. Seems like the Cape Verdeans may have had it right. One of us was stealing and hoarding food. And it was Bart."

"Are you kidding?" Jay yelled. "Goddamn it. That son of a bitch. Got himself killed, and took Jack, and almost us, with him."

"That's the way it looks. But truthfully, it's not something I think we should let out. It would just cause the families more grief. What do you think?"

Jay hesitated for a few seconds. "I guess I have to agree with you. We'll let this sleeping dog lie. Agreed?"

"Agreed."

Jay spoke softly. "Aaron and Zoe. What do you think about offering Bart's food to Mark and Jenn? We have plenty to get us to Key West. That way they might be able to continue on. They sure looked sad to leave their boat."

"I think that's a great idea," Zoe responded.

"I agree," Aaron said.

The three moved back with Mark and Jenn and explained their offer. Jenn broke down in tears. "That's so generous of you. Are you certain you won't need it?"

"That's right," Mark said. "If there's any chance you could use this food, we can't take it."

"Trust us," Aaron said. "We've got enough on board. This was totally unexpected. If you want it so you can continue on your trip, please take it."

Mark and Jenn looked at each other. No words needed to be spoken. They thanked their new hosts profusely, grabbed the bag and exited the plane. Within minutes they were back on board Trade Winds, ready to sail to parts unknown.

It took only two and a half hours for Jay, Aaron and Zoe to make it to Key West. The three, who had never visited the Keys before, smiled as they flew over the sparkling azure seas on both sides of a seemingly endless chain of small islands.

CHAPTER EIGHTY

Ben and the other men left the tower and started back to the station. The going was a little easier this direction as the current was with them. They arrived in three hours and filled everyone in on the plan. They got packed up and decided to spend the night at the station and get an early start in the morning.

Larry went about the process of organizing the tower and making as much room as he could for sleeping arrangements. There was more space on the ground floor as you entered and he cleared out some debris from the stairs.

It was around seven o'clock when he first heard it. The unmistakeable drone of a prop airplane. Larry watched as the craft did an initial pass over the runway at about a thousand feet. He ran down to the base of the tower, removed his shirt, and began waving it wildly as the plane turned around and descended for a landing.

It hit the tarmac with a screech and white puffs of smoke from each tire and taxied to within two hundred feet of where Larry was standing. He watched as the hatch dropped and three people, two men and one woman, exited from the plane. *My God,* Larry realized. *It's one of ours.*

He yelled over to them and waved. They waved back and walked over to him.

They shook hands and exchanged names. Jay said, "We weren't sure if we'd find anyone alive here. The convoluted and spotty information we've received suggested no one survived."

"There're around twenty of us," Larry replied. "We holed up in the Storm Center at the station. It got pretty hairy when it started to fill with water, but one of the men figured out how to pump it out."

"How can we pick up the others?" Aaron asked. "Our orders are to transport everyone to our Denver area office for safekeeping. As you know, we have the Regional Support Center in Boulder, Colorado. From there we'll figure out how to get everyone home, assuming they have a home left to return to. I didn't realize you had so many. Not sure we can fit all of you in."

"We'll do the best we can," Larry said. "They're supposed to be back here as soon as they can. I'm guessing it won't be until tomorrow morning."

Larry was invited to sleep in the plane with the new arrivals, and he gladly took them up on it. He luxuriated in the dry, comfortable, albeit narrow bunk he was given.

The next morning, around eleven, the group from the station arrived at the airport. Jay and Aaron organized them according to weight. They jettisoned everything on the plane that was expendable. They were still a good one thousand pounds beyond the maximum limit.

Jay called Aaron, Robbie, Larry, Sam and Tom over to a huddle away from the group. "Men, we've got a big problem here. We'd be catastrophically overweight if we tried to stuff everyone in. I don't think we'd make it off the ground, much less fly safely. I need Aaron to fly with me. Any suggestions?"

Larry and Robbie looked at each other and Larry asked, "Any idea when another plane might be able to make it in?"

"No idea," Jay replied. "Probably not for at least a couple of days."

"We can hold out that long," Robbie said. "Larry and I will stay here. No problem. Sam and Tom, how about you guys?"

They looked at each other and nodded. "We're with you," Sam said.

"Well unfortunately, we may need more than that," Aaron said. "Let's discuss this with the group."

When the situation was fully explained to the others, Ben and Valerie immediately stepped forward and offered to stay behind. Robbie spoke to Ben first. "Ben, we appreciate your willingness to remain, but you have two children who need you. The rest of us are childless. You're going on the plane."

"Well, I really appreciate that. To be honest, when I heard we were heading to Colorado, I was ecstatic. I'd like to stay there for a while and spend some quality time with my two kids. Maybe even live there permanently. But I'm willing to remain behind if you need me too."

Val and Robbie got into a heated discussion off to the side, but it was clear Val was going to get her way. The five of them would stay behind.

"That should be sufficient. Let's give it a try," Jay said.

The plane was loaded and taxied to the end of the runway. Those left behind, together with all aboard, held their collective breaths as the plane screamed down the runway and barely cleared a stand of palms well off the end of the strip. The five returned to the tower.

"We'll be fine here for a while," Robbie said. "We've got enough food and water for a week."

As they entered the tower, Sam noticed a gray electrical panel obscured by a fire extinguisher to the left of the door. "What's this?" he asked.

"Don't know," Larry responded. "First time I've seen it."

"Well I'm sure it's not going to help, as it appears the electricity is out around the island," Sam said. "But let's take a quick look."

Larry opened the panel door. All the switches but one had been tripped to the neutral position. "Looks like we had a short here. But what's this big one in red? It hadn't been turned on when the electrical grid went out."

"I guess it won't hurt to try it," Val said.

"Why not," Tom replied. He hit the switch. He hesitated, then cupped his right ear toward an access hatch laid into the concrete floor and said, "What's that sound?"

"Strange," Robbie answered. "Almost sounds like a generator."

They stood listening for a moment. Then Robbie ran up the stairs. "Come on. I think we might have power."

As they got to the main floor, Robbie walked over to one of the five computers set on a metal counter around the perimeter of the room. He hit the power switch on the one farthest to the right. When nothing happened, he went from one to the other, doing the same thing. The fourth from the end lit up and the whirring of the internal fan could be heard. In a moment the screen focused. At the same time a boom box set in the corner of the room lit up.

"I can't believe this," Robbie exclaimed, pointing to the computer. "We've got power in this thing."

"Yeah, but is it connected to anything?" Sam asked.

All four peered over Robbie's shoulder as he punched several keys and the NOAA website popped up. "Guys, we're in business. I can access and communicate with any NOAA station in North America. Let's see who's around."

He tried Miami first, then Tampa. No response. He next went to Tallahassee. Their home page coalesced on the screen.

"Okay, got one," Robbie said. He typed for a couple of minutes. Almost instantaneously responsive words appeared on the screen.

Robbie read for a minute, then said, "Apparently the Miami and Tampa stations were totally destroyed by the hurricane. Of course, Miami got it first with the fire. Tallahassee is the closest to us that's still open and online."

"What are they saying?" Sam asked.

"Give me a minute." Robbie stared intently at the screen, occasionally typing some responses. "The level of destruction in Florida, most of the Gulf states, and the entire eastern seaboard is unprecedented. Daemon went into Alabama and Georgia and northward. Eepa got the east coast. They combined again in the mid-Atlantic states and ravaged New England. Most, if not all communications are out in those areas."

"Let me take a look at the larger picture," Robbie said as he searched the North American sector. "Yeah, there's the combined Daemon and Eepa. Heading for the north Atlantic. Won't be harming any one else, at least."

"God help the British Isles if their track remains constant," Larry commented.

"Let's look around at what's coming, if anything." Robbie went to the Caribbean sector. "Just some typical tropical depressions. I'm going to go out to the East Atlantic sector. That will show us what's rolling off Africa across the ocean at us."

He hit some keys and the coast of Africa, Cape Verde, and about a thousand miles of ocean to the west popped up on the screen. Just then the four of them became aware of the gradually increasing volume of the music emanating from the boom box.

"What's that?" Tom asked.

Robbie listened intently. "Hmmm. Sounds like 'The Ride of the Valkyries' by Wagner."

The wailing successive layers of accompaniment of screeching violins and flugelhorns of the piece rose to a crescendo as they stared at the computer screen.

"Jesus Lord almighty," Val gasped. "Is that what I think it is?"

There, displayed to all of them in bold relief, were the churning, spinning yellows, greens, blues and harsh magentas of three separate hurricanes, marching across the Atlantic Ocean in unison, heading directly for them.

About the Author

Rusty Hodgdon is a graduate of Yale University where he majored in English Literature and Creative Writing. After graduating with a Juris Doctor degree from the Boston University School of Law, he practiced law for over twenty years in the Boston area. He left the practice of law and moved to Key West Florida to pursue his passion to write creative fiction. Rusty is also the winner of the 2012 Key West Mystery Fest Short Story Contest, and an officer in the Key West Writers Guild. All comments are welcome. Write to him at:

RUSTY.THE.WRITER@GMAIL.COM

Made in the USA
San Bernardino, CA
25 November 2013